Praise for Alberto Álvaro Ríos

A SMALL STORY ABOUT THE SKY
"Rios evokes the mysterious and unexpected forces that dwell inside the familiar."

—*Washington Post*

THE DANGEROUS SHIRT
"Rios continually surprises us in the way he stretches the meaning of words, turning them this way and that."

—*San Francisco Chronicle*

"Alberto Ríos is . . . arguably the best Latino poet writing in English today."

—*Prairie Schooner*

THE SMALLEST MUSCLE IN THE HUMAN BODY
"Alberto Ríos is a poet of reverie and magical perception, and of the threshold between this world and the world just beyond."

—*National Book Award Judges' comments*

"Alberto Ríos is a poet of reverie. . . . Whether talking about the smell of food, the essence of a crow or a bear's character or of hard-won human wisdom, Ríos writes in a serenely clear manner that enhances the drama in the quick scenes he summons up."

—*New York Times Book Review*

"Alberto Ríos is the man you want to sit next to when it is time to hear a story."

—*Southwest BookViews*

Other Books by Alberto Álvaro Ríos

POETRY

Not Go Away Is My Name
A Small Story about the Sky
The Dangerous Shirt
The Theater of Night
The Smallest Muscle in the Human Body
Teodoro Luna's Two Kisses
The Lime Orchard Woman
Five Indiscretions
Whispering to Fool the Wind

FICTION

The Curtain of Trees
Pig Cookies
The Iguana Killer

MEMOIR

Capirotada

LIMITED EDITIONS

The Warrington Poems
Sleeping on Fists
Elk Heads on the Wall

A Good Map of All Things

Camino del Sol
A Latina and Latino Literary Series

ALBERTO ÁLVARO RÍOS

A GOOD MAP OF ALL THINGS

A Picaresque Novel

THE UNIVERSITY OF
ARIZONA PRESS

TUCSON

The University of Arizona Press
www.uapress.arizona.edu

© 2020 by Alberto Álvaro Ríos
All rights reserved. Published 2020

ISBN-13: 978-0-8165-4103-4 (paper)

Cover design by Leigh McDonald
Cover photo by Dennis Alvear Perez
Designed and typeset by Leigh McDonald in Acie WF (display) and Bell MT 10.5/15

Illustrations on pp. viii, 106, and 139 by Jacqueline Balderrama; all other images are the
author's own.

Publication of this book is made possible in part by the proceeds of a permanent endowment created with the assistance of a Challenge Grant from the National Endowment for
the Humanities, a federal agency.

Library of Congress Cataloging-in-Publication Data
Names: Ríos, Alberto, author.
Title: A good map of all things : a picaresque novel / Alberto Álvaro Ríos.
Other titles: Camino del sol.
Description: Tucson : University of Arizona Press, 2020. | Series: Camino del sol: a latina/
   latino literary series
Identifiers: LCCN 2020010933 | ISBN 9780816541034 (paperback)
Subjects: LCSH: Cities and towns—Mexico—Fiction. | Interpersonal relations—Fiction. |
   LCGFT: Picaresque fiction.
Classification: LCC PS3568.I587 G66 2020 | DDC 813/.54—dc23
LC record available at https://lccn.loc.gov/2020010933

Printed in the United States of America
♾ This paper meets the requirements of ANSI/NISO Z39.48-1992 (Permanence of Paper).

For Lupita

CONTENTS

Acknowledgments   *xi*

The Business Card   2
1. Dr. Bartolomeo's Cure   3
The Newspaper Story   22
2. Lent and Given   24
The Marriage Certificate   43
3. Butter, Oranges, and Pink Coconut Candy   44
The Poem   61
4. A Century of Tears   63
The Prayer   75
5. The Asterisk Company   76
The Obituary, the Proclamation of a Death   91
6. The Night Miguel Torres Died   92
The Song on the Radio   106

7.   Two Small Crimes   107

Civil Registration   *123*

8.   Ten Seconds in Two Lives   124

The Map   *139*

9.   Bernardo's Corrido   140

The Green Card   *153*

10.   One Tuesday in the Early Afternoon   154

The Bill   *166*

11.   Licenciado Ubaldo Dos Santos, at Your Service   167

The Birth Certificate   *179*

12.   Curandera   180

The Photograph   *201*

13.   The History of History   202

The Telegram   *215*

14.   The Five Visits of Archbishop Oswaldo Calderón   216

The Letter   *234*

ACKNOWLEDGMENTS

The following appeared in earlier versions:

"A Century of Tears," *Indiana Review*.
"Un siglo de lágrimas," *La Palabra* (Spanish).
"Bernardo's *Corrido*," *Orion*.
"El corrido de Bernardo," *La Palabra* (Spanish).
"Butter, Oranges, and Pink Coconut Candy," *Lake Effect*.
"Curandera," *Connecticut Review*.
"Dr. Bartolomeo's Cure," *Lake Effect*.
"One Tuesday in the Early Afternoon," *Colorado Review*.
"Licenciado Ubaldo Dos Santos, at Your Service," *La Palabra* (Spanish).
"Ten Seconds in Two Lives," *New Letters*.
"The Asterisk Company," *Orion*.
"The Five Visits of Archbishop Oswaldo Calderón," *Connecticut Review*.
"The Night Miguel Torres Died," *Lake Effect*.
"Two Small Crimes," *Orion*.

I would like to sincerely thank the dedicated early readers, journal editors, and translators of the various segments in this book for their comments and gracious encouragement, and Arizona State University. Thanks especially to Jacqueline Balderrama and Irena Praitis.

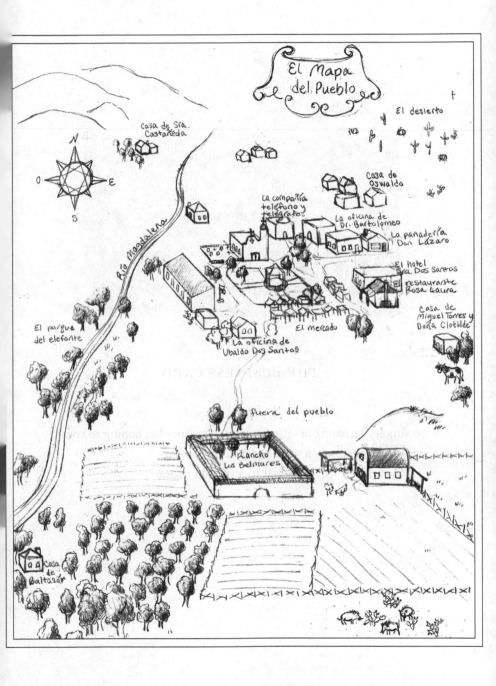

LIC. MARGARITO C. RIOS
Presidente del Supremo Tribunal
de Justicia

San Luis Potosí, S. L. P.

THE BUSINESS CARD

So simple, we hand ourselves over to someone else, hoping to speak with them even when we are not in the room.

When it works, it is equal to a trick of magic.

Dr. Bartolomeo's Cure

Narciso Bartolomeo did not start out wanting to be a doctor. He wanted to be something more enjoyable, suffering the belief that doctors only hurt people, which had been his own experience. He was born in a time when doctors did not have as many answers as degrees and certificates on their walls, and were mistrusted by almost everyone. An occasional cure—everyone expected that but ascribed it to luck. *Doctors*, they would say, as if it were a foul word, and shake their heads in disgust.

A doctor's lot had not much improved in the middle of this century as from the previous one. The twentieth century had promised everything, but once it got to work, the new century was just one more in a long line of disappointments. By its middle, it had brought war and promises. Some people thought of this as a century of tears. Narciso Bartolomeo, however, was of the opposite opinion, although he understood the vagaries of the wars in Europe and civil war here. But Narciso liked the new century's ideas and was especially fond of its promises. His hope, in fact, was to live even into the next century, and to then be cured himself of whatever might ail him at the time. It was a strong loyalty he bore to the future, and he tried to give that feeling over to others whenever he could.

Unfortunately, the workaday business of a doctor's office had little patience for promises. A cut, an infection, some pain, broken bones, colds, aching muscles, more pain—these made for a full day. And the larger issues, the chronic diseases and long deaths, the conditions people suffered, and big decisions that had to be made, all of this, all of it so regular—this began to define the years, like it or not.

On the other hand, there were babies being born, and they would get to see so much of what he imagined. He took good care of them and understood that they would be the ones to take care of him, that somewhere among them all would be another Dr. Bartolomeo, and the thought excited him.

In later years it became a tradition of Dr. Bartolomeo's to stand before his office and announce the event on the day a baby was born. He took great pride in this, and his flourishes of description and destiny became increasingly grand. While Dr. Bartolomeo knew that the child would most likely be taken to Padre Nacho to be baptized, he thought of what he himself did as a kind of baptism as well, a baptism into the new century, so that he always made sure to find some way to mention the future and science in his proclamations. A small crowd would invariably gather, people coming home from work or simply in the vicinity doing errands, or even purposefully, and when he stopped speaking there would be applause. The baby's father would sometimes follow, speaking his heart, his tongue perhaps loosened from having been already celebrating earlier in the day. It was a tradition that lasted for many years.

Dr. Bartolomeo himself did not have time for creating his own child, or rather did not have time for the person who would bear him this child. His hours had grown exponentially through the years, and his hope for a normal life diminished at the same rate. With that understanding in mind, though it was not a bargain he had understood at the beginning, he worked all the more.

Whenever he felt sorry for himself, he brought a new patient in, one more than he thought he could bear. This was not altogether an altruistic act, however. It was medicine he administered to himself in the sense that it was still irritation and resentment that he felt at that moment, but at least it was split between the two of them, and the patient got to see him who otherwise would have had to come back the next day. If he was a little brusque, he did not mean it, and the truth of that showed itself easily enough over the years. But it was a brusqueness, sometimes, that found its way into those long hours.

More than that, however, was the other feeling, which guided him so much more happily, and that was the demeanor his patients had come to expect and look for, even in the brusqueness, and they were right to look for it. That was the medicine for him, their looking for it, their asking about the future of things. Their asking him to tell them where science stood on their personal and particular matter, or how long did he himself think a cure would take, and what would it be, did he have an idea—these questions were curatives for him, and sometimes for them as well, since simply talking about something sometimes helped. It might not be immediately clear, but everything had an answer. He believed it so much that they did, too.

Narciso had wanted to be a truck driver. He understood even as a child that taking things from one place and moving them to another made the world work. Taking watermelons from the field and delivering them to the *mercado* fixed the world—the watermelons were big and green and bursting, and by moving them, now people would get to eat them and get red all over their faces and spit seeds into the wind, which would make more watermelons. It made so much sense. Who would not want to be a truck driver?

Soon enough Narciso saw that strategy at work in other things, in letters being carried from one person to the mail office, through Sr. Castillo, who carried these letters to people's houses, and then to the people themselves. Narciso, at the moment he understood that connection, wanted to deliver mail and began to follow Sr. Castillo around town to see how things got done. One thing, he could see, led to another.

In later years, when he was learning the science and medicine that would be his life, when he was being taught about blood in the body, he always imagined it—and all the other things the body circulated around itself—he imagined all of it as Sr. Castillo walking around town. It made his studies easier because he could see everything so clearly. He simply assigned the names of people's houses and businesses to different parts of the body—the head was the post office itself, which luckily enough was next to the telephone company, the ears. The brain was his own office, an indulgence that he said to himself simply gave him his bearings in this mapping endeavor. Ubaldo Dos Santos's house, the neck. The lungs were all of Miguel Torres's work, all those places to live, those small houses and connecting streets. And so on. The feet, so far away, those were Cayetano Belmares's lands, the orchard on one side and the dairy and crop fields on the other.

It was a good map of all things, and it helped him to remember both the workings of the body and something of the workings of the town itself. For a while, he believed that he was onto his first discovery, that there was something bigger, a bigger idea in all of this, a town like a body, but he hadn't had time yet to work it out.

The circulation itself of both the body and the town quickly took up the time he thought he would have for such thinking.

But soon enough Narciso saw the importance of that movement in all things, and how things needed to be connected and in good repair in order to keep the energy and meaning of that movement. Towns needed roads and workers and the post office. In people, when things stopped moving that were expected to arrive elsewhere—blood, for example, well, trouble began. And if a body were like a town, then perhaps it was like a country, or like a hemisphere, or the world itself. The idea made him giddy when he thought about it, and tongue-tied when he tried to explain it to anyone else.

City planning, thought Narciso—perhaps that would be another thing he should investigate.

❖

It was science and cities, the future, everything getting clearer, as if a great cloud were rising off the landscape, letting everyone see into the encroaching distance.

Narciso often had such conversations with the only other person who understood these things and thought this way, Ignacio Belmares, who went about building things and solving problems for the town. Narciso saw his own work in a similar light, building healthy bodies and solving medical problems. Both men fixed things and made the world work better.

When they reached this point in conversation, as they invariably did, the delight Narciso and Ignacio both felt was palpable, but the sanctity and decorum of science itself kept them from bursting out into joyous laughter. Reserve was of utmost importance— manners, the proper ways to do things. Otherwise, people in a hurry, or too loud or inattentive, made mistakes.

Narciso and Ignacio were invariably drawn to what made them happy as that particular night wore on, but reluctant—the felicitous moment once reached—to do much more than nod in a knowing way, smile, and take a drink of liqueur, preferably something from a faraway place, which helped them to dream of bigger things.

To that end, they formed a public science society, the first of its kind in town, and the first in the whole region as well, for that matter. At its height, the society counted nine members, though Narciso and Ignacio were the only two who showed up with regularity. For the others, apparently, so many things came up—*you know how it is*, they would say—that regular meetings proved difficult.

Of course, everyone wanted to be part of this enterprise, now called the Forward Science Society, not being able to agree on a single scientist to honor but all in agreement about the modern sensibility they were discussing. And many more than nine claimed to be part of the group because it clearly spoke to the intelligence of the town.

The activity of the society, however, most often came down to a conversation between Narciso and Ignacio, to which the others in attendance would defer with small agreements and raised eyebrows as their part of the conversation. Most of them would leave early, but these conversations between Narciso and Ignacio often went well into the late hours of darkness and never bored the two main participants, even as they were surprised to find themselves the only two shaking hands to say good night for the evening.

Narciso's family came from another place, his grandparents first from Italy, then his parents from South America, coming north slowly, one town at a time, doing work as tailors but always getting restless, making their way finally to this northern frontier, this wild Sonoran north that they had heard about, where everything was possible—and that was part of Narciso's story, part of how he was made. Perhaps it explained everything. His family came to this town to make things better for themselves, much the same way that Narciso now felt the echo of that effort, trying in his case to make things better in all ways.

His parents had passed away some years ago now, together. They left him enough so that he could pursue his schooling, but that was it. He was not related to anybody, so there was nobody either to help him or to hinder him. This was his life, alone, for good or for bad.

Narciso did not dwell on the past and made the most of what was offered, learning the lessons his parents had passed on to him. His family, it seemed to him, was from everywhere and knew a little bit about everything, which had been exciting to him. But small things, new things, things that his parents talked about that they had seen in their travels, these were what interested Narciso most of all. Machines to make coffee better or contraptions that helped a person sleep more comfortably or huge, golden hot-air balloons that carried people underneath them as if they were in cars but in the sky. Recipes and maps and hundred-color quilts his parents made from materials they had gathered over all these years—all these small bits of flotsam and jetsam, the sparkling gleanings gathered from a world that tantalized Narciso with their small stories and big promises: all this made him.

But paying attention, paying attention when there was something worthy, even if someone else thought it inconsequential, that is what drew him to science, and as one of its offshoots, medicine. Narciso's incessant questions about places on maps or how particular ingredients combined to make exact tastes and memorable flavors, all of this drew him down a pathway.

Even though science was his morning, afternoon, and evening, he did not discount the things he did not understand, all the stories his parents had left untold or unexplained. Indeed, he understood perfectly well how having an open, scientific mind meant looking at exactly that—what the world did not yet know and what was waiting to be discovered. Or, he would remind himself, thinking of his parents, *remembered.*

For these reasons he kept a civil relationship with Sra. Castañeda and marveled when she finally showed him her chest of drawers full of roots and dried herbs, a large brown elephant of a chest that she kept in the back bedroom of her house. It was not unlike the chests his father had made to hold the special materials and buttons and clasps and sequins and all manner of sartorial confetti for the family's tailoring business.

Dr. Bartolomeo at first tried to cure everyone who came to see him, at least that full first year, but later he began to send a few people for a talk with Sra. Castañeda, just to see if she had any thoughts on the person's particular condition, or anything surrounding it that she might know to look for and point out. He never spoke with her directly about such things, but understood that she had at her disposal some remedies that he did not. She had the past, while he held the future.

He thought of these things she took care of as diseases of the past, not simply or only as beliefs people had. The *mal de ojo*, for example, whether it was true or not, he had seen it cause many problems, which in turn led to sickness. In itself it might be nothing much, but believing in it led to restlessness and anxiety, to depression, to a lack of appetite, to fear, and then very easily to sickness of one kind or another. He could see the connection and understand the power that it held—if one believed in it, of course. He could see that if a person thought he had the *mal de ojo* and then got sick, that one thing caused the other. Dr. Bartolomeo could see that connection, though he saw it in all its intermediate steps, not as one thing moving directly to the other. Even if he could explain it, however, and break it down into its component parts as a process or like a stepladder, that didn't mean much. A person was still sick regardless. It was that simple.

Even so, while Dr. Bartolomeo believed in his more forward direction and thought of it as his province, he never forgot the feelings he had while growing up about everything that had brought his parents to this place, even if he had to remind himself. All that knowledge counted for something, if just something to stand on as one looked forward. That seemed sensible enough to him. The past had its place.

And besides, he had a great deal of respect for Sra. Castañeda's son, Perfecto, as well, and for Perfecto's wife, Berta. Both of them sometimes came to meetings of the science society, and even when they didn't were nevertheless always supportive of Dr. Bartolomeo's endeavors, which he appreciated.

Dr. Bartolomeo did, however, along with Sra. Castañeda, keep not as medicines but as necessary treatments such things as watermelon in his fancy office refrigerator. Even he understood about watermelon and the dying. A person longs for so many things, to taste them once more, most especially those things not in season. One wishes for what is not possible, after all, in that moment. Having watermelon when none was otherwise available always gave a person hope—hope and a taste of childhood, of happiness. It was the taste of another time.

His very first case was famous here. As a doctor he came back to town shiny and new. In his clean suit and with just as clean a smile and washed hands, he sparkled and had every confidence in himself. He carried a clear sense that the people in this town would do what he told them to, for their own good, of course. And he had tried to think of everything, including making an arrangement with Ubaldo Dos Santos's mother, Sra. Dos Santos, who had a small hotel. He entreated her to reserve, as much as possible, one room with two beds, but into which might be fitted four should the need for a hospital arise. It was an uneasy arrangement because no one was quite sure what that meant, the need for a hospital, but Dr. Bartolomeo offered to pay her a small monthly sum for this assurance, and that seemed like a good idea to the town generally, especially the part about him assuming responsibility for the payment personally.

Dr. Bartolomeo came to do good, his motives were pure, his attentions were thorough, and everybody already knew him.

And if they did not, his first patient would change everything. The case came to him in a cacophony of shouts and a car honking and a small crowd of people. Dr. Bartolomeo had opened his office one Monday morning after having put an advertisement in the newspaper, so everybody knew where it was.

When Dr. Bartolomeo looked down at the patchy work towel that someone had lent to the occasion of draping the patient, and with several of the people saying, "Go on, it's all right, go ahead, he needs you," he took charge, took a deep breath, and lifted the towel. He saw what was there, then looked around at the crowd surrounding him.

It was the dog Bernardo.

Bernardo had been hit by a car. It was an accident, and everyone stopped to see what could be done for the dog, but nobody knew what to do. There was no blood, but Bernardo lay on his side, unresponsive. He wasn't dead—that was clear enough. His tongue had slipped out of his mouth and was moving when he breathed, though it was a labored breathing.

When these things happened, it was generally more convenient all around for people if the impact was a little harder or the outcome a little more certain. That there might be something to do, that's when people panic. People prefer to say *if only something could have been done* to doing something. This was something Narciso later thought about, and in retrospect he understood that something very good had happened. And that he had been slow to see it himself.

"But I'm a doctor," said Narciso Bartolomeo, with all the authority of his office.

"We know," said someone.

"But it's a dog," said Dr. Bartolomeo, incredulously. "A dog!"

"Yes. And he's been hurt," said someone else.

"But he's a dog."

Everyone looked at the doctor, and for a moment the air seemed to stop moving and the noise quieted. Somewhere in the back of his head Narciso understood this to be a moment when the movement of things was being blocked, and as he took stock of the situation, he realized that he himself was blocking it. He himself, of all things, was the problem.

He threw his hands up. "Bring him in. I will take a look and do what I can. Is there an owner?"

"It's Miguel Torres's dog. He never lets him out of his sight."

"Well, somebody check on that, and send Sr. Torres over here if you find him."

With that, Dr. Bartolomeo, after giving the dog a quick check, lifted him up and brought him in his arms into his office.

When he fixed Bernardo up, giving him all the necessary stitches where he had found it necessary to open and repair his stomach and understanding fully that this was, indeed, his first patient and that everyone would be looking to see what he could do, he said that Bernardo had to relax for a few days and not exert himself, or else the stitches would come out. And he could not lick those stitches, either, the doctor added, remembering as an afterthought how the behaviors of dogs were so different from humans' behaviors.

Licking stitches. It seemed ridiculous, and anyone would understand that. But would a dog? With that thought came a nagging secondary thought: *What if the dog were right?* No person he knew ever thought to lick stitches. Certainly nobody was instructed to do that in school. But what if stitch licking turned out to be science in the next decade? It was a possibility. He understood about keeping a wound dry, but he also understood about keeping a wound clean. Which was the stronger commandment? Dogs seemed to do very well on their own. He would have to consider this later and do some tests.

Understanding that Bernardo, like any dog, would prioritize which irritation to deal with first, and not wanting him to go for the stitches, Dr. Bartolomeo fashioned a collar by taking strips of paper from the large roll he used to cover the examining table for each new patient. Hygiene and cleanliness were the first things he planned to stress to the townspeople.

Dr. Bartolomeo cut the paper strips into various sizes and then looped them around the dog's neck and sutured this fluttering mess together, since he already had his suturing needles out. He used a very thick, curved needle and a very thick thread, the thickest of each—items he had been certain he would never be called upon to use. That, by itself, made him smile, this combination of surprise and inspiration. And science.

This collar delighted his next patients, who were scheduled to be his first. The schoolchildren had not had a proper check-up in several years, ever since Dr. Cano had retired. Since these children were not old enough to remember what visits to him were like, they were cheerful as they lined up in a row.

When Dr. Bartolomeo and Bernardo came out of the examining room, there were all the kids, in a line starting in the waiting room and extending outside onto the sidewalk. But it was a neat and orderly line, even with all the fussing, all the ways children find to move even when standing still. Looking at them all in a row, one could guess all their nicknames, thought Dr. Bartolomeo, *Chapo, Flaco, Gordito, Huila, Güerita, Zarco, Guapo.*

Guapo. The good-looking boy. Dr. Bartolomeo noticed that this handsome boy also had on clothes different from the rest. Narciso noticed this because his parents were tailors, and he remembered this equation even as a child: Handsome people wear different clothing, no matter how poor they are. And they invariably wear it better. But perhaps they wear it better because someone put the time and energy into making sure that it fit. A little bit of extra color here, a better seam there—people did things for beauty.

But then they turned around and complained at how the beautiful ones seem to get everything, without understanding their own complicity. The idea of beauty was bigger than all of them, perhaps. Beauty was simply a force beyond their control, for good or for bad. But it was there. This handsome boy, *el guapo*, had handsome clothes. They fit, and they had a brightness of color that suggested how carefully they had been laundered. It was not fair, of course, but just one more item of note in the great ocean of things.

Well, all of this aside, as Dr. Bartolomeo stood there looking for how to proceed, the children saw Bernardo in his collar and laughed. Dr. Bartolomeo at first did not notice, but then acknowledged what they were interested in and raised the dog a little so that they could see him better.

"Who will help me with Bernardo?" he asked. The neat line quickly became a small, unruly crowd, everyone volunteering by shouts and the raising of hands.

Dr. Bartolomeo pointed to six children, all about the same height and build, four boys and two girls. They came immediately forward as the others voiced their dismay. But the procedure was far from over, and their attention was immediately drawn again.

"Hand me that," he said to one of the boys, pointing to a large, square piece of construction wood, one of the plywood panels that were still lying around the new office. It had been used, perhaps, to bring in the windows, or perhaps it had been the side of a big box holding some of the medical equipment. What its function had been was lost, but what it would be was everything.

Dr. Bartolomeo put Bernardo down on the waiting room couch, motioning the children to stay back. He got some more of the hygienic paper and wrapped it around the wood, taping it all neatly down with white tape. He then asked to be handed a cardboard box, instructing another of the children to look out back. He took that box and cut it into something of a triangle and stuffed the inside with a clean white blanket from one of his cabinets. The hodge-podge of things added up, and the box became something luxuri-ous, so many odds and ends sticking up and down that it looked like comfort itself, exhibiting the elegance of excess. It looked like nothing else anyone had ever seen. With that, he set Bernardo on his back, halfway sitting up, into the box, and put the box onto the plywood square.

Then he arranged the six children three on a side.

"You'll be careful?" he asked, and they all said *yes* and nodded seriously.

"Do you know where Don Miguel Torres lives?" he asked.

They all nodded their heads again.

"Then, very carefully, I want you to lift the dog, everybody tak-ing care, and then carry him over to Sr. Torres's place. Can you do that?"

They all nodded *of course*.

"All right, then. Let's go." With that, he had them lift the dog and carry it outside on this fine bed. Dr. Bartolomeo knew that he had to keep Bernardo quiet and safe, away from the stitches, and he did not want him to throw up from the anesthesia. This seemed like a good plan. And with all these children here, it was a little bit of theater as well. He needed to count them all as being on his side, as he would be seeing them all for the next—who knew?— fifty years perhaps.

As they started off, Narciso thought of Bernardo—this medium-sized, light-colored, shaggy-haired apparition—as a fine, ancient, well-fed potentate on a sedan chair carried by servants and fanned with palm fronds, but he kept the thought to himself as an amusement of his own, something not always easily explained to others. Still, it made him wish he had a camera.

But he needn't have worried. Everyone laughed and wanted to follow along. The teacher, Sra. Maldonado, said *no*, but with only half a heart. She was friends with Dr. Bartolomeo, and they looked at each other with laughter as well.

"All right," said Sra. Maldonado, "some of you can go. But those who need to leave school early today, you stay here and get checked first."

It was a compromise, and good enough, even with some complaints.

Sitting up instead of lying on his back, and groggy from the medication Dr. Bartolomeo had administered, his paws waving this way and that, Bernardo and his entourage started their voyage, stepping away from the doctor's office and into the street.

Just as the children set out carrying the dog, carefully up above their heads, a car passed by, very slowly, on the other side of the street, a car with a flat roof, the driver looking with some bemuse-ment at the dog and parade.

❖

Sra. Guillermina Belmares, who knew everything regarding this town, and everybody, and who was normally hard at work selling dairy products from her stall in the *mercado*, and was familiar with animals because her family had a dairy and raised cattle and farm animals as well, happened to have stepped away from her work and was on her way to do an errand. As she walked along the street at that very same moment, she saw what she would later describe as the most startling thing she had ever seen. And she fainted straightaway.

The details were these: As the car passed slowly in front of her, the driver looking at the dog, Sra. Belmares's view of the children was obscured. All that was left to her to see was the dog, mouth muscles relaxed from the medication and drooping open a little, giving his face the appearance of a smile, and wearing what suddenly looked to her like a royal collar, and reclining on what looked just as suddenly like a flying carpet, flying easy as anything down the street with the cars.

It was an illusion easily enough explained later, but at that moment the false impression spoke for itself with the parts that she saw. *Behold, the Great Bernardo!* one could have said, and to her it would have made a perfect kind of sense, a part of the moment that fit.

"But I saw it!" said Sra. Belmares.

What she saw was, for a half-second, difficult to decipher. It was not the evil eye, because the look the dog gave her was the only look that dogs have, finally, all love. But the dog did look at her. And smiled.

It was not *susto*, because she was not afraid; nor was the dog trying to scare her.

It was disbelief—that is what it was most and for which there are so few words, perhaps only the despairing and imploring *Dios mío, Dios mío*, which covers everything and were precisely the words she used. To that extent, she was fully in control of her senses, enough to know what to say. This was nothing Sra. Castañeda could have fixed.

And so the woman fainted. Straightaway, not two seconds after what she had seen and then thought, falling in a perfect corkscrew motion to the ground. It was a great stroke of luck that Dr. Bartolomeo was still standing there minding that the children were careful with their charge. He was not fast enough to help her on the way down, but he was there to help her up, to fan her face and make sure she was all right, or as all right as she could be.

"But I saw it!" said Sra. Belmares, again.

It was not fear, finally, that she tried to communicate when she came out of her faint. It was amazement—*But I saw it!*—yet the harder she tried to explain, the harder everyone laughed, including the doctor. Sra. Belmares took that laughter in good stead, assuming it to be a kind of amazement, too, and a good way to feel about the state of the world wherein such a thing might be possible. But whether this was the future, as the doctor so often discussed, or the past, which came to her from her schoolbooks, she could not say, not in the moment. It was simply a flying dog, one more marvel one was lucky to have seen in one's own lifetime.

When Miguel Torres showed up to thank Dr. Bartolomeo, all the fuss had died down, but a new part of the day's history began. Dr. Bartolomeo asked Don Miguel if he would mind very much bringing Bernardo back, or letting the children bring him back. He would explain later. As Dr. Bartolomeo had taken such good care of Bernardo, and since it was the doctor who was asking, Don Miguel agreed readily.

For the sake of Sra. Belmares, who did not understand why everyone was laughing, the doctor decided to reconstruct what had happened, taking into account everyone's stories, even to having the children repeat the performance.

When he explained it to the children, telling them what Sra. Belmares had seen, they laughed as hard as they could and were eager for the reconstruction, telling everyone they knew to come and watch.

Bernardo was now king of the town, or the grand pasha or the venerated caliph, the poobah, the *magnífico*—the children came up with many names, very much impressing Narciso, as this was an indication that they were paying attention in school, which made him feel even better about the future—and everyone wanted to hold Bernardo up high and be part of the story. Bernardo himself, once he was feeling better and no longer groggy from the medication, was not eager to cooperate at first, but he was a good dog, and happy enough to be easily persuaded to help the children in their own happiness. It was a good day.

And when they did carry him, all under the watchful eye of Dr. Bartolomeo but with everyone in town there to watch as well, and with street vendors, having arrived out of nowhere, selling sugared plantains and cucumbers with lemon and chili, every flavor of *paleta*, and others selling leather belts—where does everyone come from? wondered Narciso—Bernardo, as it turned out, had a big grin naturally, and because of his coloring it was better seen when he was held up high and people had to look up to see him. That part of Sra. Belmares's story reproduced itself easily.

"That's it," she said, standing there as well. "I saw that dog laughing. I told you." That was enough for her, and she nodded her head in a firm *yes* to show she was right, and everyone agreed because they could see it, too, plain as anything. The part about the flying carpet, that part didn't matter so much to her, not with everyone laughing so hard. The explanation was a ridiculous waste of time but good enough—even she could have explained it, and people could get on with their business, she said.

"But I saw it," someone from the back of the crowd mimicked, a little cruelly Dr. Bartolomeo thought, no matter that everyone laughed and that he himself had the urge.

It did not happen that way, Sra. Belmares would claim thereafter, and with authority. But everyone who had been there knew.

And in the annals of the Forward Science Society, which Dr. Bartolomeo was careful to write down for posterity at the end of each week, even many years later the four paragraphs concerning the possibility of a dog flying on a floating carpet were the most read and the selections always referred to when someone was telling the story of this town.

The curious last chapter of Bernardo's part in the chronicle came later, however, when somebody looking through the notebook, kept rather casually in the town's small memento museum, ripped out the unnumbered page with the third and fourth paragraphs of the story, which were Dr. Bartolomeo's very good, succinct, and scientific explanation of what happened.

People remembered for a while that they had been there, those two paragraphs, but they were no longer in the society's journal, written out. All that was left was Sra. Belmares's colorful and clear telling, and since she was well regarded and knew everything else concerning the details of the town's history, and was quoted widely elsewhere regarding other details of the town, the first two paragraphs remained as the day's full and permanent account, as written in his own hand by Dr. Narciso Bartolomeo himself.

CLUBS, SOCIAL EVENTS

Women's Page

MRS. TOM SCHMIDT

Hospitality Night Program At Army Post Meets With Success

"Hospitality Night" at Fort Huachuca met with great success last Friday evening when the visitors who attended the dance came laden with home-made cookies and cakes to be served to the boys during the intermission period.

Over 500 soldiers were served, and to many it was the first of home-made "goodies" in many months.

Residents of Bisbee, Douglas and Nogales participated in the program. It is planned to make it a monthly occasion.

Already residents of Douglas are making a monthly "hospitality" trip to the Fort when they visit, sew and exchange ideas on the various parts of the country.

———o———

Hollywood Visitor

D. W. McLean of Hollywood arrived yesterday in Nogales for a visit. He formerly resided at the ranch of General and Mrs. Lowell Rooks.

English Girl To Become Bride Of Nogalian

Miss Agnes Christine Fogg of Warrington, Lancashire, England, bride-elect of Alberto A. Rios, son of Mrs. Refugio Rios, 107 West Street, arrived in Nogales Monday. The couple plan to be married in the near future.

Miss Fogg arrived in New York City September 23rd aboard the S. S. Media. She was met in Salt Lake City by her fiance. This is the first time the Rios family has seen Alberto since he left for England three years ago with the U. S. Air Force. He was recently discharged as a staff sergeant.

———o———

Welsh Rabbit is delicious served on toast or crackers; it's also good served on hot cooked drained elbow macaroni.

THE NEWSPAPER STORY

Everybody reads it. This is even more true if what one is reading is toward the back, where the real news in a small town is reported. All the front matter comes from somewhere else, that big front page of make-believe. But a small note in the obituaries or the engagements or the "who is visiting town" sections—these are the real news, and the smaller the bigger.

A small town is no less the small patch of sky
Above it,
Even in the smallest part of that sky a thousand stars,
More, even—a million, like words,
Some shining, some behind others
But so many, always, before and after us
So many pinpricks and moth-holes, glitter and sand,
So much,
A campfire doused into risen sparks.
A small town makes a small scar in time,
A stopping place, uneven, if just for a moment,
A moment—which in small towns is called a hundred years,
Just for a moment, this place in time, these people,
These stars, this brightness you see and which we think is
The sun and the moon and the stars and the eyes of owls
All drawn together
But the daytime of a small town
Is made as much by all the lives
Having been alive here, right where you stand,
Bright every one and even now.

2

Lent and Given

On the first day of Lent, their small Catholic town caught fire with the holy business of giving things up. Had people planned ahead, the way old Padre Nacho had been suggesting, as he always did when his flock became impassioned, they might have been more reflective. But year after year, his calls for temperance at heightened moments fell on deaf ears, maybe because Padre Nacho himself got so worked up about moderation.

Everyone, like it or not, fanned these flames in this part of Sonora, in northwestern Mexico—who, after all, had ever heard of not giving something up for Lent? It was like a school project and they all were young again, wanting to please the teacher, but a school project that was also a race.

So the competition to give things up began, and to give up something better than someone else.

"Gum," said little Ernesto, a sincere second-grader, before school, feeling good that he thought of something first.

"Candy," declared Lichita, a fourth-grader who couldn't let a second-grader top her.

Soon all the elementary schoolchildren had sacrificed their favorite food—upping the ante to cookies, cake, ice cream, or *gorditas*, or chicken and rice, and even beans, and so on, with no end in sight.

Until they went, "Oooh," on the playground when Ulises, in sixth grade, said he was giving up eating entirely. But he was the school clown and chubby, so opinion was divided if he won or not.

Adults were no less resolute.

"It's desserts for me," said Ulises's father, Sr. Torres, the garbage man, to anyone who would listen during his early-morning route. The dirt from his job blended with the residue of Ash Wednesday so convincingly on his forehead that some households speculated maybe he had returned to Padre Nacho for seconds.

"Yes," those who were awake answered him. "Desserts. That's good, Sr. Torres. But it's meat for me," they would say, meat or beer. Always something a little more than whatever Sr. Torres would offer up. He was only the garbage man, after all.

As lunchtime got closer, food and drink all started to take shape as something beyond generics. Meat became hamburger. Soda evolved into Coca-Cola. Dessert—well, there were so many. Which one?

"What do I do here?" asked Guillermina Belmares, who managed the *mercado*. Were fried plantains sprinkled with sugar desserts, or fruits helped along?

And candy took on names of a very large family, each with its own unforgettable face—*cajeta*, fudge, *paletas*. "Candy" as a concept was easier to give up than "Hershey's bars." Something specific raised the stakes. Hearing "Hershey's bar" made a person want to eat one. That made this giving up of things more difficult, as everybody suddenly hungered for things they seldom thought to want.

❖

The sighs of what the town was giving up put a small breeze into the air the first days of Lent. People walked around as if hung over, unable to believe what they had done the night before.

But what had they done?—not dance on top of the bar while everyone clapped. Restraint, not abandon, caused this hangover.

As things heated up, people gave up more: perfumes and baths and outings and music and sex and everything else, a piece at a time. Pretty soon, if it was in that town, someone gave it up.

The schoolchildren, too, thought of new things to renounce beyond sweets—stuffed animals, toys, games—but it was too late. Kids knew that once you said something you couldn't take it back, unless a grownup said to. But when the schoolchildren finally imagined the idea of giving up laughter, the very suggestion made them giggle, defeating the purpose.

And relieving Ulises, the comical sixth-grader. Sort of. His father, Sr. Torres, the garbage man, told him to stop fooling around—nobody can give up eating for Lent!—so Ulises switched to joke-telling, but with a caveat: joke-telling during class. That would be all right.

Finally, everything was heard to be given up, until the last person—the town's lawyer, Ubaldo Dos Santos—had no choice but to give up sin itself.

Everyone applauded. But they also were envious. Not only did he find something really great to give up, but it made him famous, too. Some people have all the luck, they would say.

This giving up of things was especially hard on the merchants. "Giving up" is the opposite of "I'm buying this," and even sales were seen only as temptations. People would walk quickly past threads and fabrics at the Marisol and the boot sign in front of the narrow Hermanos Celaya shoemaker's shop.

Don Noé, the butcher, was hardest hit and could only throw up his hands. "Candy," he would say. "*That's* something to give up. It rots your teeth."

❖

All this might explain the strange story of Sr. Oswaldo Calderón Segundo.

Or Sr. O, as people began calling him almost immediately after his birth. His mouth kept opening in what looked like wonderment, like surprise, so that he seemed to be saying "oh" to everything and everybody. In elementary school he became the teacher's pet because of this, the instructors feeling flattered, and in middle school bullies and clowns alike preferred him to witness their mischief because the automatic "oh" equaled something like applause.

He was "Segundo" not from his father, Horacio, the bookkeeper, but from an almost brother, also named Oswaldo, who had died from a too-small heart a few years before. Horacio and his wife, Flora, the seamstress, wanted to keep their first child alive, and this was their way. Oswaldo felt like he had a twin somewhere, which was all right with him.

After Dr. Bartolomeo announced in front of his office Oswaldo Segundo's birth, Horacio and Flora carried the newborn to the church. They wanted to ensure that this new Oswaldo was put into the world the right way, fearing they had done something wrong the last time by waiting a few days.

As soon as Maricela Blanco, Padre Nacho's clerk, read his birth certificate aloud when they were registering his baptism, the baby's fate was sealed. *Oswaldo Calderón Segundo*, Maricela Blanco started with a serious face, but by the end of the name her face contorted with amusement. The infant made such a loud and visible "oh" that she could not help herself.

"I will give up *fotonovelas* for Lent next year," she said afterward to Padre Nacho. "I'm so sorry. I didn't mean to laugh. I just couldn't believe it. He seemed to know his name, right then and there."

Her laughter had been contagious to others but disheartening to Oswaldo's parents, who tried to be stoic. After a few moments, however, Oswaldo's parents ended up with slightly bent lips themselves and then gave in to laughter.

"What should we do, then, to repent?" asked Flora as the family walked home, Oswaldo in her arms. She suggested that perhaps this boy was doing the work of two, and that everyone saw it, including the boy himself.

"Nothing. It's too late," said his father, and that was the end of it. "Little Sr. O here will have to find the answer to that."

Some people were confused when they heard his name, thinking it was "Señoro," a cross between *señorito* and *señora*, and a curious new word worth discussing, but they refrained because they didn't want to make trouble. That's how it was with Oswaldo— perplexing no matter which way he turned.

After finishing high school Oswaldo worked through the years at one thing and another, all basic, and was good at most but not great. This adequacy explained his living arrangements—he made enough money to live on his own, which he began to do with his parents' blessing after he turned twenty-one, but only could afford to rent a one-room afterthought of a house around the corner from them.

Even when he was young, and certainly when he got older, Oswaldo could be depended on when there was a house to build or furniture to move. When a strong wind knocked things down, he helped to pick them up. It was not uncommon to see the middle-aged everyman almost anywhere doing something that had no exact name. People realized pretty fast that "laborer" wasn't right because sometimes he didn't, in fact, labor at a task. A few observers floated "handyman," but that suggested Sr. O was dexterous, and while sometimes he was, sometimes he wasn't, so that got nixed too, not so much because of the logic, since they didn't know exactly what *dexterous* meant, but because of the person who conveyed it: Ubaldo Dos Santos, the lawyer. Not to see Oswaldo on any given day was stranger than seeing him. One supposed him equal in this sense to the town's trees or buildings: invariably there, even if only in the background.

In this way, and after so many years, Sr. O became invisible for much of the day. Nobody was unkind or inhumane—he was a regular person in church and in the evenings and when he shopped. And women, when they noticed him, always offered a smile, but as if toward a puppy or a harmless stranger just passing through town, so Oswaldo never courted or married, though he would have liked to. If he had a job to do, people saw but didn't see him. Still, the townspeople were goodhearted and did their best to say, "Good day," to him or give a nice nod of the head. But when Oswaldo was at work, and when the town was at work, people easily looked right through him. After many years of this, even his parents, who later both passed away peacefully of old age, one within months of the other, did not necessarily see him. They loved him, but they didn't always look up.

Dogs, too, let him pass by without raising their heads.

❖

Lent lasts for forty days and forty nights, which is how people always say it: "Forty days and forty nights." But as even little Ernesto the second-grader said, all those numbers sounded like they needed to be added together. Forty of this and forty of that made eighty separate things, totaled Lichita the fourth-grader, doing the math for Ernesto. So Lent, especially in the middle, seemed like forever to give up things, for kids and grownups alike, and something like hell happened to time. There may have been a lesson in that, but it got as lost in the middle as did everything else.

Then the townspeople found out something else they didn't like. At Sunday mass about one-quarter through Lent, quite nonchalantly, as if everybody knew this already—which they did but always forgot—the priest told them that Sundays don't count in those forty days and forty nights.

The word *lent* means "lengthen," Padre Nacho reminded them, and stands for that time in spring when the days grow longer.

"The original period of Lent was forty hours, as hours were measured then. It was spent fasting to commemorate the suffering of Christ and the forty hours He spent in the tomb.

"In the early third century," Padre Nacho finished, "Lent was lengthened to six days. In about the year 800 it was changed to forty days."

He did not elucidate, even though it seemed to everyone that someone had some explaining to do.

Oswaldo's countenance—"Oh!"—spoke for the congregation, himself included.

Nobody said anything about it. And everyone went around smiling. But that's not how they felt, especially at home, where they spoke their minds. Even the goodhearted people, and that was mostly everyone, got short-tempered and unsure. But their upset was not noticeable in public, unless one went to Don Chuy, the barber, in which case the honesty of his shaking hand drew a little blood now and then.

This was why people painted their walls and cleaned their houses and washed the dogs during Lent—as elaborate ruses to divert attention and make good things stand out. The louder and shinier and bigger the good thing, the better.

This worked well except for Oswaldo. Sr. O started to see things, even as he himself was not seen. Oswaldo had always seen things, of course, but these new things were different. Sr. O started to see people breaking their promises. Catching one person is not so much and doesn't amount to a great deal. But what about three, seven, or ten? Sra. Dos Santos, who ran the boarding house and was the sister-in-law of Ubaldo the lawyer, for example, ordered an *agua de manzana* because how could something called "*agua*" be soda, after all? And Sr. Jaramillo, the mortician, went back on his word not to complain because exposing bad manners is simply proper etiquette.

After a week or so of moving around invisible like a ghost, Sr. O had seen, as far as he could tell, everyone do something to the left or right of what they had promised—including the priest, who, when hungry, was not always patient or forgiving when listening to long confessions. Each night Oswaldo fell asleep reciting this extensive and still-growing list.

Sr. O thought to reassure everyone by giving a little smile or shrugging his shoulders, but nobody saw him. As was their habit, they saw through him. Sr. O figured that nobody was worried, since his knowing didn't seem to have any effect on them. Doing whatever they had done—breaking whatever promise they had made—didn't matter to them, he surmised. So Oswaldo learned a great lesson. And with this knowledge he changed the town.

His idea was simple. It was almost scientific in its deductive reasoning, something that could have come from the records of the Forward Science Society, or from Dr. Narciso Bartolomeo himself, who was not only the town's doctor but its philosopher as well, and who cut back on pontificating with his index finger for Lent, though he did so quietly as a nod to his dead mother, not to science. No one had asked Oswaldo what he gave up for Lent, as they had not seen him. But he had given something up, all right. He decided to give up the giving up of things.

❖

Rather than taking away, his must be a route of excess. At first this seemed like a trick, but the logic was clear enough. When people found out, they thought about it and talked about it, and finally shook their heads *yes*, like it or not. Giving up the giving up of things: that was something, and so it counted.

Because Sr. O's charge was to indulge where others could not, he gained a sort of authority, though people were slow to realize it. Ghosts have power, after all, whether one believes in them or not.

"They do, too—ghosts count," insisted Gabriela, the high school senior class president, to her little brother Ulises, the primary school clown, when walking the sixth-grader home from school one day, forgetting that she wasn't going to be a know-it-all for Lent. Since she was a straight-A student, that put an end to that, especially after their father, Sr. Torres, the garbage man, told them no fighting at the dinner table. Fighting dishonored their beloved dead mother, Fernanda, who went to heaven much too early because of the cancer; and the towns-people always agreed, but this was too sad for them to talk about, except to praise Dr. Bartolomeo for his bedside manner, Sr. Jaramillo the mortician for his handiwork, and Padre Nacho for the eulogy.

At first what Oswaldo tried was small enough to ignore. The tongue tore off one of his work boots, and he did not have it repaired, much to the bafflement of the Hermanos Celaya shoe-maker's shop. Oswaldo put on cologne to work the odd jobs he found. He stretched the four or five rubber bands that he would use later in the day around his right ear instead of putting them in his pocket.

Then he ate dessert for lunch. He ate this meal at Don Lázaro's bakery, which Oswaldo had all to himself—no waiting—on a Thursday almost midway through Lent.

On Friday he had breakfast for lunch, but since townsfolk were all in their houses, at work or school, or at Rosa Laura's restaurant, nobody saw him. On Saturday, when Sr. O continued to upend culinary traditions, some people noticed. They noticed, however, because the proprietor had told them, even though Don Lázaro had promised to give up gossiping but didn't in this case because it was for the town's own good, he said.

Padre Nacho, who eventually found out just about everything because of confessions, shook his head, not just at Don Lázaro but at the whole town. And at Oswaldo most of all.

Oswaldo became a regular at the bakery for lunch, and even a few times for dinner. After the late afternoon crowd, the bakery was again empty for dinner, and the place was his. People who hadn't given up sweets for Lent started dropping in for dessert later in the evening, as Oswaldo lounged with a full belly, and thought at first that he frequented the bakery to make a virtuous point because he always left without seeming to order anything. They nodded their heads and looked down, a little embarrassed at themselves.

After some days of this, Don Lázaro and Oswaldo became friends, more than they had been, anyway. As Oswaldo ate one thing, then another, Don Lázaro began to bake savories especially for him, like giant empanadas with several portions of pineapple filling. This saved Oswaldo time because he could eat just one for his meal instead of many small servings, which is how empanadas normally came.

When Don Lázaro baked him an enormous pretzel, however, things changed—not on account of the treat, which Oswaldo found much to his liking, but because of something Don Lázaro mentioned casually.

"Pretzels," Don Lázaro said with a nod of his head, "they're perfect for Lent. Did you know that? The Germans made them like they are. The crossed arms of the dough were intended to look like a Christian at prayer, with palms on opposite shoulders and forearms crisscrossed." Don Lázaro crossed his forearms thusly.

Oswaldo had not seen it before, but he saw it now. He even said, "Oh!" Suddenly, the bakery felt a little closer to the church. Oswaldo excused himself and left, as he was not so confident in his plan to go quite so near to God with it.

Sr. O took up residence the next day at Rosa Laura's restaurant. He ordered dinner for breakfast, then returned in the evening to request breakfast for dinner, and he had Coca-Cola both times.

There was meat in his dinner order, noted Gabriela, the straight-A student and high school senior class president, interrupting her birthday celebration. But nobody was listening because her little brother Ulises wanted to do the same thing as Oswaldo, and because their father, Sr. Torres, told both his children to stop it. Then the birthday cake came out and they forgot about Oswaldo's supper. Especially since Sr. Torres couldn't eat even one bite because he had given up desserts for Lent—meaning more for Ulises, the chubby child chirped. But first he had to help blow out all the candles, Gabriela insisted in her know-it-all voice, causing Sr. Torres to tell his children to stop it again because their beloved dead mother, Fernanda, wouldn't like this, and the other customers nodded their heads and said quietly to each other that this was too sad to talk about, but what a caring doctor, and the mortician did such lifelike work, and the priest's words touched them still. Oswaldo agreed, to himself.

At church that Sunday, Sr. O felt better about things, and braver, having had the opportunity to digest his thoughts. During the service Oswaldo took a deep breath. And then he did it. He prayed to be rich. When no thunder struck, when no walls came tumbling down, Sr. O added: *To be rich rich rich rich.*

Oswaldo knew he should run this by Padre Nacho, and maybe he would. In time. Meanwhile, the people in town began to look at Sr. O. They could see his smile kept getting bigger even as theirs kept getting smaller. Oswaldo became not a man in a circus but a circus of a man: himself the thing. He was the dancing bear and the clown on stilts, the strongman with the mustache and the bearded lady, the jugglers and the acrobats, the motorcyclist in a cage and the human cannonball. Sr. O was everything, but nothing for long.

Then he wore his one suit to work, which on that day was cleaning out sludge from the alley behind all the stores on Obregón Street, and the sight of him dumbfounded Don Noé, the beset butcher with few customers. The next evening, Oswaldo strolled around the perimeter of the town while reciting the sole poem he knew, and that only partially, much to the consternation of Sr. Jaramillo, the mortician, who changed his mind to a degree when it dawned on him that he had another example of bad manners to complain about. During siestas, Oswaldo engaged in calisthenics, a regimen Dr. Bartolomeo found out about when giving him a physical but didn't know what to do about it because regular exercise was a good thing.

All this soon became a show to the children, a fascination to the adults, and a story to the newspaper—though one it could not publish, said Sr. Velez, the editor, on the phone from the city, whenever townspeople would call from the community phone at the *mercado*, because who would believe such things? So even when people talked about what Sr. O did, and no matter how hard he tried, Oswaldo stayed invisible.

"*No me digas,*" one neighbor would say to the other after hearing of the latest escapade. "I don't believe it!" The person would shake her head *no*. What Oswaldo was doing wasn't being done. It was that simple. "Whoever heard of something like that?" her acquaintance would echo, both shaking their heads *no*. That moment was bigger than a judge's ruling in a court. If people talking across their backyards decided something, or if the consensus at Don Chuy's barbershop did, that was it. Whatever the newspaper or the mayor—who gave up campaigning for Lent, except when he didn't—or any other official said was irrelevant, no matter how long they talked or how big their words were.

"Perhaps someone should ask Padre Nacho about this," the neighbors inevitably said, since this could be a matter for a higher authority, but without volunteering to bring it up to him.

Besides, it was already too late. The next week something else started to happen, like an earthquake. It was a quiet tremor, to be sure, because this was a nice town, but there it was.

People began to help Oswaldo in his giving up of giving up things—not by stripping him of possessions or otherwise making him poorer. The exact opposite. They heaped upon him their temptations.

People did it perhaps out of generosity—if they could not indulge, at least someone could, and they could watch. Or perhaps they were afraid that he had seen them lapse, even though they pretended not to notice his watching, and hoped the gesture would keep him from telling on them. Maybe they were just considerate. Or maybe this was a sign of their reverence—each gift, each item they left him, a kind of prayer. They could have been spiting God, too, but only a little since it was a good town.

Regardless of why, it simply happened. And the more it happened, the more it happened even more.

Things began slowly. Somebody slipped him a Coca-Cola, and then another, and another—though from the third onward Oswaldo asked for an orange Fanta instead. He started to find cookies on his doorstep. Next, chocolates stacked by the door at lunch, then a variety of meats at dinner, including, by the end of the first week, goat, beef, quails, and what smelled—*Oh,* his face said—like aging deer.

Just about none of the townspeople could afford much, and no one owned a television yet, not even the doctor or lawyer or mayor, so what each brought him was small. But a lot of people bringing even a little adds up. And with so many people knowing, or suspecting, that Sr. O had seen how they had twisted Lent, they brought him not just one small thing, but a small thing every day. Except, of course, for Padre Nacho, who felt he had nothing to give and wanted no part in this anyway, and a very few other important people like the doctor, who needed his possessions and didn't believe in what he called nonsense, though he said it quietly, sometimes pointing his index finger, to be sure, because he could not help it, but at the same moment remembering his dead mother.

Soon Oswaldo had many more of things than he could eat or use: rabbits and salsas and sweet *jamaica,* shovels and umbrellas and fancy hats. A purse, worn but still nice. He wasn't good at smoking, but if he wanted to look like Pedro Infante or Jorge Negrete in the movies that the townspeople occasionally went to in the city, some needing to hitch rides with others, Sr. O now had cigarettes and cigarette holders. Also at Oswaldo's disposal: a pair of binoculars, several radios, a plaster Virgin of Guadalupe, and red lipstick.

He did not complain, even with the work of taking care of everything becoming his job then, for Oswaldo was getting *rich rich rich rich,* by the town's standards anyway. Though he did wish he were a twin since there was so much to partake in. Or that he were a bookkeeper like his father had been, for there were so many entries to keep track of. The bicycle was handy, and the flashlight worked. The sheep needed to be fed, but there was food enough among the offerings. Some things came in pairs: dice and cards; shirt and pants; crutches. The stockpile was a sight to behold, though at night much of it was a nuisance, and sometimes a noisy nuisance. Even Paquita the cow mistakenly found her way into the mix, ushered along by the barking of Bernardo the dog after happening by this circus and wanting to join in.

The lawyer, Ubaldo Dos Santos, who professed no sinning, had to agree that Sr. O bested him at Lent. And Sra. Dos Santos, his sister-in-law, who ran the boardinghouse, raised her glass of *agua de manzana* to Sr. O at Rosa Laura's restaurant one night.

Oswaldo wished he could tell his parents about all this, but they had died many years ago. He shared the news anyway at the tasteful gravesites arranged for by Sr. Jaramillo, the mortician.

The other person Oswaldo wanted to fill in also had passed away long ago: Maricela Blanco, Padre Nacho's clerk, who, though she didn't mean it, had sort of laughed at his baptism, as Sr. O understood things.

❖

Oswaldo had not taken up cursing. He didn't have the stomach for it. But that didn't stop others. After a week of things mounting up, there was no getting around his house and its treasures. "What the hell!" said a startled Doña Clotilde, the new postmistress, when she walked by. She couldn't help herself. But nobody heard. She looked around to be sure, crossed herself, and surveyed the house again.

Just then, Sra. Jauregui, the aged widow who weighed nothing, came by and threw her hands up to her face.

"*Madre de Dios,*" she gasped.

"Yes, that's just what I was saying," said Doña Clotilde.

When Oswaldo stuck his head out to see what the fuss was about, he had to crane his neck to see over the deposited bounty. He couldn't keep up with things. Bottles of Coke stuck out like horns from a big pumpkin that also featured two eyes made of prunes that had dropped from a bag and a mouth made from a wriggling worm that had beaten Oswaldo to this dinner.

The two women were already walking backward, away from this apparition. Oswaldo sticking his head out from between its horns made them scamper.

"It's the devil!" shouted Sra. Jauregui in between breaths.

"It better be," said Doña Clotilde.

Pretty soon Sr. O had so much stuff mounded and bundled and piled that he had to build a fence, and then a second fence, but the profusion spilled out beyond his yard.

Things got a little scary when a determined Chucho Reyes, the baker's helper, tried to steal something. But it turned out that the small stove had belonged to him to start with, so nobody was sure what to do. Townspeople who caught him dragging it down the street demanded an arrest. But Officer Maldonado discovered upon investigation that the well-meaning soul simply got carried away in the hoopla of giving up and needed the appliance after all. When Chucho Reyes replaced the stove with a painted breadbox, the matter was quietly dropped. The outcome met the approval of Padre Nacho, who had been asked to intervene by Oswaldo even though everyone knew the priest had no jurisdiction here. Nobody mentioned the stolen stove again.

Except Padre Nacho. With everyone so interested in Lent, he had them where he wanted them. Or did he? People dragged themselves to church but rushed over to Sr. O's at word of something new being left.

That's when things changed altogether.

In place of a sermon, Padre Nacho decided to read the newspaper aloud on Sundays. Besides big people like the doctor and lawyer and mayor, the priest—or rather the church—was the only one who could afford a subscription, or who bothered to subscribe, anyway, so almost everyone depended on him most of all for details regarding the world. The radio worked well and gave the town its immediate and loud news. But the newspaper, as read by Padre Nacho, gave meaning to current events. A well-enunciated *and* or a crucial *therefore*—these nuances made all the difference.

He had tried sermons for decades, but there wasn't much to be said for their success. Then again, since it was a nice town, some credit was due to Padre Nacho, Dr. Bartolomeo would philosophize, soothing the priest in one way but not in others. The stifled yawning and polite smiling, the occasional snoring, and the elbows into the rib cages made the parishioners look gruesome to Padre Nacho. Like a horror movie, he told Oswaldo on afternoons when Sr. O helped out at the church as Lent wound down.

"Sra. Jauregui is so goodhearted. But when she starts to lean over falling asleep, I hold my breath," he would say about the aged widow who weighed nothing. "Or Doña Clotilde," the new postmistress, he would shake his head. "When she takes a deep breath and knits her eyebrows in concentration and bites the insides of her mouth, her eyes bulge out so much that she looks like a bull spotting the red cape." The two men would laugh, but the vision unsettled them.

"You should try something different, you know, on Sundays," said Oswaldo one afternoon late in Lent as they scraped wax from the altar candleholders in between snacking on one of Don Lázaro's pretzels. "Tell them things they don't know."

"But my son, I tell the stories of God."

"And it's a good thing, of course. But even I know those stories, Father, sir," said Oswaldo. "And you tell them over and over. I like them, to be sure." Here he made the sign of the cross quickly. "But, forgive me, Father, don't you think, well, something new, something new wouldn't hurt?"

The priest said nothing but nodded his head. The next Sunday Padre Nacho began his sermon by pulling out the newspaper from the shelf on the lectern. He put his glasses on and his elbows up, folding the paper first one way, then another, until he got it straight, with the front page under his scrutiny.

The editions found their way to him in bundles of several days, as the circulation department would not deliver every day just for the likes of him. On this Sunday he found himself reading about last Tuesday, although nobody seemed to notice or mind.

The tenor of his stories, however, was everything. George VI had died and his daughter became the queen, Elizabeth II. The NATO conference had approved a European army. The AEC— whoever or whatever that was—had announced "satisfactory" experiments in hydrogen-weapons research. Eyewitnesses told of blasts near Enewetak. He wanted to ask if anyone knew where Enewetak was, perhaps Gabriela, the straight-A student and, after all, high school senior class president, but thought better of it.

That week, Oswaldo continued to reap the benefits of everyone's Lent, but the donations tapered off, which didn't bother him given all he had to curate.

The next Sunday, Palm Sunday, which was when some townspeople liked to debut their new footwear from Hermanos Celaya shoemaker's shop, Padre Nacho announced that Albert Schweitzer had won the Nobel Peace Prize and that he did his medical missionary work in French Equatorial Africa. Padre Nacho saying he was a good man made people remember that name.

After Padre Nacho got started with these new Sunday readings, everybody began to listen and put Lent, about over, back into proportion. Everything was righted by Good Friday. Or it could have been Easter Sunday. But it was one of the two, the townspeople agreed, because both made sense, and that was good enough—even for the priest. And for Sr. O because he got to keep all that had made its way to him.

The church put the world into context. Or, wondered Dr. Bartolomeo, raising his index finger since he also was the town's philosopher, was it the other way around? The townspeople couldn't decide and didn't care. Besides, they came to realize they liked both answers here too. Everybody being right sat well with the town.

Oswaldo sat in the front pew, every time. He had the leisure to be there, and to keep helping, since now, as things turned out, he was one of the richest people in town. But he would have been there anyway. A good story, after all, is a good story, and gives up nothing.

Parroquia de la Purisima Concepcion

CERTIFICADO DE MATRIMONIO

En la Parroquia de la Purísima Concepción en _Nogales Sonora_

a los _30_ del mes de _Noviembre_ del Año de mil novecientos _cincuenta_

_____ contrajeron matrimonio el Señor _Jesus_

Urbina y la _Sra. Refugio_

Martinez

Fueron testigos _Santiago Ayala_

Ma. Jesus Varela

Ofició el Presbítero _Ignacio de la Torre_

y en la misa de velación, el Presbítero _Ignacio de la Torre_

Doy fé de que este asiento aparece en el libro de matrimonios núme-

ro _6_ página _45_ partida número _516_

Nogales, Sonora, a _15 de Enero de 1966_

El P._____

THE MARRIAGE CERTIFICATE

The laws are suspended on this day, on this day of happiness, but not the required forms that document it. On this day, even the laws of physics are argued, as someone invariably tries to fly, and succeeds. Wings come in the form of good feeling. Sometimes a refreshment helps.

But the forms. They are forms. No curlicues. No champagne toasts. Just blanks filled in, the institutional memory of marriage. No dancing.

The Office of the Registrar does not care for dancing.

3

Butter, Oranges, and Pink Coconut Candy

D on Perfecto Castañeda went to the market to buy some white cheese, as was his custom on most Tuesday mornings. He intended to buy the salty kind, the rancher cheese, not the creamy kind. He liked the taste of salt, even though the smoothness of cream in the mouth—or in cheese or in coffee or in anything else—this was not a taste he would choose to give up. Still, salt, salt was his longtime secret. Everyone knows about cream. But salt: salt always needs a special kind of attention, an attention Don Perfecto was willing to give. Even thinking about salt made his mouth water as he walked, which only underlined its attraction.

Acorns and nuts were like that as well—*bellotas*, the small, brown nuts, smaller than acorns, that fell from the black walnut trees that grew in the hollows of the hills, the *nogal* trees. They needed perhaps even more attention than salt, as salt was easier to come by than *bellotas*, *bellotas* and a growing list of other small wonders: mountain onions and buttermilk and roasted pumpkin seeds and *ciruelas*, the dried plums that sometimes cracked a tooth. These things were all tender in the world, hard to like at first taste but then tender in the heart for years afterward. Everybody remembered them, but in a busy world few people took care of them, finally. Some things like this had already disappeared, some of the old tastes he remembered from childhood. Their flavors had died, just like people he had known. Even their names were difficult to remember. Keeping these things in the world, thought Don Perfecto, this was his job—his job and his dinner.

As he thought about it, some apples, of course, some apples were already gone. He remembered some very particular green ones that had grown near his house when he was young. They were nowhere to be found now, no matter how much he looked for them. In those years so long ago there were two trees, next to each other, that had given such fruit in the summers of his youth that they were his youth itself. They were wild apples, and never grafted, which was the tragedy. When he talked to farmers through the years, he learned that the apples would never be found again. Apples grow from tree to tree by grafting, but not seed to seed, which changes them into some other kind of apple, a child apple recombined into an apple someplace in between the tastes of its two parents. Spinster apples and bachelor apples, these were the ones that needed some help to carry on in the world, but so rarely did anyone understand. Don Perfecto himself was a bachelor and knew something about this state of affairs.

Some medicines, too, were gone to him, but only because he had lost his mother, Doña Armida, who had both an eye and a hand for their incarnations in the hills and gardens around town. She understood and recognized roots, could hold their ugliness in her hands, and she could sort through leaves and stems with easy authority. She knew what to take from animals, from science, and from the earth itself, one thing not more or less important than the other. She could make the world seem right, and was so good at making the planet revolve smoothly that, until her passing, Perfecto had never thought to suspect that this world might be capable of acting otherwise. That was her way with things.

If Perfecto had tried to pay more attention to her, he might have learned more about the gifts abundant in the hills and scrub, the healing ingredients that were so plentiful because no one else knew what to make from them. But Doña Armida would go out at night as well, and he couldn't see what she was doing at all. What good was there to be learned from that? She would simply reach into dark places and come out with something in her hands and a smile on her face, a white root or a particular spider, a small creature sometimes alive enough to make even his mother nervous to hold it. That's not something to learn by seeing. It was something to learn only by doing, and he had neither the inclination nor the bravery, not then and not now.

With Doña Armida gone now, however, he was sorry he hadn't tried, and understood only more how good a mother she had been to him. With a thousand teas of *hierba buena* and *manzanilla, hierba cana* and *hierba de la princesa*, with *hierba doncella* and the dark *hierba mora*, which could only touch the lips for a half-second, the *yerba marina* that came with the sailors and the *hierba mate* that came from far away, all of these with their rules and etiquette for tasting or putting on the body, with her hands stained ochre and pink from the early fall leaves in the desert, with the herbs she put in the food—*they're good for you*, she would say—the *romero* and sweet basil, with the plants she pulled up right from the ground and then turned into dinner, the *verdolagas*, and the *tuna* fruits she pulled off the cactus and de-thorned for the family: With all of this, Doña Armida had kept the vagaries of life at a distance, though finally at a great cost to herself.

But that was a long time ago.

Don Perfecto was thinking of her this morning as he asked for the salty cheese he had come to the mercado to buy.

"A kilo," he said to Sra. Belmares, who nodded. A kilo was what everyone asked for. He could have simply nodded, and she could have simply guessed.

That's how clear the world was here. Who, or why, would anyone want to do things any differently? What would be the sense in that?

❖

But which was it, then? Was the world clear and good and staying the same, or different and rude and changing all the time?

The answer was Berta Maldonado. After her, the answer would be clear. In fact, after her, there turns out to have been no question. Nothing would be the same, though perhaps for different reasons, reasons having little to do with things lost. Whatever he imagined romantic in things as they used to be or staying as they were, well, it soon enough changed. And soon enough it was not his mother he was thinking of.

Srta. Berta Maldonado, curiously enough, also shopped for cheese on Tuesday mornings, though her predilection was for the creamy kind. All the years since her childhood, Berta, who had herself learned from her own mother, had shopped at the market early, almost always arriving by seven in the morning. Don Perfecto had always preferred to shop at eight.

Curiously enough, in recent months, both had been shopping on the half hour between seven and eight, both of them in the *verdolagas* and *piñon* and live parrot aisles at about 7:30, both of them shopping for what was normal in a kitchen, both of them shopping for themselves, as they each lived alone these days, both their mothers having known each other and walked out of life almost together, unwilling to stop a good conversation.

Sra. Belmares, the cheese vendor, whose family ran the dairy, was not slow in noticing, and even less slow in saying something.

She said something even when she didn't know but only suspected. She said something even when she didn't suspect but thought it should be so. On occasion, she simply said something for the sake of saying something. Of course, regarding Perfecto and Berta, she did not say anything to Don Perfecto or to Berta, Berta whose mother and she had been close enough friends that they called each other *comadre* and baptized several of each other's children.

And what she said came straight from the dairy—*like chickens and roosters,* she said to Maricela Blanco; *like a bird and a bee, as they say,* she said to Flora, the seamstress who took orders once a week; *like a cow and a bull,* she said, but quietly and only to herself— herself and the few passersby who happened to know what she was talking about, if only because it was all she'd talked about these last months. And she would wink at them, which was like underlining the meaning of her whisper. Everyone would laugh and nod their understanding, to which Sra. Belmares would always add, with emphasis, *What is taking so long?*

Sra. Belmares was not the only one. Everyone knew that Perfecto and Berta would find each other, but the game was still being played, and everyone wanted to join in. The only ones who didn't know about Perfecto and Berta were Perfecto and Berta, who still barely looked up at each other, and when they did, quickly looked away. Perfecto would always feign a sudden, polite cough, while Berta would invariably trip on something.

With his coughing, which required that he avert his eyes politely to the side, Perfecto never saw Berta trip. Berta, making the noise she did when she tripped, never heard Perfecto's respectful cough. In their eyes, each thought the other faultless and, mortified at their own behavior, hurried off toward some other imagined necessity—a kilo of coffee for Perfecto, a small bag of green lemons for Berta.

It was the same every time, for each of the last several months, every Tuesday morning. Had someone thought to call this ritual a dance, everyone would have paid to watch, and gotten their money's worth. Everyone had heard about Berta and Perfecto—or Perfecto and Berta—by now, and many had found a way to maneuver themselves into the small crowd that now formed, innocently it seemed to Perfecto and Berta, on these mornings. But it was a dance and a party and a show and a soap opera and a song readying itself to be written and a movie, and a good time was had by all.

That is to say, a good time was had by all who understood the words to this play. The adults had all seen it before, but it was an old classic and never seemed to wear out its welcome. The children only frowned and complained about being dragged to the market. Their crying and sniffling and shouts to each other helped keep the deception fresh.

At a tender moment, when everything seemed to get suddenly quiet, when Perfecto was turning the corner just at the same time Berta, carrying a papaya or some plantains, rounded the same corner—at that moment, just when the play seemed to find its climactic moment, a dog would run off with a carelessly held bag of chicken, or a parrot would decide to suddenly sing the entire Internationale, or a bus would go by clouding everyone in a sooty mist. It was always something like this that would seize the moment from the two main actors, and the crowd would laugh, understanding that this was not after all the final act, and that their secondary roles were not yet in jeopardy.

But one Tuesday morning, enough was enough. Sra. Belmares called to Perfecto, "Don Perfecto, won't you come over here for a moment?"

Perfecto thought it plain enough, this invitation, and went easily toward her.

"And Berta, you come over here as well."

With that, everyone moved in, not just Perfecto. Everyone wanted a front-row seat. Berta, at first, could not make her way through the crowd. Everyone was facing Sra. Belmares, mesmerized by the alchemy of the words she had mixed—Perfecto and Berta. They were so anxious to see what happened next that no one looked behind them. Berta stood there, the dried shrimp stall on one side of her and the *aguas frescas* stand on the other. Berta, too, wondered what all the fuss was about. She thought she had heard her name but now suspected that she had misheard, because everyone seemed so interested in something else, something certainly not involving her.

But when Pedrito, a son of the belt-maker, saw her and said, "There she is," trying to be helpful, Berta understood that she had been right the first time. She was being called.

The crowd all laughed and made a pathway for her.

All this fuss, she said with her furrowed brow and shaking head, which only made everyone laugh even more. She would have turned and left in that instant if she had seen Don Perfecto or had heard Sra. Belmares call to him first. But the crowd and been too noisy, and she walked to the cheese counter to see what the matter was and if Sra. Belmares needed some help.

When the two saw each other, Sra. Belmares held her hand up to say *wait*, and she came around in front of her stall. Don Perfecto started to cough, and Berta tripped over somebody's feet, somebody standing right beside her, but so close that even though she tripped she could not fall.

Sra. Belmares held up her hand again, to quiet everyone. When she held the hand up, it was with such authority that everyone who had gathered behaved like schoolchildren and the market became quiet. But the world was the world, and played its part, too. A car suddenly honked loudly. Sra. Belmares kept her hand up, moving it in a *wait, wait.*

One of the recently added portable walls in the new dress area decided it was too heavy, someone having thrown a dress over it in the search for another. It fell with a loud, hollow sound, a different kind of sound because of all the clothes hung on it, so that everyone was tempted to look, but Sra. Belmares kept her hand up and moved it even more, the hand itself also loud, *wait, wait, wait.*

As the crowd grew, someone took Berta's place by the *aguas frescas* stand, but after a few moments got jostled and reached up a hand to grab onto something to keep steady. The hand knocked over the big brown-liquid *cebada* container, which—thank heaven— was not made of glass but of plastic. It fell with a dull sharpness that sounded like getting hit in the stomach, a *huh*, and then took a bounce. The sweet *cebada* drink began to spill all over the area. But someone righted it, and a tragedy was averted. What would have been the talk of the day was reduced in that moment to almost nothing, a small irritation.

Sra. Belmares stood her ground, holding her commanding hand high and waving Perfecto and Berta closer to her with the other one. Now, at last, everything and everyone quieted. Sra. Belmares nodded her approval to the crowd—it was a full crowd, now, that had gathered, people having had enough time to drag the entire town here. And nobody wanted to miss this, whatever it might turn into.

Sra. Belmares had never been a matchmaker before, or perhaps had simply never had the chance. That was about to be rectified, and everyone knew it. Almost everyone.

Don Perfecto kept looking around to see who all the fuss was being made about. Berta, not able to trip, stood up straight, which meant to her that something was wrong.

Sra. Belmares spoke.

❖

What she said didn't amount to much. "Your mother, Doña Rosina, and I," she said to Berta, "we were friends since childhood. You know that."

Berta nodded.

"And your mother and I, Doña Armida, God rest her soul, she was raised in the mountains, but we all knew her," she said to Perfecto. "She knew about cattle and was a help to me more than once. She knew about animals and about the mountains."

Don Perfecto nodded to say he remembered. He used to come here with his mother, though he liked staying at home better even then.

Well, this was nice, but what was happening? Perfecto looked around and saw the crowd, so many faces, all of them smiling, but he wasn't sure at what. At something behind him, he thought, and so he smiled, too, and turned his head. But there was only Sra. Belmares looking back at him, and nothing behind her. Just her standing there with her hand up. He wished he were at home now.

He suddenly felt like he was underwater, and that all the sounds of the market and the people and the world were distorted and all the movements he made were laborious and dreamlike. In this momentary state, he turned and saw Berta. Berta! Even in looking at her for only those few seconds his slow movements provided, he had already in this moment looked at her for longer than he had dared before this. He did not mean to be rude. At all costs, he did not want to be rude. At the same time, his head would not move quickly, as if he were somehow not quite in charge of it. He wanted to apologize to her, but his mouth would not open. It said something else, something he could not understand.

As he heard the story later, he did move slowly, and it was odd, and everyone agreed that it was indeed dreamlike as he fell to the floor in a faint. He was the talk of the town. His fainting, and then what happened next.

❖

Don Perfecto was not a sickly man—his mother had taken care of that. Doña Armida had a cure for everything. And he understood the value of walking, something he did all the time. Indeed, he himself had never gotten into a car. Everything he did, he did himself. And for his mother.

This was difficult when his mother became sick, as he had to repeatedly climb the hill to bring the doctor.

Dr. Zamudio said the same thing every time—*Doña Armida, you don't need me.* She knew more than he did, he said, and meant it. He had, in fact, called on her more than once to help with patients who believed in the old ways and so understood her kind of science. Dr. Zamudio understood this and had been raised this way himself, even though he was now a product of this new century and its schools. Still, he came from the mountains, too. His mother and Doña Armida were distantly related. He had not forgotten that.

But when her cures reached their limit, Perfecto looked for anything that would help, even a doctor. He was a good son, and lived with his mother for all the years of her life. His father had gone to the war and never returned. No story of him ever returned either, and sometimes Perfecto thought that his mother's walking through the mountains was to look for him, that he must be somewhere out there.

Perfecto never knew him, never saw a picture of him. He had only the picture his mother drew for him in their conversations, but in those pictures he was her husband, not Perfecto's father. Perfecto didn't know what his father looked like, even with all his mother's stories of this handsome and brave man. Perfecto imagined that his father had a mustache, a big one, like all the men in pictures from the Revolution did, but he had never asked his mother directly. She liked talking about his eyes instead.

Perfecto was forty-one when his mother died, and in all that time he had helped her and taken care of her and did what she needed done—even as she was sick she was still helping others to recover from one thing or another. Perfecto took care of her, but, in truth, he understood after she was gone, she took care of him. After her death, people starting addressing him as *Don* Perfecto, now that he was the head of this house, and in recognition of what he had done in making his mother's life a good one for as long as he could.

In all this work of taking care of each other there had been no time for anyone else. For the last few years he had read the newspaper to her at night and taken her on walks during the day. Perfecto did the household shopping in the mornings, but always with a tempered plan. The walks with his mother took hours because she would stop at every available green possibility, a wild plant here, a misplaced herb growing there. She would often collect enough of one thing and another that she made dinner from the bounty, dinner and medicine.

But now he had fainted, and in front of everyone. It was a disgrace to the memory of his mother—this is how he felt.

With regard to feeling, however, and his feelings in particular, things were now more complicated.

Sra. Belmares, on seeing Perfecto melt to the ground, pushed Berta in his direction and told her to help him.

"How?" asked Berta, who didn't know what to do. And, standing in front of Perfecto, knew even less what to feel.

"Lift his head," said Sra. Belmares. "Rub his face."

Berta looked at Sra. Belmares, then at Perfecto.

At that moment, as with every other time she saw him, she fell. But this time, she fell *to him*.

She slumped to the ground next to him and drew his head up into her lap. She did as Sra. Belmares had instructed, rubbing his face and trying to fan some air to him. At that moment she wanted all the air in the room, all of it, for him. She took his head in both her hands and said his name, *Perfecto*, just to him, too soft to wake anybody, but so loud in its quietude as to wake the soul of anyone who understood.

And then she kissed him. It was a cure as much as anything else, the only medicine available to her, the only remedy. She kissed him. If he were dead, it was a kiss good-bye. If he were yet alive, it was a kiss to reach something in him, and she called on all the stories she had ever heard about bringing somebody back to life. She drew on the stories of her childhood, the fairy tales, which she had read a thousand times and believed.

Nothing worked. And yet he still breathed.

This was something more serious.

"Don't let his mother take him," Sra. Belmares whispered to Berta. "She's here somewhere. Do it again." Sra. Belmares looked at Berta and nodded to Perfecto's still face.

Berta summoned her breath and her bearing, rubbed his face again but this time with her thumbs behind his ears, and she kissed him again.

It was enough.

Sra. Belmares did not waste any more time. She commandeered a group of men to pick Perfecto up and get him into a car—she didn't know—and to take him home. And *Berta*, she declared, "Berta, of course, you have to go with him and make sure he's all right. We'll check on you later. But take care of him."

Who else could be sent? Sra. Belmares, though she may not have been able to say what she wanted to say in gathering everyone, at least got to accomplish what she set out to do. Sending Berta was the logical thing to do—everyone would understand that. Don Perfecto would need someone, and everyone else needed to go home, to their families, to make lunch and dinner, to tend to their business.

But Berta had only herself, the same as Don Perfecto. Everyone understood this and was more than glad for her to take care of him.

And, Sra. Belmares guessed as well, Berta wanted to do this. She wanted to do this even if she didn't know she did.

Sra. Belmares did what needed to be done: she gave Berta permission. Everybody gave her permission. Yes, sending two unmarried people home together, this was something, said Sra. Belmares, very quietly. "But the circumstances, they call for something, something extraordinary, I think. It's not even a choice. This has to be done.

"Don Perfecto, he is the least of things," Sra. Belmares continued to Berta, who could not believe her ears. "Food, somebody to make it and then to give it to a person, that's always the best medicine, the first cure. Don't you think, Bertita? Go with him. He'll be fine with you there. He needs you. But you have to go with him. And don't hurry. I'll take care of anything else."

In that moment Sra. Belmares performed a marriage.

Berta picked up the things that Perfecto had been carrying, marshaled the men together so that they would carry Perfecto without dropping him, then followed as they took him to a waiting car someone had offered. It was that simple.

He needed her, according to Sra. Belmares, and Berta responded. She didn't know if she agreed or not, but she could see how anyone would need help at a moment like this.

Perfecto, for his part, was waking up and starting to fuss. Sra. Belmares hurried everything along and didn't give him any kind of a chance to speak up, even as he was pulling out of his daze.

❖

Perfecto read a great deal and knew about more cures than he thought, simply from being around his mother. To his surprise, some cures came in the form of stories, stories he knew that had been told to him by Doña Armida, not to help him in the moment but for him to save up, to use later, to use now.

Berta had come to help him, but he didn't need help. That didn't mean he didn't need Berta.

When they got to his house, and after his genuine amazement at the ease of riding in a car, Perfecto and Berta found themselves, after all this, alone in his house. The men had tried to move Perfecto into the bedroom, but he had insisted that his reading chair in the living room would be suitable, and that's where they put him. He was able to walk, but they had gone to so much trouble by this point that he felt he needed to let them feel useful. They carried him to the chair, under Berta's directions, and arranged him carefully as if he were an old man.

When everyone had left and it was just the two of them, Perfecto looked up at Berta.

He stumbled to speak, to thank her, to be amazed that this was his house but that there she was, Berta, sitting in it.

Perfecto at first wanted to apologize, even though that was not true—he was not unhappy at this turn of events. He wanted to explain, to be sure that Berta would not leave, but he didn't have any explanation for simply the two of them being there, together. He wanted to do something, something regular, something to take care of the moment, but this was not fixable in that way. This was different altogether.

And Berta nodded her head to say *no*, she didn't need any explanation. She was as surprised as anyone to be sitting in this living room, surprised but not unhappy. If she dared to think it, in fact, she felt quite the opposite—happy, but that was not the right word either. She was both happy and in the right place in the world, and in the right moment.

Someone had remembered to bring the market bags Berta and Perfecto had been carrying with them, so they had cheese—two kinds. They had oranges, pink coconut candy, and butter for tortillas—*the colors of the morning sky,* Perfecto would later say. They had the garden outside and what Perfecto had in the pantry. They had the afternoon and the evening and the night. They had each other.

Their first night together was all stories, their best stories. They had no words for the day, but they each had words they had been saving for someone. They had saved them up over twenty years, at least, stories that in another marriage would have been spread out over all that time. But tonight, this honeymoon was full. And it was stories first—everything else would come later.

"My mother, Doña Armida, told me a story, once," he said to Berta. "It was about a man, a man in the United States, from the South, very rich. He owned a large ranch, the kind with a big house, and he had many servants. There were fields everywhere, and he was very successful.

"When his daughter was going to get married, because he loved her very much, he wanted to do something special. He thought about this and then he made a plan, which made the wedding a great success. He bought a boatload of spiders from China—China or somewhere like that, but you know how everybody always says China—I don't know if it was China, but it was around there—and this man then let those spiders loose all along the mile of road leading to his mansion.

"Then the man ordered sacks of gold and silver dust all the way from California. Using fireplace bellows, his servants blew the brilliant dust onto the webs the spiders had built, creating a sparkling shade under which the two thousand people who came to the wedding walked to reach the altar that he'd built for his daughter in the front yard of the house."

Berta's eyes were big. It was a big story, and he told it very well, as if he had been practicing.

"That's what Sra. Belmares has done today." Perfecto suddenly looked shy, but said the thing he felt. "I wish I could have done this for you just like that man, but what's important is that it has happened."

"I am very happy to hear you say this," said Berta, and she meant it.

Sra. Belmares thought about this in only one way, the same way everyone else did. That Perfecto and Berta were not married but now would be: It was a straightforward corrective, like a laxative, or like putting an animal down when it's too old and sick, or like angling a road so that the rain will flow down the sides.

It's doing the right thing, thought Sra. Belmares, or really just letting the right thing happen, and she said it to anyone who would listen, the right thing as much as possible, for personal reasons that anyone would understand, or for the common good, but it was the right thing to do, the only thing to do. And nothing was, in fact, being done. Perfecto and Berta had always been married, whether they—or anybody else—knew it or not—married, but in search of each other.

Whatever made this happen, whatever caused it to be, whether it really was Sra. Belmares or some other natural force of nature, it was a necessary thing, for the good of everyone. The town council might have voted to do this, had they thought of it. It would have been their job, really, fixing what needed fixing. Anyone could have directed the mayor to the problem.

It was settled, then.

Berta going home with Perfecto was the right end to a good morning, no matter the circumstances otherwise. The marriage was done, and felt as if it had been in effect for years, a marriage good and true, long and proven, love and salt. Any ceremony would come later, soon. But the real marriage, it was old news.

Had a twenty-year-old child walked out of that house, no one would have been surprised. That no one walked out, not for the next week, surprised no one either. It did not surprise them, but it did make them laugh.

de la Capital y regresarán hasta el próximo lúnes.

Saludos para todos en general y para tí y mis adorados hijitos
las caricias de siempre de parte de su padre que los adora.

Tayo.

Margarita,Margarita,Margarita de mi amor,
Inocente florecita de un jardín encantador.
Margarita,Margarita,Margarita de mi amor,
Con tu sonrisa se quita la pena de mi dolor.
Señor don Tunejo,orejas bonitas,
Sin ellas te dejo,si no mete quitas
Si no me te quitas sin ellas te dejoooooooooooo
Duérmase mi niña,porque ahí viene el coco uy uy uy
Se come a las niñas que duermen muy poco.
Si esta niña se durmiera,
En su cuna la acostara,
Con su colche la cubriera,

Para que no se resfriara,
En seguida me saliera
Y desde afuera vigilara,
Que nadie ruido le hiciera
Para que no despertara.
Pero si se despertara,
Porque es una papelera,
En mis brazos la arrullara
Hasta que al fín se durmiera,
En su cuna la acostara,
Con su colcha la cubriera,
Y desde afuera vigilara
Que nadie ruido le hiciera.
Usted es una papelera,
Mona de Guadalajara,
El que no la conociera,
Pueda ser que la comprara,
Pero si la devolviera,
Porque al fín no la aguantará
La tirarían para afuera
Que el Sultán la pepenara.
El Sultán,taran tan tan,
La niña quiere comer,
Pero no se la darán,
Porque eso no puede ser.
El Sultan tarán tan tan,
La niña quiere almorzar,
Pero no se la darán,
Aunque tenga qué ayunar.

THE POEM

My grandfather wrote individual songs for each of his seven children, which he played for them on the mandolin, composing them first as poems. He most often wrote when he was very far away.

That he would want his daughter to sleep, to be warm, to be safe, that is a father—even if there is a mention of the dreaded *cucuy*, who eats children but who, really, gives a parent on invoking the name loudly the chance to tickle their child, turning mock fear into laughter and making the world right in a calming embrace, right and ready for sleep.

Sleep, my little girl, because there comes *el cucuy*
Who eats little girls who don't go to sleep.
If this little girl would just go to sleep
I would put her in her crib,
And cover her with her blanket
So that she wouldn't get cold.
Then I'd leave
But from just outside I'd watch over her
Making sure nobody made a noise to wake her.

4

A Century of Tears

The late afternoon light was falling into the water as Cayetano Belmares watched from the doorway. He expected steam to rise, most of all where the sun touched the ocean, or what looked like the ocean: in this light, the great wheat fields in the distance looked like a grand body of water, golden water, and the small undulations caused by the breeze looked enough like waves, waves as he remembered them from his youth, on the visits to the ocean that he took with his parents. That was a long time ago, but he never forgot the water.

The light fell, but slowly, like an enormous day falling altogether, all of it, whole, coming down on fire with itself. The colors in the sky seemed to float in a dull after-dusk of flame, filled with the slow-moving stuff that hangs in the air after an explosion, or like the seeds of the cottonwood in season, that desert snow of fluff. The small gathering of clouds that were in the west this afternoon, this early evening, they carried fire with them the way people carry water jugs—on their backs, slumped over, the heavy water everything. Looking into the sky, that side and corner of the sky, was like looking into a photograph of the day whose corner had been ignited by a match.

Maybe he was exaggerating, thought Cayetano. It had been a long day. Everything was tired, the whole world, and Cayetano Belmares most of all. The fire was dying, in the day and in himself. But it was a fire, had been a fire. That much was certain. He had started the day with an energy the opposite of what he felt now, the way he always did. So strong at the beginning of the day and then so tired at the end of it—this told him he was alive and that all was right in the world. Energy at the end of the day always meant that something didn't get done, and that turned into worry, and that turned into unhappiness and difficulty sleeping. No, tired was better. Tired was good.

The color the sun made in the clouds and on the far distant horizon was nice, but the heat wasn't. This was the desert. It was summer. These kinds of sunsets were old news. Only Cayetano paid attention to them anymore. Beauty wasn't hard to come by here—ice was. Ice and cool places and fresh breezes. Work was good, but a person would feel better being near something cold, which was always a danger. Something cold brought work to a halt. People knelt before cold drinks, at least here on the farm. And it was not the drink—the drink didn't matter, lemonade or tea. It was the cold. And the cold made things happen, but not what anyone would think. Nothing got done on cool days. They were too rare to pass up, so that people got lazy and nostalgic and wanted to go on picnics.

Hot days were regular, and people complained, and everything moved in slow motion, but work got done. It didn't make sense to Cayetano Belmares. It seemed like things should be the other way around, but he kept this feeling to himself. He might not understand it, but he knew he could count on it.

The cows, too, the cows and other animals, the same thing happened with them. On hot days, they simply did whatever they were told, too uncomfortable and tired to do anything else, to do anything that required exertion. Even complaining was too much work. To complain meant taking in enough breath to breathe out loudly enough to be heard—even the thought of complaining seemed as if it weighed a thousand pounds. But on cool days they had a different energy. They began to think for themselves, which always caused trouble.

That was the thing about summer. Everyone seemed to complain, or meant to, or tried to, but nobody ever got around to it until winter, and then it was too late. And that's what winters became—everybody complaining about summers, saying what they did not have the energy to say two months earlier. So, in summer, fences got mended, crops were seen to, the cattle never ran away, and work simply got done—if only because not-doing-work was too much work.

Cayetano looked into the distance, at the clouds, then turned around to look into the door he was entering. Outside was outside, and work. The clouds were far away. Inside, though, inside was something different. For a moment, from having looked into the light of the setting sun, he could see nothing but blackness, and then everything with haloes. He closed his eyes for a few seconds to find his way in the darkness.

❖

But it was not what he saw with his eyes that guided him. It was dinner, with its octopus arms of good smells, all of them calling to him, waving him over as an old friend, whispering to him in the way that arms might, rough-housing him over to his chair at the table but with gentle, siren-like touches all over him, hot and cinnamon and *calabasitas* and rice and meat and goat and honey and *chicharrones* and iced *horchata* and beans and salt and chile and yellow cheese and potatoes and creamy farm cheese and onions and garlic and surprise, but not too much surprise. The smell of dinner may have entered him through the nose, but he felt it all over his body. It made his own arms rise to the occasion, fork in one hand, tortilla in the other.

Time, at that moment, was that moment, all of time frozen. The whole day resolved itself into sitting down and taking a first bite of food—that first taste a barometer for the work of the day. It was not the setting of the sun that told the day's story. It was dinner.

And when Cayetano missed it, he was unhappy and unbalanced. Sometimes someone wanted to say a prayer, which was all right, if it wasn't too long. At least dinner was still in sight. But when he had to miss it for other reasons, when he had to wrap something up and take it with him on some emergency or another, it made him sad. It made his body sad. And the day, on those days, could not find its proper finish. No dinner meant that the world had gone wrong.

Not altogether wrong, of course—he knew the sun would rise the next day and life would go on. But for the moment, and the moment was everything, life did not seem so certain. The taste of nothing is what he felt, though he had no words for the feeling. No words, but no confusion either.

When dinner was on time and good, though, he ate, and in eating he felt good and right, and when he finished he looked around the dinner table at his family. That was his prayer, the feeling he had right then, that all was right with the world, and that this feeling was worth having.

The immensity of this feeling was in relation to how, before he ate, he was blind, blind in the sense that he was so tired from working so hard all day, and in the heat especially, that he could make no sense of the world until after he had cooled down, eaten, had something to drink, and let his eyes adjust to the evening light after having had them so wide open all day in order to see what was what—what needed to be done, who needed help, what was that cow doing over there, when did the buyers say they would be coming, didn't that over there need a little extra water? His eyes looked in a thousand directions during the day, never stopping, so that when he walked in the door at night, came into the one room and looked only at one thing after clearing his eyes—the dinner table—it was an enormous relief.

It felt good to stop looking at the world and start feeling it.

That's what work used to be, thought Cayetano—feeling the earth, the animals, the plants, everything with his hands. But the farm had gotten too big now and was a ranch and an orchard as well as a dairy—it had always been a dairy, but it was more of one these days. People wanted everything and always needed more. It was a good life, but hard on any given day.

Hard on him, and hard on his family. *It's a good life,* he would say, and everyone would agree, but he wondered sometimes.

Though his hands were empty, they were full. He had regular calluses on his hands, the kind that meant hard work, but he had special ones, too, crueler ones. These others were the ones that came from handling so many rawhide strips, which Cayetano used to bind everything on the land—fences, animals, bundles of wood. He had these calluses on calluses in the thick part of his hands, the saddle between the thumb and first finger of each hand, that webbing that spoke to him of water yet again, and childhood, as if he were some fabulous sea creature, the way he imagined, out in the blue waters and swimming into the secret underground pirate caves. But now the webbing was rubbery and thick, a little yellow and always dry.

Cayetano had these extra kinds of calluses also on the insides of his knees from riding his horses, from keeping something still

while he worked the leather straps with his hands, these knees giving him the feeling of four hands, which made him even stronger.
And he had more calluses here and there, depending on the season
and its particular requirements. He was his work, and his body
gave itself over to this life, wholly, altogether, all the time.

In its fullness his body sang. Hard skin against seasoned rawhide, the sound was a music, an old song to Cayetano whose words
he knew. He caressed his wife like no other man. His caresses were
hard to the touch but soft to the heart. His wife knew it, but so did
the others, the animals, the orchard trees, the house itself when
things went wrong and needed fixing. They all knew his hands.

It was a kind of happiness.

And though there was hardness, beauty entered those hands
easily, the same as with his eyes. What his eyes sometimes saw, his
hands sometimes felt.

It was a beautiful ranch to the eye, but more as well. Anyone
who stayed here came to understand that the ranch, when they
touched it, touched them back. And it was Cayetano's hand that
reached them.

But if he spoke with his hands, Cayetano was not nearly so elo-
quent with his words, or in the regular ways of things. He loved
fiercely but could not say it. He built this ranch instead, and planted
the orchards and kept the dairy. He did what people wanted and
needed, and found his life in this way, and went from being young
to being old.

And because this life was easier to live but more difficult to explain,
at least for Cayetano, he lost some parts of it, a son leaving for the
city, another son working hard but not understanding the work,
just doing it, which was no good to Cayetano at all, not what he
wanted for his boy. And another son who did the work but had no

words. He loved the ranch and the trees, he understood this in the ways that Cayetano did, but he was quiet to the world even as he was intense in his own. Everybody worried for him, for what would happen to him. This boy was not angry or sad. He was somewhere lost in between.

And then there was Cayetano's wife, Guillermina. The dairy had been in her family for many years, and Cayetano was happy to make it part of their lives, to continue its operations and its family name.

His wife had all the words and told all the stories and took care of other people coming to visit—enjoyed it even, which was something Cayetano did not understand—and as her job took on not only the duties of the household but of selling things from their dairy stall in the *mercado*. Cayetano's hands and Guillermina's words had always been a perfect marriage.

Except for one day, one very long day, one day with no dinner. The personal quietude with which Cayetano approached all things and the great storm that was Guillermina, two things that normally went together so well, one day did not. Quite the opposite.

So many events had occurred on their *rancho* through the years, so many births, so many deaths of animals, a young boy's death by accident in the orchard, their children dispersing this way and that. Their general prosperity did not give a full report regarding their troubles, but it was like that with anyone. They were luckier than most, and said it to each other in their private moments, he with a nod at the end of the day, she with a quick massaging of his shoulders.

But tonight, tonight when Cayetano walked in the doorway, there was no dinner.

Guillermina saw him at the door and came to him, saw his face but shushed him, caught his elbow and guided him into the room. The table was not set at all—it still had the tablecloth on it and a vase with flowers—and there was a visitor, who was, it looked to Cayetano, eating a small something on a small plate that nonetheless looked delicious.

When Cayetano walked in, the young man holding the plate and wearing a tie tried simultaneously to stand up, put the plate aside, run a hand through his hair to comb it, and smile. He accomplished two of those four things, the plate and the smile not faring nearly so well as the standing and the combing. Luckily, Guillermina had already made her way over to him to bring him to the table, and she was able to catch the falling plate.

"Don Cayetano," said the young man, at the prompting nod of Guillermina. She also nodded to Cayetano, and her nod sat him at the dinner table, as it had so many times before, but this time for a different kind of dinner.

But who is this woman? wondered Cayetano. Guillermina was never this quiet, this accommodating, this—dared he say it? *This nice.* He meant her no disrespect. It was that she simply was the one who got things done in the house, and this was not normally a quiet or an easy process. Indeed, it was rarely anything but the opposite, with a great fussing and a great expense of emotion to get everyone to do what needed to be done.

I don't need to listen to this boy, thought Cayetano. *I know what he will be saying. I don't know what words he will say, but I know what they will mean. How he says them will be like anyone.* He will say, "We are going to float on a golden boat down a mighty river, a guest of the gods, everywhere, food at our left, drink at our right, animals all healthy and happy around us. We will float, and nothing will be needed, no call for us to help, no bleating goat, no lowing cow, no shivering horse, no yowling dog. Nobody will need us and we will need no one. We will reach for grapes and cheeses and pomegranates-already-peeled. And plums. Our glasses will be filled with something new to drink, something cold, something that has no name. Around us it will be day and night both, stars in the sky but enough light to see everything. We will float, just float. That will be our job, and everything will float with us. And flowers, all around wherever we go, in the water. It will be like the gardens in Xochimilco, the ones everyone has heard about from everyone who has traveled south, but better, better than those gardens. And the scent of so many flowers will rise and float with us, too. Flowers. But I want them to be the kind that smell good because they will stay with us for a lifetime. These are the flowers that grow inside you and become your memory of things, that wonderful scent. I want it to be a wonderful scent. Help us with that."

Well, he won't say that, thought Cayetano, *but he will say the equal of it.* The words were what Cayetano thought he himself would have liked to say when asking for the hand of Guillermina so many years ago. But her father, Don Martín, scared him very much in that moment. What if he had said *no*? Or what if he had gone to some trouble to make things rough? It would have changed everything. Don Martín's saying *yes* made all the difference in the world. It mattered. And why should he have said *yes* beyond faith in— Cayetano didn't know what. It could not have been faith in him, not yet, as Cayetano had done nothing to warrant any kind of faith beyond simply being a hard worker and his promise to continue.

But that was it, perhaps. Maybe that's all there was. What else was there to say *yes* to? There wasn't much. It was an act of courage, perhaps more on Don Martín's part than on Cayetano's. It was an act of courage stemming from the look in Don Martín's daughter's eyes as much as Cayetano's own, and most probably Don Martín took more from her look than from his. She was his daughter, after all. She was his daughter, and she was asking him to let her go. The feeling was confusing, more than Don Martín had ever thought he would feel, and it made him sit down under some minor pretext. They loved each other, so how could she want to leave? The question, that question, resonated louder than the request Cayetano was making.

And now that same moment was calling to Cayetano, calling him to courage with the sides of the table reversed. And the feelings of confusion and of needing to sit down overwhelmed him as well.

Marta came into the room. Marta, his little girl. For this moment, none of the other children entered into the conversation, not Ignacio, whom Cayetano had thought would be the first to leave, not any of the boys. The universe at this moment consisted only of Marta, Guillermina, and this boy. Cayetano felt overwhelmed again, beyond needing to sit down. Whatever he felt didn't seem to matter. He could see that they were all set on this. It made him feel quiet, as always. He felt this way not because he had nothing to say—quite the opposite. But silence had always served him better. He understood this. His words were always better understood in what he did instead.

Cayetano knew this boy Julio, though not well. Tragic circumstances had drawn them together, however, and apparently even more so Julio to Marta. When they were all young, Julio's family had come to pick fruit from the orchards, as many families did during the harvesting season. Julio had a large family, the Calderón family, and they had spread out in every direction. His brother Oswaldo, however, had an accident—he fell from a horse and died right there. It was a very sad occasion, and there was nothing more to be done. Dr. Bartolomeo had been called, but it was too late, and indeed his being there even at the moment it had happened would not have changed the result. The boy hit something with his head.

The two families, through fate, had been closer thereafter, though Cayetano's relationship had been with the parents. That left the children of both families to go off and play together, which is how Marta had met Julio. Cayetano wasn't certain of this, but he understood it right away, once this boy was introduced to him and once he was sure of the boy's parents. Julio himself was grown up now and not at all the skinny boy who had tried to help. It was Julio, if he remembered correctly now, who had helped Marta take care of Baltasár, Cayetano and Guillermina's youngest child, who took the accident very much to heart—not with tears so much as with his life. The boy was quiet already but became even more so afterward. Though it could not be determined precisely, it seems that Baltasár had seen the accident, though he could not articulate any specifics. He was not very good at speaking, and especially not to strangers. But even Marta could get very little out of him more than his wide eyes and down-turned mouth.

Marta through the years had taken particular pains to guide and help her youngest brother, this boy Baltasár, who needed extra help. Across many seasons she had shown him the ways of the orchard and helped him find work to do there, ways to help, which he took to with a fierce energy. His quiet had been so long thought to be like Cayetano's, but too much so, and the boy had difficulties. Marta had helped him find an Eden among the trees, and they built a small house for him right in the middle of it, a place Baltasár liked to stay. If Marta left, Cayetano was sure the boy would not come back to the house—not because he was unwelcome, but because he too would know something about confusion and feel that something was wrong. He would not understand his sister going away.

That made this moment doubly hard for Cayetano. Everything he understood—the ranch, the dairy, the farm, the town, the whole universe—everything was interconnected, and even one little change affected everything. But how could he say this to Marta?

And, as he thought about it, even to Julio, who was Cayetano so many years ago sitting in a chair and at a table much like this one.

Cayetano would find another way, Cayetano and Guillermina and the rest of the family, they would find a way. Baltasár, too. Cayetano knew this was the great rumbling movement of things, the same as what turned the day into night and night into day, these big things that he loved so much. This movement was what made his world his world, and this was part of it. He loved it all in its best suit of clothes, but in this moment it was hard to see. *It is a good life*, he used to think, and now it became even more clear to him. *It is a good life, but hard on any given day.*

After having been asked to give his blessing to these two young people and to let them go, Cayetano sat for a few more moments, calm but not looking straight at anybody, not even his wife.

His life was quiet and his place in the universe small. This had already been a century of tears for the world. In this small moment he could change that.

THE PRAYER

It is made of so many things, a prayer, so simple in structure but of a magic: invoking its words, one is moved into the black place behind closed eyes. Right then, we free the something else in us and let it go looking for what it needs.

So often a prayer is for someone who has gone. Those many words are the gasoline in a time machine's engine, which in those moments always runs in reverse.

5

The Asterisk Company

The wet-wool drear of the afternoon was wearable, a coat thick enough to hide in, substantial enough to button. Headlights weren't enough, though they were everywhere. Night was where day was supposed to be. On this afternoon, a slow storm nosed itself into everything, from the cracks in the sidewalks to the conversations in the taller buildings.

Because of the thickness of the clouds, those on the streets who saw lightning saw its normally sudden light blurred from a sharp fork to a dull spoon, a spotlight wide and awkward. The impact was almost humorous if one stood long enough to look at it. The lightning through the serious clouds was like some cheap theatrical effect, reminiscent of flashlights flickering on and off behind cotton sheets in a third-grade play.

The thunder as well was quieted by the thickness of the air, though in that humid wool a clear if ominous bass sound kept gunning like a distressed car engine trying to start, shaking everything that could be shaken. The few people watching the storm could feel the thunder in the hairs of their arms, a slight quiver with every disquieting rumble.

Everyone except Ignacio ignored the storm as best they could, the way they always did. What might have signaled the end of the world some centuries ago was now just a nuisance. Water was just water, and tomorrow it would be something else—too little rain, too much wind, not enough wind, too much dust. The world itself was a little boring these days, and people had turned to other things.

This is what shocked and thrilled Ignacio most. In the country-side, where he came from, and where the desert was much more in evidence, weather meant everything. One lived—or died—by it, and animals too, the cows and the horses especially. The chickens managed, and the wild animals, the coyotes and the lizards and the bears and the rabbits, they all seemed able to find their way in the desert. Still, for Ignacio and his family, for the big animals and the fields with their crops, a thunderstorm like this meant everything.

Here it meant almost nothing; people simply seemed annoyed. Ignacio's impulse—which he held in check because no one else seemed inclined to do the same—had been to remove his clothing and stand in the rain, freed from the burden of having to carry so much water to a bathtub the way he had to at home. Standing in it was what he would have done not even two months ago.

But he was here now, and glad to be here even if he didn't always understand everything.

Where people on the *ranchos* were always looking for ways to better channel the water and feed the crops, here people were always looking for better ways to ignore it, better umbrellas and windshield wipers and rubber boots that they ordered from cata-logues, catalogues from places that must have already solved the weather and moved on to other things. That was the direction Ignacio wanted to move in.

At home, everything moved in circles and went nowhere. The crops were planted, the rains came, the wheat and corn grew, everyone ate, and after eating they were strong enough to go out and plant crops again. *What kind of life is that?* wondered Ignacio. Here in town, one thing led to another, and nobody knew what would be coming next. A person had to be smart here, and solve things as they came, not rely on old answers.

This was the life for him.

Science and *cities*. Words like these had kept Ignacio awake as he was growing up. The desert had given him all the room in the world during the day, but at night too, so that his dreams were big. All that room simply served to show him everything he did not have—he and his family, of course, and all the others who worked on the *ranchos*. But he felt this absence more than others, he could tell. His dreams had all the room they needed, without anybody else needing the dream space, as they did not want the same things he did.

When he walked around the ranch at home, chickens clucked, donkeys brayed and babies cried, dogs barked, and bats fluttered away, all wing and movement, igniting the darkness with sound. They were the sound of movement itself. But it was a little sound, and donkeys and babies and dogs and all the rest, they were a small concert, not at all like the great and constant noise of the town, cars at all hours, music from some buildings, tradespeople moving their wares, grocers and fish sellers at three in the morning getting ready for the next day in the *mercado*.

It all left Ignacio breathless.

The problem, however, was that Ignacio had no particular plan. In all his dreaming, and in all his breathlessness, sorting out the thing he actually wanted to do had escaped him. He felt sure it had no name, so he had no way of dreaming it, only that it existed, whatever it was. And coming here to town, coming here to stay, this would be the first step. The next step would present itself. And it did.

The rain. There it was, free to everyone, which was not the case with very many things in town. But the rain, right here, what more could he ask for? This was what he had been hoping for, a moment in which he could try *science*, the word he imagined defined moments like this. All he had to do was to connect the free rain to something that people wanted, and that would do it. Towns and cities were all about things being connected, he thought, one pipe to another, or one wire, one brick, one street. But a lot of them, and they all had to fit or the point was lost. It was like a big puzzle but with straight lines.

On the *rancho*, one thing fit with another by luck, and usually only once. Nature never worked with straight lines. And that was the problem. Everything was crooked or bent or curvy, and no two things were ever alike. In cities, things just fit together like magic, and they were all the same. That was a kind of heaven, thought Ignacio, things all fitting together and working, and when something didn't work, knowing right where to go to find the thing that would work. Everything behaving—the world behaving. That was how to move forward, all right.

Ignacio had a pencil, and he found some discarded paper, which he tore and folded into a notebook. He punched holes through one side of the leaves of paper with the point of that pencil, then he found some loose pieces of string with which he tied the sheets together. It all worked quite well, and he discovered at the same time that the trashcans behind buildings were good places to look for things. .

He proceeded to write his notes on the subject of rain, a word he wrote on the first page, and then wrote over it again to make it darker.

Rain.

This was his science book, the way he had learned in school. He had been the only one to pay attention. Now it would all make sense. He began thinking, in the serious way that had impressed his teacher each of the several years he had been in school.

Rain. It didn't taste very good. He had certainly learned that as a child, collecting rainwater and drinking it that first time as if it were a great treasure. After that, after spitting it out, Ignacio understood why the rain barrel was used only in emergencies. And he wouldn't be able to afford any sugar or anything like that to improve it. He could put some water into stronger tequilas or *pulques*, but he would still have to buy the tequila, so that wouldn't work. He wrote this idea down, followed by "no."

Rain didn't smell very good. That was the next thing he thought of. More accurately, it didn't smell at all. It made other things smell better by waking them up—the creosote, the roses—but the rain itself didn't have anything inside it that would do the trick. He wrote this down next, also followed by "no." As he wrote it, however, he had a side thought, which he made a note to come back to.

The note was "Lemons." All this thinking about smells made him remember what it was like to walk under a lemon tree just past the season, with all the lemons that had gone unharvested—too bad for them, and too bad for the family whose job was to sell them, but so many always fell—crushed by his feet, bringing an overwhelming scent into the air, a wonderful fragrance that always made him feel good. Very good. He made an asterisk next to "Lemons." And when he saw the asterisk he had drawn, he thought, *That's a good way to remember something.*

Rain did have an interesting sound, Ignacio thought, one that he used to enjoy back in the country, especially when he was trying to fall asleep. But here, the sound of rain just seemed to irritate people, telling them that they would have to look out not to get wet, not to get muddy, not this and not that. And when they got inside their city houses, they couldn't hear the rain anyway. This did not seem like a promising idea. He wrote it down. Another "no." He wrote these notes down so that he would not think about them again, which would be a waste of time.

But then he furrowed his forehead. Perhaps rain could somehow be made to play music, the way someone strikes the keys on a piano? Raindrops all seem random, but perhaps, perhaps there was something to discover here. He put a line through the "no" and put a question mark next to it. *Maybe.*

Rain looked like what it looked like, which was like rain. There wasn't any other way to describe it. It did make other things look better, much like it helped things to smell better. But rain by itself looked only like water. Water sparkled, but there didn't seem any easy way to wear it, like a ring, for example, or to use it as a paint, as it would dry out.

He could change its color, perhaps. That was an idea. Almost anything could change water's color. Maybe he could find a pleasing hue and sell colored rain as a cleanser. That was a good idea. A determined color. An uncommon color. This might work. It would need to be a very persuasive color, and one that didn't make things worse than they already were by staining. Still, it might work. He wrote this down as his first good idea, putting an asterisk next to it.

Another asterisk. He liked the way they looked, and with two of them now, things were adding up.

What about the way rain felt? People could take a bath with rainwater, as he had in the countryside, but where would he store it? Besides, someone already provided that service, more or less. Running water was built into most houses here, and sewers. More or less. Certainly running water was part of all the newer houses, which was the direction Ignacio saw himself moving in—forward, toward the future.

It was the same with ice. Somebody already made ice, and the ice plant, which provided ice for the railroads to keep the fresh produce the trains carried from going bad, often created something of a shower under the ice chutes if one were inclined to try it. But it was cold water, as Ignacio learned. Very cold. Anyway, Ignacio didn't know how to make ice, so it was just as well. He wrote down "Bathwater," then "no." He wrote the same for "Ice."

But what did rain feel like? It felt like something. This idea stayed with him for a while and filtered through his thoughts. It could feel like fingers touching you all over, like a cat's paws, he supposed. People would like that. But that's really just a bath, a bath or a shower. Or wet—would people want to feel wet? Swimming? In a lake? A swimming pool—that might be a good idea. He put an asterisk next to "Swimming pool" but imagined right away that building such a thing would be too expensive. Next to the asterisk he also added an "X," which was, in combination, almost as definite as a "no," but not quite.

People might like to feel wet, even though they spent so much time working at the opposite. Could rain make people feel dry? That was more of a long-term question, something to think about. It was just what he loved best, something that suggested its opposite, a nod in the direction of impossibility, which is most certainly the exact place people did not look for solutions. But he had an open mind, which was the only way to be modern, especially in a scientific age. He put an asterisk next to "Wet and dry," just to keep his options open. He had heard of "dry cleaners," after all, though he wasn't quite sure what that meant.

What else, he wondered, was on the far side of "wet"? Could there be something in that direction that nobody had thought of? Just the phrase "dry cleaners" was a start, but he needed to work with water. Wet cleaners, well, that was just water. But it did point back to his idea of selling something colorful and relying on the fact that water cleaned things. But perhaps there was something more than that in this direction. What was the opposite of dry cleaners? Wet dirtiers? Would people want something made dirty?

Nothing came to mind, not immediately. People wanted things clean, after all. Germs and stains and bodily fluids—cleanliness was not hard to understand. Still, perhaps. Not clean but dirty.

No, nothing. But he liked the idea and direction. And besides, it made him laugh.

Ignacio's mother, Doña Guillermina, had given him some money to come to the city. She was the only one who understood. His father, Don Cayetano Belmares, didn't know what to make of Ignacio at all and didn't think about what he would do with his future. Don Cayetano simply assumed that Ignacio would work with his brothers, taking care of the *rancho* along with them. It was simple. He didn't think Ignacio was either good or bad at doing the work that needed to be done, but he did think that he would be there to do it.

That was the thing. Ignacio's leaving would surprise his father. But just as a lame horse has to be put down, thought Ignacio, there would be no reason to discuss the matter further. If he was gone, then that was that. His father would see no use in crying about it. Don Cayetano understood how to keep a *rancho* working, and sentiment had little place in the equation. He was not a cruel man, not at all, and Ignacio loved his father. He had shown Ignacio how to do so many things. But Ignacio also understood that he would not be missed by his father, not in the way his mother would miss him.

Doña Guillermina knew what was coming and had managed to put enough money aside to get Ignacio through a first week in the city, but only a first week. After that, he was on his own. It was the best she could do, and Ignacio knew it. His father would not have been angry about this arrangement, but had he known about it, he would have been quick to point out how the money would be much better used. And he would have been right, regarding the *rancho* and Ignacio's family. But sometimes a little bit of risk might be a good thing.

Ignacio hoped so. He would do his best. But even if things worked out, he was pretty sure he would not be going back. He would go to visit, of course, and if he got rich then he would certainly help out, but that was it. Ignacio believed that his future was here, and he would make the best of things no matter what came his way.

But a week's worth of money, it doesn't ever last a week. Money is curious that way.

And it's especially true when the matter has not been simply science and cities, but someone, as well. Ignacio had met someone his second day in the city, someone like him who had come in from the *ranchos* looking for work, staying in Sra. Dos Santos's boarding house. They had met at dinner, which Sra. Dos Santos served every day promptly at five-thirty.

Her name was Isabel, and she liked to hear about science.

❖

But Isabel was not why Ignacio had created his scientific note-book. Not exactly. It's true that he might not have created it quite as quickly had Isabel not asked what he was doing, but he would have done it in good time. It was certainly in his plan. His Plan.

Isabel liked hearing about that, as well.

Because he grew up in a household of brothers, which was a good thing on a *rancho*, Ignacio was not used to being around young women, and Isabel was certainly that. Ignacio was used to loud dinners and everything else that went with getting the work of the place done by the end of the day.

Isabel, on the other hand, was very used to being around young men and was surprised at his reticence. She'd grown up just the same way he had, with a houseful of brothers, loud dinners, and work to be done.

Regardless, Ignacio was shy and not sure what to say to her. So he talked about his book of science, perhaps a day before he actually had created such a thing, but in so doing gave himself a direction and a plan. It was not a plan for immediate work, perhaps, but that's what comes of talking to a young woman, his mother would later tell him. Ignacio was not sorry. What his plan was, at least as he told it to Isabel, was to find an idea—and not just any idea. He did not want to just sign up for a job like anybody. No. He wanted to start big, which was the only way to start—if you were Ignacio, who was a boy talking to a girl.

I have an idea starts the conversation, and her eyes get wide. After that, the only thing to do is to actually find an idea and start big. Otherwise, who knew what would happen, disappointing a young woman? Ignacio did not want to know. He had read the word in school, and his teacher was fond of repeating it. And Ignacio had taken the word to heart. But now, the word needed a definition. It was up to *science* to save him.

❖

Ignacio was a thin, gangly boy who grew into an even thinner, gangly man. He never worried too much about clothes, because everything was too big for him. When he walked, his pants followed a half-second later. When he got dressed up in the clothes he got from his brothers, who liked dinners so much they often had two, he never understood why they complained so much about their ties and how they strangled them. For him, it seemed whimsical, this bit of cloth hanging from him like a limp flag. Nothing strangled him, and that gave him a different outlook on the world.

And it was this gangliness that finally gave him the answer he was looking for.

Eating dinner at Sra. Dos Santos's boarding house was a formal affair, everyone dressing up in some reasonable version of civility. Ignacio had brought with him one suit, which he thought he might use for church, but which he needed to wear each evening for dinner, or else go hungry. It was this one suit, in fact, that first brought him into conversation with Isabel, though she would not say so.

She understood his situation almost immediately, as soon as she saw him wearing the same suit for a third evening in a row. Two times, that was nothing. But three times—while it may equally have been nothing—spoke loudly to Isabel. She herself had been given enough money by her parents to buy some dresses, and along with what she already owned, these were enough to give the illusion of variety. But for Ignacio, the idea of variety apparently did not present itself. Regardless, Isabel could see that Ignacio's simply wearing a suit seemed to satisfy whatever requirements Sra. Dos Santos had. She seemed content enough.

But Isabel understood what wearing a suit three times in a row meant, or would mean. She believed he would wear it a fourth time and a fifth, and think nothing of it. She knew her brothers very well.

She tried to find a way to bring up the point, which is what led to their first conversation, which, as things turned out, was everything.

She tried to be gentle, but he took offense, that first time.

"Of course I have another suit. Why would you ask such a thing?" Ignacio was red-faced, speaking a little too loudly after she had taken the care to whisper her concern.

"I'm just so curious to see you in another color," she responded.

"You are?" he asked, believing the flattery she had perfected when trying to persuade her brothers to do one thing or another. So far, he was just like them. But that would change.

With that they began to talk, and Ignacio, while not changing his suit—since he didn't have another one—did change the color of his shirt, which was perfectly appropriate, and which got a nod from Sra. Dos Santos. It was not much, but also everything. It was, Ignacio would later understand, the smallest things that brought them most together.

She didn't care if he had another suit, and neither did he. But she cared for him, and he cared for her—that was the real conversation, though it did not consist of words. It was instead a small feeling, a feeling that started to grow. This kind of conversation seems very quiet to the outside world, but to Ignacio, and to Isabel, it was as loud as the rain.

"I have an idea," said Ignacio. He said it first to Isabel, to practice, Isabel standing there with her long, black hair, her big eyes, and her eager smile, which she tried to hide.

"Be serious," he said to her in as stern a way as he could. But with her, sternness simply made them both break out in laughter.

"Really," he tried for a third time, "I have an idea. And it's from my suit. You know how it doesn't fit?"

Isabel tried to pretend that she didn't know what he was talking about.

He frowned, and she frowned back, and they laughed.

"Okay, yes," she said. "And?"

"My brothers are all heavier than I am. And that's what made me think—rainwater is heavy."

This was not the direction Isabel thought the conversation would take. But she was patient.

"Water weighs something—a great deal, in fact."

"I remember carrying water in buckets from the river to the house," said Isabel. Everyone remembered that. As it turned out, nobody in the city was so far removed from the countryside that they did not understand that work, and remember with some vibrancy the pure weight of water.

"The city is in such a hurry to make more of itself that buildings are going up all the time. Why not use water as a machine to help the process?" Ignacio was visibly excited by what he had said, but Isabel had no idea what he meant. The best and the biggest and the most important ideas so often begin in exactly such a manner.

But Ignacio was already sketching in his scientific notebook, using the blank space that was supposed to be for ideas and simply drawing one thing after another in the place of the words he had first imagined would serve him. But these drawings were simply another kind of language, words too, but not heard—these were words to see.

Ignacio remembered something from school—though it was unclear to him in its details—a reference his teacher had made to Archimedes and how he said that he could lift the Earth if he could find a place to stand and a lever to do it with. What Ignacio thought of wasn't that, but in remembering that idea he came up with his own. He knew about pulleys and work-saving mechanisms, from the block-and-tackle contraptions for loading hay into the barn to the various ways of controlling animals when you were the only person around.

And here was the thing. Water weighed something. It was like his brothers. An empty bucket weighed very little, but a full bucket—that was altogether different. It was like his brother Armando wearing the suit that Ignacio now wore. Ignacio was the empty bucket. What Ignacio designed was as simple as that.

The city was always building, and there were always obstacles to be moved—old tree stumps, trees themselves, pylons from old construction, all manner of nuisances. Ignacio designed a big bucket, sometimes a very big bucket, connected to these various objects with a whole array of pulleys. At first he thought he could wait until thunderstorms filled the buckets with water, but he soon realized they never would. He would have to find a way to carry the water—which he did, or rather, which his workers did.

They filled and filled the various buckets attached to various obstacles, and, slowly, these obstacles began to rise out of the ground in deference to the weight of the water in the buckets. It was science, perhaps, but Ignacio just thought it was an idea that nobody had used yet. And it worked. Before too long, and thereafter for many years, these water machines could be seen all over town. They never worked quickly, and didn't need to. Building new things, even in a city, took a long time. Sometimes a thunderstorm did indeed fill the buckets enough, and on those afternoons one could hear all sorts of things being lifted out of the ground. It was a circus of sudden work, and a whole year's worth of effort was accomplished in one very wet cloudburst.

When an afternoon like that happened, Isabel said it was not unlike each time one of their babies came.

When interest in his water machine waned, Ignacio moved on to sun and wind machines, which also found some success. They were always replaced by bigger machines from bigger companies from bigger places, but for a while all of his machines found some use. The curious thing, as even Ignacio came to see, is that he did not work with straight lines the way the big companies did. He worked instead with the crooked lines of what his town needed, for itself, things specific and particular to this place in the Sonoran Desert, and that was his success, however limited.

He became a scientist of sorts, by observation if not by training, and his enthusiasms were always contagious. He wanted to move forward, that direction always clear to everyone he spoke with. And he never wavered in his earnestness, which was also persuasive. He made enough money to take care of a family in the city, but not more. His time for building his machines was short, as his ideas gave everybody else ideas, but for that while it was enough. They made things happen. Some years later people would still see remnants of his personal machines in curious places, always identifiable because of the large asterisk he painted on each of them.

He never could convince Isabel to try one of her deliveries with a system of pulleys and other devices, all designed to help. "Designed by a man," she would say and kick him out of the conversation.

While his time was short in scientific time, it was long by all other standards. He lived to a time when his kids called him *papi* and his grandkids called him *tata*, his friends called him *compadre*, and his wife called him *viejo*. It was a good life, a city life, and just what he'd always wanted. One thing stayed with him, however, from childhood. Wherever they lived, Ignacio planted lemon trees. When he first proposed to Isabel, it was in a scent of lemons, and when he died, it was lemons everyone remembered, lemons as much as thunderstorms.

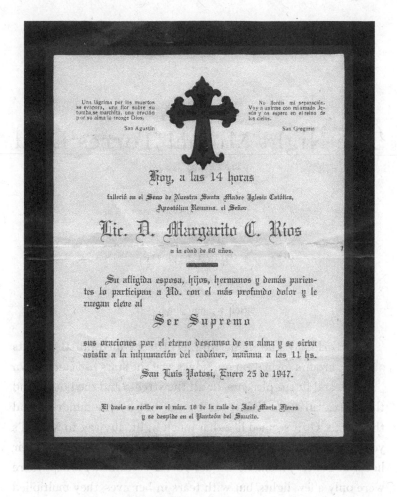

Una lágrima por los muertos se evapora, una flor sobre su tumba se marchita, una oración por su alma la recoge Dios.

San Agustín

No lloréis mi separación. Voy a unirme con mi amado Jesús y os espero en el reino de los cielos.

San Gregorio

Hoy, a las 14 horas

falleció en el Seno de Nuestra Santa Madre Iglesia Católica, Apostólica Romana, el Señor

Lic. D. Margarito C. Ríos

a la edad de 60 años.

Su afligida esposa, hijos, hermanos y demás parientes lo participan a Ud. con el más profundo dolor y le ruegan eleve al

Ser Supremo

sus oraciones por el eterno descanso de su alma y se sirva asistir a la inhumación del cadáver, mañana a las 11 hs.

San Luis Potosí, Enero 25 de 1947.

El duelo se recibe en el núm. 18 de la calle de José María Flores y se despide en el Panteón del Saucito.

THE OBITUARY,
THE PROCLAMATION OF A DEATH

These announcements, they cannot be more serious, no matter how funny the person was. The obituary column is common now in newspapers, but personal notices used to be equally common. The words in an obituary, the proclaiming of a death, they have to be filled with the person who is gone. But only the good, only the plainest language, only the honorable actions.

People may be all these things, of course, but they are always more. A lifetime more.

6

The Night Miguel Torres Died

Curiously, the night Miguel Torres died, all the lights around town went on. It was as if the stars had come down and lit the place up, lit all the streets and the houses and the stores, all these lights one by one but by the hundreds and thousands. Or it seemed like that much light, anyway, to Miguel's young wife, Clotilde, who was looking out the window of their house at the very moment Miguel Torres screamed. Perhaps there were only a few lights, but with tears in her eyes, they multiplied into so many, and all of them at that moment.

When he screamed, so did she, which made even more lights come on, real or imagined she could not say, even when she thought about it later. The scream he made in that instant as a man old before his time was, she imagined, not unlike the scream he made as a newborn child. And those two screams made a set of bookends for his life, which otherwise had been a quiet one.

Clotilde did what she could, but she was young and didn't know much in the way of caring for other people. It was of no consequence to Miguel, this bothering of whether she could or could not take care of him, not any longer. She had been a joy in his life, caring for him more than he could have imagined or hoped, and that was enough. It made anything else bearable, anything.

It was not enough for Clotilde, however, who took to heart the charge she now had in these last weeks. She did and was doing everything possible, everything that could be garnered from the doctor and from Sra. Castañeda, who knew about other ways to cure people, and from Clotilde's own common sense. And praying, too, through it all, praying when it was the one medicine left. What a curiosity, she thought, that this sequence of difficult events should draw her even closer to Miguel, that illness made for a kind of love. This was not a Paris kind of love, not like in the movies, but it was what Paris meant.

She sang to him, she rubbed his head, she brought him soup and red rice with peas and lemon. She brought him watermelon, or what she could find since it was not in season. Everyone knew about watermelon and the dying. The curious thing with all this screaming and all the lights coming on is that her scream was very loud, and it made sense that someone would be curious and turn on their house lights. But his scream was very soft, almost inaudible, a simple sigh. And that was it. It may have been a word, but so many of his words were sighs at their best, thought Clotilde.

But if the sound he made was stillness itself, she nevertheless heard it as a scream—that loud, that much, a sound that filled the room and filled her as well. This is how she remembered that night, but it was not the only way to remember it. The sigh, the lights coming on, the neighbors coming over, the ambulance, the long night, the next day. These were all Clotilde's ways to remember, but Miguel Torres had a mind of his own, and he wanted this night to be remembered in a very different way.

❖

Miguel Torres knew he was dying, even though the doctor generally said otherwise and was very optimistic sounding in the carefully chosen words he used. Dr. Bartolomeo was known for his positive demeanor in all things. He was a devotee of science and absolutely believed what he was saying. And it was that spirit that made him dislike circumstances when things did not work as they should, or could. He was always certain that there was an answer to be found.

"You're too young," said the doctor, even though he looked like a child himself to Miguel, who understood he was just saying that to make Miguel feel better. It was cheap medicine. Miguel trusted Armida Castañeda more, with all her roots and herbs and applications. She was of a generation he understood. She never tried to say if someone was sick or not. Quite the contrary, she often seemed to take the other view, just nodding gravely when people explained their situation. She just listened and then tried to fix whatever they said they were feeling. That was her specialty—not diagnosing, just fixing.

The last time Miguel had visited her, telling her over some coffee about how tired he was feeling, she had given him some ground powder to add to his coffee in the afternoons, and this had helped him quite a bit. That was a very different thing from what the doctor was always trying to do, with tests for this and tests for that and hitting his knee with a little hammer. Her nodding after listening was all the test there was.

Miguel understood what all those words meant from the doctor, however, all the "we'll see how this works" and "perhaps another test will show us." What more did the doctor need? Miguel knew it was something, even if it had no name. Perhaps being introduced face to face with whatever he had was exactly the wrong idea—face to face they would have had to deal with each other and get on with things. At least this way, without knowing, Miguel perhaps had a little more time.

He would go and see Armida again, get some help, and then he would make sense of the world. Or rather, he would make sense of Clotilde, who was the world. If he could take care of her, he could take care of the world, and that's all that needed to be done. If he could take care of himself along the way, that would be a bonus.

Taking care of himself, as things turned out, was part of taking care of Clotilde, at least according to her. This is why he kept up his visits to the doctor and didn't mention so much his visits to Doña Armida. Clotilde thought that doctors were the most modern thing—all those shiny medical instruments and a waiting room and a nurse. These were all very up-to-date ideas, and she would hear of nothing else.

Clotilde did not discount God or religion in all this, but—and it surprised Miguel to hear it only in that he had not heard anyone say such a thing, and so he admired her all the more—*this thing of religion and church, everything that people did, all the sacrifices in the name of Christ, one might be better served in admiring them rather than imitating them.* It made Miguel laugh when she asked where the police were when Christ was being hauled off to be crucified. She was not, as it might sound, uneducated—she meant this as a real question.

All this was easy enough, thought Miguel. He was starting to think of a list of things that would make Clotilde happy, with the ominous overtone that these things needed to keep her happy even if he was not there to be happy with her. She would feel good that she had given him good advice, young as she was. If his seeing a doctor made her happy, then that was it. Done. His job now was to think of the next thing for his list.

Of course, making Clotilde happy was not an easy thing—that is, she was happy when he was happy. He was fortunate in this circumstance because she so willingly believed this, but he knew it was unfair. Still, he understood his greatest gift, now, to her. His would be a happy death after a short sickness, a grace, a good life finished well.

No complaints.

❖

Miguel Torres had been raised by poor parents and had a mean early life. He sold homemade and found and natural items wherever he could and was happy for whatever luck would give him. He did all manner of small work, like it or not, getting paid at the whim of whomever had hired him, though so many would say they had promised no such thing, even after he had finished a hard day's labor.

He worked to please and was doing so even now, all these years later, but for another reason altogether. His was no longer a mean life, and he wished that lot on no one. He helped to end that misery where he saw it and he could, and was followed by the *chicle* and shoeshine boys all around town, known to them all as a soft touch. They could come to him with their stories. He didn't talk very much, but he listened very well.

"When I was young," Miguel Torres told Clotilde one night, "I had three friends. One of them was a dog." The dog, it turns out, was Bernardo, Dr. Bartolomeo's first and most famous patient. Bernardo spoke always with his heart. The other friends were Martín Dos Santos and Cayetano Belmares. All three became something, but they each chose different paths.

Martín became a *licenciado*, a lawyer, who, regarding his own practice, specialized in nothing in particular but knew the law regarding all things generally. It seemed always enough in this town. How he got the money to go to school and get this training was something of a mystery, but considering how hard he worked, which Miguel himself had witnessed many times, it was not surprising that he had managed it. Martín had a vocabulary of words as extraordinary in number as stars in the sky, which explained a great deal. Martín could always be counted on to say something.

Cayetano Belmares, on the other hand, stayed outside town building a *rancho*, the Rancho los Belmares, that over the years included not just cattle but chickens and a dairy and an orchard, with a few fields, now, of wheat and corn, and whatever other enterprises each year suggested. There was always something new, a new fruit, a new cheese. People, when they had time, went out to the orchards in season to pick their fruit fresh, bypassing the *mercado*. Cayetano worked all the time, and people saw him only rarely these days. Cayetano, unlike Martín, spoke best with his hands.

Miguel himself bought and sold properties, which in the beginning of the town's becoming modern was lucrative enough— everyone who wanted a shop came to see Miguel. But the big businesses had not yet come in, so he was always working with friends, or friends of friends, and could always be counted on not to charge an exorbitant price. It kept the town happy and working hard. Miguel, people said, spoke with his heart.

In all these ways of speaking, these three—Miguel, Don Martín, and Cayetano—told the story of the town. And when each married, though it separated them in everyday things, they took care to be sure that all of them were all right and there to be counted on when the sun rose.

But hard work is what Miguel counted on now—not the hard work of driving cattle or speaking to the government, but the hard work that sometimes must be done between and for friends. If he were going to die, he needed to count on somebody to do the abiding work he himself was no longer capable of doing. He needed as well to trust that it would be done, which was almost as difficult as the work itself, giving over that confidence to someone else.

Death might be a mystery, but understanding what the dead want was no such thing. The idea was simple: Miguel wanted to take care of Clotilde even after he died. Whether he would be around to do it himself was uncertain. If he could will it, he would be there. But he understood he was not the first to feel this crush of feeling. It would take more than that. He would try to be there but would take the better precaution as well to put in his place what would be left of his hands and his heart and his good sense.

Miguel was not a person for great plans, and when he was, they were not for himself. A great plan was rarely a great plan for one-self. When people called something a great plan it was usually because they themselves or someone they cared for had benefited from it. Miguel was a person for simple plans, and that is what had gotten him to this point in life, reasonably successful in all things. His greatest joy was to do things that were right in front of him but which he had chosen up to then not to do, for whatever reason. He could feel in himself the moment of suddenly turning around and saying to himself, *Wait, I am not yet finished.* In those moments, in coming back to something everyone else had abandoned, in that small work he found so much of his life, and its goodness. Unfinished business was the way of the world, and taking care of it, most especially in the simplest of life's dealings, was his way of living.

It was precisely that approach, imagining what he could do and wanted to do but had not yet done, that helped him to find Clotilde. And Clotilde, now, was that unfinished business.

The plan, in the tradition of the best he had done in his life, was simple, without decoration or worry or loose threads or uncombed hair. It was simplicity itself. He would first call on Martín Dos Santos, who would give the instruction to his son, Ubaldo, who now carried on the family tradition. But Martín would understand the importance. Miguel would call on him to help devise what could be devised regarding the care of the living by the dead. Some money. The house. A circle of friends to call on. No regrets beyond loss—Miguel wanted that, all those things, put in writing. Miguel wanted to help in this regard, perhaps most in this regard, this helping after he could not be there to help.

He was not a big talker, but he wanted no mistake made regarding what he would have said had he been bold enough. He wanted his words to carry the profound gift—the soft charge—of telling Clotilde to move forward, to walk past him when the moment came, to walk past him and into the many years that would follow. He would tell her this. He would tell her this himself, with words. But his words were so few that some might mistake them as being inconsequential or slight. Perhaps even Clotilde would make that mistake. So he wanted to tell her in writing as well, to give her every permission, every license, every document. He wanted her life to be as big and as long as it could be. He wanted her to be listening for that life, that long life, in his words. These would be the words that would say he loved her.

Martín would find the language to keep this promise and make this life he imagined for her. Cayetano, on the other hand, would find the work that needed to be done, and do it. He would work to make things right. And he would know why work was what needed to be done, every bit as much as words and promises and ideals. He would understand the doing of things firsthand, himself. Cayetano was always where things needed to be done, doing them. No words. That is how the two of them had always spoken to each other.

And that was it. This was his great plan, to do a simple thing—but to do it. To attend to its details, sign everything that needed signing, give everything that might be given. To do and not simply to think. And then to trust that she would do the best she could, but that he would have helped. Miguel would exact whatever promises he needed to exact, but more than that, he would tell his story plain and true to his two best friends from childhood and believe that the goodness he felt in those days they felt, too. Even now. Especially now. It was uncomplicated faith.

It was all so simple, but he was desperate that its simplicity not be misconstrued. Miguel Torres left a will filled with the will to continue, to do what he had done all along, to help in the ways he could, best especially at the smallest ones, helpful most in the half-inches of life's movement. To this end and finally, along with the time it took to explain himself, Miguel left a will with his friend Martín Dos Santos that said only *help her in any way possible.* Next, Miguel left an instruction with his other friend, Cayetano Belmares, which said, again, only *help her in any way possible.* These instructions were too simple to misunderstand.

Miguel and Clotilde had met but didn't know it. That is, they had been introduced, but in a hurry, in a crowd, and with inaccurate names for each other. She thought he was a Rafael and he thought she was a Matilde. There was no time to look into each other's eyes as their friends dragged them off in opposite directions. It was the circus, and everybody was excited, everybody in town on the high wire themselves with the work that night of getting into the right seats, quieting the children, buying sodas and fried plantains rolled in sugar.

Everybody looked at the tableau of marvels waiting to be used, trapezes tied in a bunch at the top of a structure of metal bars, a colorful ring made of decorated wood, not more than two feet high and bedded with straw, empty cages off to the side, leftover confetti from previous shows, the smells of animals, but not animals from around here, an occasional roar, motorcycles revving somewhere in the distance, which was a roaring sound itself, a clown walking through the crowd making fun of this and that and getting made fun of in return, grandparents with big eyes and children with big eyes, paint everywhere, wires everywhere, wires and ropes, all this inside a very big small tent, a dirty canvas affair held up by all manner of beam and hook and anchoring sandbag.

Music started and everyone began to applaud. They had met each other but had met someone else as well, and it was the someone else who took charge of things at first. Those two people who met, Rafael and Matilde, those two others, perhaps they went off and had a wonderful life together. But Miguel and Clotilde as Miguel and Clotilde did not think of each other again, if indeed they had thought of each other at all, so that when they met for a second time it was as strangers, but only to each other.

Everyone else assumed that they already knew each other. It made them both shy, because each thought the other remembered what they did not. And facing each other, foursquare and with those eyes and that hair and that mouth, who would forget this? They were shy, slow to say what they did not know but eager to find out.

Some things happen this way. They married quickly, feeling almost immediately that once they took good measure of each other, being apart was the wrong state of being. Miguel was older than Clotilde by some years. While Clotilde was no child, she still sometimes relied on things from childhood, but the best of them—that trust, that excitement, that obsession, none of which was betrayed by Miguel, none of which was he even capable of betraying. Miguel was not much of a man, as it turned out—he was instead that same boy he used to be, just grown up. They found common and good ground. Their marriage lasted several years, but it was what felt like the longest part of their lives. What they had together was so full that the empty years counted for not nearly as much.

But what was in a day? What made this life? It was not much, thought Miguel. And that was the key. It was getting up, having breakfast together, brushing his teeth, putting his jacket on, going to work, coming home and seeing Clotilde's face before anything else, having supper, talking, and reading. It wasn't much more than that. Those were the best days, when they were not much more than that. Anything else, days when something else happened, only served to take them away from what they loved most. It was the boredom of a wonderful life. In this sense, nothing happening was the best news of all at the end of a long day.

The night Miguel Torres died, all the lights in town went on, but then Clotilde Torres closed her eyes, and they all seemed to go off. It was that simple, open eyes and closed eyes. What her husband had done, she could do. In the darkness from closing her own eyes she could see darkness and then into the darkness, and knew the place of dreams. It was always dark at first, but that wall went away, and everything offered itself. The world of dream—she would find him there.

"Miguel Torres," she would say every night before going to sleep, "I am looking for you."

She imagined she would find him with his dog, Bernardo. In their lives together, Miguel did not say much, but what he said he meant. Regarding Bernardo he said almost nothing, which she understood as gauging the depth of what he felt for that dog. It was enough that she wished she had known the animal herself. Perhaps, she thought, she would one day find Bernardo in another dog, and if she did she would take very good care of it.

If there were ways to think about Miguel, this was a good one. She could recognize the things he left behind easily enough—the house, his shoes, his toothbrush, the dominoes, the lean-to in the yard—but she was more surprised by all the feelings he left behind, which seemed to be hiding behind doorways and under tables no less than his shoes and his dominoes. It was not just the things, but what held the things together. It was not simply ownership that made a person say *that was his toothbrush.*

Miguel had led a life of small kindnesses, and along with the material things he left the kindnesses as well, in places where she would find them. They came to her as memories at first, then as stories other people told her about Miguel, and then as simple feelings, moments of understanding regarding what he would have done in a given moment or what he did in fact do. She herself was not always as generous to the moment, as her sadness sometimes made a noise.

Sometimes it was enough noise to wake up the dog that was not there.

❖

The town with its illnesses, thought Miguel, the things that lived inside people—the minute beasts and the fernlike growths and the wobbling floors that dead people stood on—they made for a different world, not just the world one saw when looking at everyone as if nothing were the matter. In this way, there was never simply a day of errands and shopping. Illness made this town two towns, one inside the other. And each person two people, or a hundred, all inside the one. Illness was its own gossip and talked about everyone.

Illness was everywhere but never told its story, too busy for words, which is what people were left with. Illness quietly and over the years simply changed the town, the shape of the town, the movement of the town. It made the town limp. The town had, as a result, been turned into a gathering of monsters, thought Miguel, a gathering of insects, a place that could no longer recognize itself.

One understood this immediately when looking at the man who was now a caterpillar, Sr. Urquidi, who dragged himself, his legs no longer legs. Sra. Jauregui, an unmistakable butterfly who weighed nothing and flitted all about with an attention that weighed the same, everything fluff, one moment moving on almost immediately to the next. The moth, Don Chuy, who was thick and had to work hard at what he did, had to work hard at sustaining flight, which did not come naturally and which is why he breathed hard all the time. Doña Celestina, who spun webs, catching whatever and whoever walked by her front porch.

They were everywhere, the things people had become. The gnats, those children running here and there and in everybody's way. The mantises, always hungry, always planning. The mosquitoes, those people who made business deals without telling a person everything, and at the right moment and in a single instant hurt them. The ladybugs, sweetness itself, so many more than one might suspect, like Berta Castañeda, thought Miguel. And, for that matter, her husband, Perfecto, ladybugs both.

There were the walking sticks, who blended in and were always simply somewhere around, the people who were neither loud nor quiet, black nor white, tall nor short. The bees, those hungry young men who came in from the fields and the faraway *ranchos* and *campos* and *llanos* and *montañas*, always looking for work and not afraid to do it. They could be counted on. Cayetano's sons were bees.

Even health was a kind of illness here, an affliction inexplicably visited only on some. It was an affliction in that those who worked had to work hard, having to do the work so many others could not. And there was a great deal of work in this world.

And there were all the rest, the other illnesses and their pet people, the afflicted who became the worms, the ticks, the beautiful green *mayates* and the curiously articulated potato bugs, who could roll themselves up into a protective ball. All of them, and so many. The people he knew and the things they became, it was all something to see. And, he understood, he was no different from any of them.

This, this was the circus, finally, thought Miguel, the real circus—not that crude entertainment he and Clotilde had seen so many years ago. These people around him, they were the true daredevils and acrobats, living their precarious and delicate lives, doing in these circumstances the extraordinary work of picking up the simplest of things, mustering up the sheer will to walk a few steps out into the yard or onto the street. These were the bravest ones. These were the real lions. The tigers and elephants.

All of them, the whole town, lived in a century crazy for names, thought Miguel, the names of things that were, that existed, that were all around, a century hungry for what-was-causing-what, giddy for knowing. It made sense. From knowing came the next step: *all the answers*. But in between, in between was only that— grayness and half-light, the liminal flap of the butterfly's wing in a light wind, hope and hopelessness both, but neither quite. He, Miguel, was just one more in this gray light, inhabiting a life whose address in time was in between.

What made this life worthwhile came in a small voice from somewhere in the distance: "Miguel Torres, I am looking for you." It was a quiet sound, and just what he hoped to hear.

Once the century itself started looking, the answer was always in view, but not within reach. It was always just ahead. Dr. Bartolomeo always had news of that news, and the counsel to others that the answer was so close, and that one must be patient and try to hold on. It was coming, the answer, but not yet. In that middle distance between the old centuries and the new science that everyone was talking about and which was in all the magazines, Miguel Torres died. Ten years later he would not have.

THE SONG ON THE RADIO

It played what seemed like every five minutes on the Spanish station KXEW.

"Café Combate" was not a song so much as a commercial that had a song in it, and not even a song so much as a jingle, but one of those jingles that's like a thorn under your skin. It was so simple, about coffee, about drinking coffee. It was a jingle that everyone could sing, a jingle that would stay alive into the next century, and whose power nobody could explain. Its opening, *Café Combate, la gente toma, / Café Combate, de rico aroma*, was what everyone remembered, even though there was much more to the song.

But perhaps that was after all the essence of coffee itself, coffee and the break one took in order to enjoy it.

A coffee cup raised to the lips: It was a celebration of the half second, of the first sip, welcome, loud in its simple quietude, a personal secret in a public moment.

7

Two Small Crimes

Sra. Clotilde Torres had woken, rubbed her eyes, with some difficulty got herself up from the bed, put her feet into her slippers, went to the bathroom, then to the kitchen to start the morning coffee, no different from any other day, she said. She had opened the kitchen curtains, looked out at the crabapple tree in the yard—it was all just sticks this time of year, no leaves, no fruit. It was a drawing of a tree, really, an idea.

"I know what you mean," said the officer sitting across the table. "Trees aren't really trees in January." Sergeant Maldonado and Doña Clotilde were drinking the coffee she had just mentioned. The coffee had been sitting in front of him awhile now and was probably cold, though he didn't say anything. He began to bring the cup to his lips, prepared to compliment the taste regardless.

"Let me warm that," Doña Clotilde said just at the same moment he thought about it being cold, as if she knew what he was thinking. Florencio Maldonado could tell that Doña Clotilde knew how a kitchen worked and how all the things in it should behave. She was like his own mother that way.

He protested her offer to bring some more coffee, but not much. Before he could say anything further, she got up and brought the pot of coffee to the table, poured him some, and waited for the steam to rise.

"I think it's still hot," she said, but waited for the steam to be sure. In this chill morning kitchen the steam showed itself quickly, a swirl and a jerk as it lifted itself from the cup, its movement remembering the jarring addition of more coffee. "It's like me getting up out of bed, fighting with the covers," she said. "A little bit of fight, anyway. It looks like courage, don't you think? That's why I like to drink coffee in the morning. It gives me something."

He laughed a little, seeing clearly what she meant in the unsettled rising of the steam, the coffee itself still moving a little in his cup. Coffee had always been simply coffee for him. The stronger the better.

"I smell my village in that cup. It's something from a long time ago." Doña Clotilde said these words aloud, and they startled her. She didn't intend to say this to the officer, this little boy Florencio trying to look so grown up. Her village was far away from her now. He wouldn't understand.

But Florencio Maldonado did understand. He had come from a small place, too, though he was very young when his family left to come north. It was really his parents who had come from that place, but he had heard about it often enough. *Our village*, they used to say. And he remembered.

"I know what you mean, Sra. Torres," said Florencio.

"Please, call me Clotilde," she said to him right away. "You've known me since you first came here."

"Doña Clotilde, then." Florencio Maldonado nodded his head. That was certainly true—their families had known each other for many years. They had lived on opposite sides of town, but that didn't mean much in a place this size, even if it thought of itself as big, certainly as bigger than a village. People just knew people. And if they didn't know somebody, chances were excellent that they knew about them. One could know all sorts of things about a person without ever having actually met face to face. So much police work operated that way.

The coffee was good. But now Florencio had to take a breath and get on with things. It was taking that breath that always turned him back into Sergeant Maldonado.

"Well, we should get down to business, shouldn't we?" said Doña Clotilde, faster than Florencio could say it. She could see the fullness of the breath he took and understood perhaps even better than he what taking a breath like that meant. It was just as well. She had been about to do the same thing, to take a deep breath herself. She was in no mood to dawdle either. This was not about coffee and small villages, after all.

On the other hand, Clotilde was not anxious to explain her situation to Sergeant Maldonado, this child. He looked like a man, but she had known him for too long. *Where would I start? How much would I tell him?*

Sergeant Maldonado took out his notebook and a pencil, about to ask her what had happened.

That's how it is, isn't it, thought Clotilde. *A notebook and a pencil.* She would have taken out a frying pan and some butter and asked, *Where's the chicken?* They simply had different ways of looking at the world.

❖

She had already told him about the regular part of the morning, how everything was like it always was, and how she did everything she always did. Clotilde was thankful he had not rushed her, and the coffee was a nice distraction. But now it was time.

"I'll tell you about the second thing first, if you don't mind."

"Of course, whatever you'd like," said Sergeant Maldonado. "Any order, as long as it's an order of some sort, will be fine," he added, pleased with himself to sound so wise, and to have thought of it just like that. He would try to remember this remark. It would be helpful to him in other cases as well. A simple statement, but useful—he liked those things best of all.

Clotilde could see the flicker of satisfaction that he felt, and could appreciate it. He sounded like a fine policeman. He was a good boy.

"I lost my husband," began Clotilde. This time it was her turn to take a deep breath and be serious. "The dogs are gone, too. The house needs repairs, as I'm sure you've noticed. I've lost so much, and it doesn't stop."

Sergeant Maldonado looked down, not straight at her. He wavered in his policeman sensibility, and for a moment went back to being Florencio.

"But that's not a crime, is it? I mean, you know what I mean," said Florencio.

"No, no, I was just saying, losing so much. It makes losing something small seem so meaningless."

"Not at all, Doña Clotilde. Did someone take something from you?" So that was it, thought Sergeant Maldonado. Someone stole something from her. Well, they would hear from him, she could count on that. "What was it? Tell me what happened."

To ask an old lady what happened, that's a big mistake unless you really want to know everything. Police say they want to know everything, but it's not true. The moment they bring an old lady in and she starts to tell them everything, they are sorry.

"Or rather, really, don't worry about everything. Just tell me what it was. Something outside? Or did someone break in?" Sergeant Maldonado wasn't sure what he wanted to hear and was also a little nervous about how much. He had other cases to work on as well, after all.

He was, curiously, suddenly nervous, though he tried not to show it. Was it better to hear everything, even if it took all day? Or better to hear a boiled-down version and depend on the teller to choose the important details? *There's no winning in this*, he thought. Or else the answer was clear, but it was not what he, or anyone else for that matter, wanted to hear. Listening to everything, start to finish, was the only solution. But the time it would take—who had time like that?

"No, nobody broke in, not exactly like that. But someone did take something."

"Ah," said Sergeant Maldonado, and thought *now we're getting somewhere.*

"But don't think that will answer anything," said Doña Clotilde. "It won't. And that's the thing. This is a little bit, well, a little bit delicate, I think. Am I able to confide in you?"

"Of course, Doña Clotilde, of course," said Sergeant Maldonado, but he said it more as a reflex than as something true.

"It's just, well, someone took my cow."

"Well that's something, something very clear. We can do something about that," said Sergeant Maldonado, invigorated by this clear-cut state of affairs. A stolen cow, that was serious, and reasonably easy to solve, at least if past history were any indication. Stealing a cow, that was serious business.

"A milk cow?" he asked, to be sure. Otherwise, he thought, somebody would be enjoying a good dinner tonight, perhaps. It happened from time to time, people taking, or rather *finding* a cow or some cattle, and proceeding to make short work of things. A little extra in the butcher shop or a truck driving around offering some "surplus" meat—he had seen this before.

"Yes, my cow, Paquita. Maybe you remember her? She's been here a long time, though I keep her in the backyard. You've seen her, I think."

More than that, thought Florencio Maldonado. He had once, how could this be said? He had once *borrowed* some milk from her. One cow gave enough milk for many people, after all. He was sure she hadn't missed it. And there was more.

"I'm sure you remember her," repeated Doña Clotilde.

"Someone stole Paquita?" asked Sergeant Maldonado, surprised. People stole animals in the abstract, as far as his experience went. They found cattle, or they shot something from the road and ran away with it. But someone's personal cow? He had never heard of such a thing.

And Paquita. Of all the cows in the world. He had a history with that cow. *Florencio, Florencio*, he thought to himself, loudly enough that he was afraid Doña Clotilde had heard him. His story was something more than the milk he had *borrowed*. That cow had been a part of his life.

❖

That cow, as things turned out, had been part of everybody's life. Everybody knew Paquita, but not for any regular reason, not because people could see her grazing by the fence or because she was paraded around town or anything else like that, not any of the ready reasons one might know a cow in this town. Quite the opposite. Everybody knew Paquita because they were not supposed to. She was a secret cow, and everybody knew it. That's how secrets were around here.

Nobody really knew why Paquita was a secret, simply that she was one, and that they had to take care not to say anything. That's what they said to each other—*Don't say anything.* Otherwise, of course, everyone would know. The fact that everyone already knew was not the point. Everybody was always interested in keeping a secret.

Paquita was a handsome cow, handsome as only small-town people can understand. A dull white with black continents on her back, she wasn't used up or on such a production schedule that she became a machine more than a cow. She had time for talk, which is what everyone understood her flicking of the ear and quick raising of the tail to be. She had time for thinking, which is what they understood her idling into the field after a particularly long conversation to be. She had time to understand happiness, which is why people milked her, which was an additional benefit of the moment and also saved them a little bit of money. Most important, however, she had time to listen, which was the point. Listening was everything. And curiously, that sense of listening was in her eyes.

Who else had the time, after all? Finding someone to listen, really listen, someone—or in this case something—who could take in all manner of confession and make no judgment, whose flick of the ear, in fact, suggested that the person keep on doing what brought them there to begin with—finding this grace was an enormous boon to people. The priest, Father Gagnon, should have been the one everybody confided in, and he was, to a point, but not to the extent to which people bared their souls to Paquita. Father Gagnon knew everybody, and could not on occasion stop himself from raising an eyebrow at one thing or another. His raised eyebrow, it was clear, was not the same thing as Paquita's flicked ear. One was a blessing, more of a *carry on* and *it's all right, it's all right,* while the other was simply what it was, a raised eyebrow. While everybody liked to listen to Father Gagnon speak because of his strong accent, which came from somewhere nobody could quite remember, they did not equally like to hear him speaking directly to them.

So, depending on what a person needed to say, some Saturdays had a line of people outside the confessional, and some days—it need not be a Saturday, as Paquita did not keep a schedule in the same way that Father Gagnon did—a line of sorts formed behind Clotilde Torres's house. For the first few years, Doña Clotilde and the visitors ignored each other. But as time wore on, she started to invite people in, and made coffee and tea and had some small cookies always at the ready.

For this kindness she would find mysterious packages at her doorstep, cookies and replenished coffee and sometimes food, whole dinners even, with notes on how to heat this or that or how to refrigerate it properly. Sometimes she found money. Any given item wasn't much, but at the end of a month, things added up. In recent years, in fact, *added up* was an understatement. It was how Clotilde Torres made her way in the world.

But there was more to this story, and that was what was going to be difficult.

She looked at Sergeant Maldonado.

"Someone stole Paquita?" asked Sergeant Maldonado again, and it was clear that he was surprised. Any other cow, that would be one thing. But Paquita?

"You know about Paquita, then?" asked Doña Clotilde.

"Oh, well, you know, I've heard things." Sgt. Maldonado moved around uncomfortably in his chair, looking stern but not directly at her, keeping his eyes on his notebook.

"She's just a cow, a cow that I've had for many years, though that may surprise people. But who doesn't have a cow, really?" she asked. It was common enough. Not everybody went to the *mercado* to buy everything. Some people still lived in the old way, trying to make everything they needed.

Sergeant Maldonado was sure that she was going to tell him about some other cow, even though he had never seen another one in the field behind her house. Paquita—that was ridiculous. Nobody would steal Paquita. Nobody. And for what?

"Well, that's the one thing, of course. Somebody seems to have stolen her. But the other thing I need to tell you, well, Florencio, you're a big boy now."

He looked up.

"Well, you're going to ask me about Paquita, I know. But you have to help me with this, I think. The thing is, Paquita was not, may not, was not exactly mine to begin with."

Sergeant Maldonado's eyes widened.

"You may still have another search for a cow somewhere in your records, I don't know," said Doña Clotilde. She tried to be matter-of-fact even as she revealed something of her darkest secret. But she knew enough about cattle to understand that there were papers involved, and brands, and that sort of thing. She was not an expert, but she knew that much. Everybody knew where cattle came from, which cows and bulls were related to what particular cow and bull parents—that sort of thing. Clotilde Torres had always lived in fear that somebody, somewhere, kept meticulous notes on these kinds of things. A missing cow, especially a milk cow, would be big news in a small town. And perhaps in a neighboring small town as well. Or on someone's *rancho*. She knew that. Very big news.

But she knew something more, as well, which she very much hoped she would not have to say, no matter how big a boy this Florencio was now. The crime at hand seemed to be someone taking Paquita, and that was just how she hoped to keep it. Anything more, well, what was the point? What was the point, really, after so many years?

❖

Paquita carried everybody's secrets with her, so the necessity of finding her right away was clear enough to Sergeant Maldonado. It was not as if the cow could speak, of course, but the weight of all those stories, that meant something. People could point at Paquita and say, *there they are.*

For some, she was a sorrow eater, taking the hardest stories in and keeping them safe. That sadness would have eaten up other people had they been told, and needed tending, which Paquita did very well. Those eyes said that she understood and that they could leave this or that baby with her, which is to say, this or that baby's death. It was not fair to Paquita, but those who left her with these stories could not have gone forward otherwise. She understood. The sound Paquita sometimes made, that lowing that filled the air with its surprising volume and low tone, that sound was her record-keeping.

And for others it was love, so much about love. Who else would have the patience to listen? It was so often unrequited love, but no less painful or thrilling or hopeful. It was this love mixed into her among the other stories that gave Paquita the strength to stand. The love stories, and there were so many kinds—even the stories of the babies were love stories—these gave her the belly that she carried, and about which she did not complain. She simply opened her eyes all the wider and took in whatever came next.

And there was more, though nobody dared think about it. There were other kinds of stories in the world, stories that were perhaps not so much about love. She carried these, too, with no more complaint, though she would shift her weight from time to time in response to the heaviness of standing in one place to hear what needed to be heard. In those moments, one supposed, nobody would be surprised if she were dreaming of being a horse. But she said no such thing and stayed where she was, every time.

How this all started, even Doña Clotilde could not say. It may in fact have started with her, shushing Paquita when she first arrived, calming her, pleading with her not to make any noise. And she had listened. That was perhaps the beginning of everything, the story Clotilde herself told Paquita that first night, all those years ago.

"Yes, yes, I know about Paquita. Well, the Paquita I know, that's what I know. I don't understand about another cow. I'm not sure what you mean, Doña Clotilde."

"Would you like some more coffee?" she offered, to make the story as plain as anything, regular, as easy as saying *yes* to a next cup of *café con leche*, which everyone loves. It was the best plan she could come up with.

❖

"I was a young widow—I don't know if you knew that. I was young, and my life was happy, and then, you didn't know him, but my husband died. Don Miguel. It was simple, nothing complicated. Miguel was older than I was, and he just died, a heart attack in his sleep, and that was the end of it, his life and mine, over in the failing of a single heartbeat. I took it very hard, but in time things got slowly better. It's an old story. I loved him very much, which always makes things harder. Love should make things easier, but it doesn't work that way." Doña Clotilde got this all out quickly. Sergeant Maldonado started by taking notes but then just listened.

"After some time went by, a year maybe, after all the *pésames*, the *I'm sorries*, after all the food baskets and invitations to dinner, after the flowers and all the offers of help around the house with this and that, after all that, things began to run out."

"You mean the money?" asked Sergeant Maldonado.

"The money, things in good repair, the future. It all began to simply run out."

"Ah," said the sergeant and nodded his head.

"Cayetano and Miguel had been friends since childhood," said Clotilde, "and Cayetano used to spend time over here when he was on this side of his *rancho*. Their place is so big, now, that it took a lot of time for Cayetano to look over all his land and do the work that each part of it required."

"It *is* a big place," the sergeant agreed. "I have gotten lost there myself, in the orchards picking fruit. Keeping things in order all over that place must be a big job."

Doña Clotilde nodded. "I look around my own kitchen and understand that—each corner here needs something in just the same way, a spoon needing to be put away, a spot of something spilled on the floor needing to be wiped up, the broom needing to be returned to its place behind the door. It never stops."

"Never," added Sergeant Maldonado.

"There is a hill in between his land and ours, and Cayetano would always take the time and trouble to make that ride over here to visit. It was very nice of him. Sometimes Miguel was in town, at work, and it was just the two of us. We would have coffee and talk about things, and I would tease him about how he was *Don* Cayetano now. And we would talk about his family, and his love for the world. That was always the curious thing to me—Cayetano, you'll find this out when you speak to him—Cayetano was made for this place. All these small hills, all this heat, all this work, it's all him. They are not separate things. They are all him."

Sergeant Maldonado nodded. Everyone knew that about Cayetano Belmares. He was always at work.

"Well, after Miguel passed away, Cayetano kept visiting, and he could see that I was nearing the end of what I could do for myself. Miguel had left me a little bit of money, or rather, he had left it in our jar in the kitchen, our emergency money, but that was all. His work gave us enough money to live on, but not much more. Like everybody. Like your own family, Florencio."

He understood.

"That's when Cayetano offered to do something, but I said no, it was asking too much. He laughed it off and said he knew just what would work. It's hard to argue with him when he sees how to fix something."

❖

"We were friends, it's true, but even so, giving—lending—a cow. It was his idea. He would lend me the cow, and he would say to his wife, to his cowhands, that it was lost, that it had somehow wandered, but that he would find it, that he would look for it, that *this and that and another thing*—and somewhere in the gray of so many words and weeks it would be all right. His wife and the workers must have missed the cow terribly, but I couldn't think about that. Cayetano said he would take care of things for the time the cow was gone. I listened to him, and believed it. I was crazy with myself, with what I was going to do and how I was going to live. I would have done anything," said Clotilde, and stopped for a moment.

Sergeant Maldonado did not rush her. He felt the moment as well.

"I would have done anything, and this was simply what there was to do, too easy almost, but harder work than one would think."

"Making Paquita move, I can imagine."

"Yes. It was me, in the night. I was the one who led Paquita from the far pasture around the small hill over to my small yard. I tell you this now, but I've never told anyone else. I entrust this information to you, Florencio."

Sergeant Maldonado shifted nervously in his chair again.

"Our walk took all night and part of the next morning. Paquita did not know how to walk to a new place, and I had to show her. And the harder work of disguising her, of making her into another cow, that was something, and it started right away. I used coffee to stain her hide and different things to make the black spots look different, grease and oil at first, then later some paint. I kept it up for many years. Every morning, I made her up more than I did myself."

Sergeant Maldonado was smiling, could not hold back a laugh.

"Well," continued Clotilde, "Cayetano came by later to check on things and then kept coming over, the same way as if nothing had happened and he was looking for Miguel but found only me. A year later, one day, he came over as usual, but it was different. I think it was different. We had some coffee. It was early afternoon, and he happened to be on my side of his world. I asked him in, and we looked at each other, for a very long time. It was not more than that, but it was something strong. What we did not do is what we did. I was a young widow, as I said, and what we did not do was a very big thing to do—that is, *thinking it* was so strong that it stayed in the air. It was not the first time, not exactly. After that, though, he did not want to take the cow back at all. And he never brought Paquita up again."

"Ah," was all that Sergeant Maldonado could think of to say. He was glad, for once, that she did not stop speaking.

"But I have lived in fear all this time. You see how it has made me so quiet all these years. My fear was not of Cayetano coming to get the cow, but that something would happen to him, and that someone else would find out—his wife, Guillermina, most of all. You know Sra. Belmares, I think? Who doesn't. Nobody would want her to find out—I think you understand that. Nobody would want her to find out for so many reasons. But more than that, I feared for Cayetano himself, in that losing him now would be like losing a second husband. He had taken care of me that much."

"Ah," said Sergeant Maldonado again, repeating himself.

❖

"So there you have it, Sergeant Maldonado. Two crimes. The first is that I need to report that Paquita is missing, but I cannot, as you now understand. That, after all, is the second crime, though it happened first. Since I have no Paquita, you know, everybody, well, nobody will say that I do—so that to claim her I would be admitting to more than will be helpful, don't you think?" Doña Clotilde did not wait for his answer. "There is the little matter of a brand, after all, which the coffee stain will keep covered for only so long, and only then from the eyes but not the hands, which will feel it easily."

"A brand, then?" asked Sergeant Maldonado. This was unfortunate.

Doña Clotilde nodded. "Yes. However, for all practical purposes, I am saying that there is no Paquita. She does not exist. But you must find her."

"Ah," said Sergeant Maldonado once more. Now he understood.

Or rather, he understood that he did not understand, not everything, nor did he want to. He had enough to go on. A missing cow. That part was simple enough, and something he could take care of. He told her as much, and Clotilde smiled, grateful that Sergeant Maldonado did not repeat back to her the whole story he had just heard.

And he meant it, he said to her with a sure nod of his head. He would help. A missing cow was easy. "Cows wander away sometimes, especially when they aren't tied to anything. You don't have a fence?"

"Well, a fence would mean that I had a cow," responded Doña Clotilde.

"Yes, I see. And you yourself can't go looking for a cow if there is no cow to look for. You are just hoping for life to continue as it has."

"Just as it has."

"Well, if I were looking for a cow, there would be many possibilities here. The moon leads them, or the smell of food in the air, some other animal's food, so that they are led in that moment like anyone would be." He would find her. This missing cow, especially with its brand, would be easy to find, but returning it to its owner, that would be difficult. A brand is a brand, after all. But if it was on loan, certainly that was a different situation.

The brand aside, still, and he repeated it, a missing cow, he could help with a missing cow.

And he wanted to. He already knew how. The trick would be to approach Paquita the way everybody did. Approach her from her left side and speak into her left ear. Then wait for the ear to twitch, to say *all right*. Whatever was on her right side, Florencio understood, had nothing to do with the town, and the twitch of that ear was simply the twitching of an ear. He had no business on that side of the world, no business and no interest.

"Don't worry," said Sergeant Maldonado to Clotilde Torres as he stood to leave and walked slowly toward the door. "Don't worry." As he walked, he looked around at the things in this small room, all of them quiet, the candles and the photographs, the doilies on the chairs and the old radio in its cabinet, all these things, all of them, holding their breath. "You've told me what I need to know."

CIVIL REGISTRATION

We keep important papers. But sometimes there is a fire, or a misspelled name, or a lost suitcase, or a misrepresentation. Sometimes, so simple and sensible a thing as moving a document from one place to another—*how logical at the time!*—loses it forever. And this, which cannot be explained: it sometimes gets put in the trash by someone trying to help, so much does junk mail look persuasively official, that quality of green ink with black, that spiraling effect along the border.

Still, years later, so many things turn out to have survived.

But as it also turns out, passed from mother to daughter, so much about a document can be misplaced again.

8

Ten Seconds in Two Lives

Julio saw Marta in the rearview mirror, standing there in the cold, as he stepped on the brakes to back up slowly. The brake lights shone on her as much as on the driveway. He saw her in that moment bloom rose against the gray, ruby against the fog. Rather than any ghostly appearance in that circumstance, bundled up, cold, covered, Marta was instead suddenly more alive than anything else he had seen. The red shining on her showed him life, life itself, something alive and not withering, something warmed up in spite of the hard, cruel cold. The whole event was not more than ten seconds, but sometimes ten seconds is enough to last a lifetime.

The cold was a stranger to the desert, not a regular visitor, and unsettling every time. It was always the news when it arrived, on the radio, in the newspapers, in every conversation. Nobody had the clothes for these few days, which came around only once every several years. This kind of cold, the unexpected visit of an inconsiderate cousin from far away, this kind of cold was colder, in that there was no real way to prepare for it. And to have made plans, really, it would have been a waste anyway. A few days, that was it. One could put jackets on top of the blanket on the bed, wear pajamas under clothes, stay inside—none of that was so difficult.

It was the heat one had better be prepared for. And here was the thing—Julio, seeing Marta, stopped feeling the cold, just like that, in that instant and from there afterward. No cold, not as long as she looked back at him. And she was looking at him when he saw her in the red light from the brakes—that was the sharp part of the feeling he felt, her eyes, looking at him.

Had he been a child, he might have construed this as the *mal de ojo*, some kind of evil eye, the way he looked at her and she looked back at him, and the way that moment seemed unshakeable, as if some kind of light traveled between them, a light having nothing to do with the brakes. But he was not a child, and this was as far away from the *mal de ojo* as could be, but just as strange. Love at first sight. It was that exactly, even though he already knew Marta, and even though they had already been dating. This was something else, and everything. It was love at thirtieth sight, which, thought Julio, was probably more rare than the first-sight one.

Or really, it was at five thousandth sight, something more like that. They were married, now, for almost a year. And everything was good, very good, so this way of seeing her came as even more of a surprise.

He didn't know whether to say anything to Marta about it. He didn't know if she felt it, too. And if she didn't, he didn't want to know. If she did—well, yes, but he couldn't take the chance. And besides, he felt it enough for the both of them.

After Julio backed carefully out of the driveway, which was so narrow that only one person could get into a car, when he was far enough and slowed to a stop, still staring at her even though she had averted her eyes to the ground—perhaps simply because of the cold—Marta got into the car on the passenger side. This was not their car, and they were both taking great care not to do any damage. They drove slowly and looked more carefully at corners. They parked far away from the front door in the store parking lots. They had the car for a couple of days, taking care of it for a friend, but with the bonus that they got to use it as much as they wanted. During these several cold days, it had been a great help.

Their own car was an incorrigible teenager of a thing, unreliable and disaffected, never working when they needed it to. But it was all they could afford. The irony was that spending money on its troubles is exactly what kept them from getting a better car. They didn't know what to do about it, so that just when they would decide to sell it, or hope that someone would haul it away, it suddenly broke down, right at that moment. And it was smart—if they were on the edge regarding their budget, then it would only be a small thing, a door handle or a gas cap. It seemed to be able to break in relation to how much money they had or were about to have.

That was their car and this was this car, thought Julio, this car on a cold night with Marta and nothing more to do except some evening errands, all simple, and maybe some dinner if there was enough money left over. Dinner with his beautiful wife.

The thing about beauty and his wife, and why he hadn't quite thought about it that way, nor did he think that others did, was that those ten seconds in the red light were his, suddenly and absolutely. Even if he were a painter or a sculptor or a photographer, he could not pose her in that position to make the moment happen again. It was those seconds, and though he didn't know it yet, they would last him a lifetime.

And at the slow rate things were moving in their lives, this seemed like a long time. Work was good, but not great. They had enough to eat, but not to feast on. They had enough clothes, but not more. They had a house, but a very small one. In all things they were at the start of something, the start of a life, but they could not seem to get it into the next gear.

It had been a headlong rush for so much of their lives, at least in these last several years, that moving slowly now seemed wrong, a wrong turn, a bad sign. Julio could remember so easily asking Marta to marry him—after, of course, asking her father. He remembered how her saying *yes* had made him feel, then their wondering about what they would do once the initial happy days settled themselves. They moved into the boarding house in town at first, trying to save money while Julio found work doing a variety of small jobs. But small jobs meant small money. His brother came to town to do the same thing, and had more luck, so that Julio worked for him for a while. Then Julio heard about the group that was going to cross the border, and like Marta saying *yes*, this made him feel something.

It had an effect on Marta, too, once he explained things. Leaving town for good did not excite them, leaving their families and everything they had known, but what they might encounter, what a little bit of imagination might gain them, they both felt that. The feeling was not excitement, exactly, but more like need. It was a direction much more than geographic. It was a direction in their minds, and once they imagined another world it called to them like a magnet might speak to a nail.

And after all, they were young, they were in love, and they were—in that moment—the definition of what was new in the world. To live somewhere new as well, this only made sense. The United States—it was what the *rancho* was to his father, thought Julio. It was the future. It was the risk worth taking, and hard work was the way to make one's luck. Julio had no reservations about that. His father had taught him not to be a stranger to hard work. In fact, his father had taught him not to even think of it as hard work. Whatever needed doing on any given day was simply what needed to be done. There was no time for *hard* and *easy*, which just got in the way every time. There was only ever *next.*

❖

All that was a long time ago now. Getting here had been, finally, uneventful. He and Marta read about people getting into trouble crossing the border all the time now, but for them it was not like that. With the help of Licenciado Ubaldo Dos Santos, the town lawyer, they had worked hard at all the papers they needed to get into the country. And then they waited.

They took an English class, and then another and another. And when the waiting was over, they simply came across, new citizens, just like that. There were a thousand details, but each one was simply the next one, neither harder nor easier, not more aggravating or less aggravating, more time-consuming or less time-consuming. In fact, time itself was not time itself—it was simply one more part of the process, as if it were a box to be checked on a white piece of official-looking paper with twenty other boxes requiring consideration, filed among twenty other pieces of paper equally boxed.

What kept them going was that they did it together. They practiced words on each other. They filled out forms together, and they laughed. There was not much to laugh about, but that didn't stop them. They worked and they laughed, and this was the secret they found together regarding this particular moment in their lives, but it seemed to apply to everything else as well.

Licenciado Dos Santos had counseled them to have patience as well, patience and a little more money, first for one thing and then another. And then another. Throughout this process, a little more money added up twenty or thirty times became something other than a little more money, and this always meant more work and more time. But if Licenciado Dos Santos found a problem each time, he also found a solution, and they were ready. They worked, they stood in lines, they mailed off letters and forms and fees.

That's what Julio had found so attractive in Marta, her willingness to do what needed to be done, just the same way he felt about things. Getting things done felt good, but not everybody moved through the world in that way. Licenciado Dos Santos seemed to share that feeling, however, so Julio felt he had come to the right person. The *licenciado* had a reputation for being thorough, which was good, as there seemed to surface so many legal nooks and crannies that, without him, would have drowned them. They were willing to swim, long and hard, but they needed someone to keep them pointed in the right direction.

But they had gotten through it all. The paperwork, the lawyers, the offices, the governments, the federal people, the state people, the local people, the Border Patrol, who were a government all by themselves—they had gotten through it all, and now they were on the next step of things.

After all that, the next step seemed like a step backward, or a step in place, at most. They felt now like they were on a treadmill, one of those machines Julio saw when he looked in the window of the health center. If all those people were doing something that put all that walking to use, well it was an idea. But somebody had the better idea of work belonging only to the one person, with no impact on anyone else, and maybe that was the way to go. Work for one, like dinner for one. Personal things. It made Julio laugh. Personal bridges, personal streets, personal everythings. Maybe it's what he wanted, too.

None of that mattered right now. He and Marta had a car tonight, Marta was suddenly beautiful to him, and the night had just started. Maybe the next step wasn't such a big one after all, not what he thought it would be. Maybe it was simply a step he had missed, and that's what all this moving in place was all about. Maybe the step was Marta.

He turned to look at her again, and she smiled at him. It was a nice smile. Maybe personal things were something to think about.

❖

They had each other, after all. Through everything they had each other, and together they had worked in the world and done things for other people and done all right for themselves as a consequence. But each other—what had he done for Marta? All the work, the paychecks, all that, of course, but the question nagged him beyond those things. There was the baby, the idea of a baby, of course, and that would be something, but that did not seem to be happening. No baby so far. And it had been awhile now.

They could go to the doctor, but that cost money. And what would the doctor say, anyway? They could or they couldn't. It was that simple. If they could, then it would happen, and if they couldn't, then that was that. Julio knew that Marta wanted a child, but that she was afraid as well, a life so precarious. They had left a world where a child would have been welcome and welcomed, first with a big announcement in the town by Dr. Bartolomeo and then a baptism and all the rest. They had left that behind. Marta was right to be scared here, honestly. They read about so many things happening, so much fear. Working hard was the easiest part of it all.

There was this other thing about having a baby. He wasn't sure if he wanted one. In his heart he knew a truth that in public, and even in private to Marta, he betrayed, always saying he would work hard and take care of them and be strong. But the truth of it was, he was not a man, just a boy who had grown up. Boys want a lot, and he had worked to get all of those things, but the going was slow. That time didn't add up to suddenly becoming a man. And the slower it got, the less of a man and the more of a boy he felt. He couldn't come up with the answers for what to do differently, so that things would get better.

On the other hand, thought Julio, *we are not who we were.* He was not the boy he had been, and she was not the girl who laughed at him. That was a long time ago, it seemed. They had changed, the world had changed, and the answers had changed. Hard work used to be the answer, but now it seemed like hard work was just hard work, and that doing it only meant more of it.

That's why Julio had listened to Hector Alegría, whose car this was. He had lent it to them.

"It's going to be a cold couple of nights," Hector had said. "Go ahead. I won't be using it myself." He was going on a small trip, he had said, work of some sort. And the car, well the car was just there to be used.

"Better to get it running than to let it freeze out on the street," he had said.

It made sense to Julio, who was glad to help out. "No good to let it sit there," he had agreed. They both laughed. Julio wanted to use the car, and Hector knew it. But Julio would never have dreamed of asking, so the offer came as something of a gift. A welcome gift. Here, after all, was something Julio could do for Marta. It wasn't much, but it wasn't nothing either. A nice car for a few days could help them see what was possible for them, possible and not far away, Julio hoped.

"If you'll just do one thing for me," Hector said casually, a seeming afterthought.

"Of course," offered Julio.

"I think you might like doing this. It's nothing. It's easy. And they will probably give you a tip for your trouble, like a pizza guy. If they do, keep it. It's yours."

"Well, that would be even better. No problem."

"There's a small package in the trunk. Could you take it to the address that's written on it? It won't take even a few minutes. But don't do it until Friday."

"Done. Don't worry about it," said Julio. It was the least he could do.

❖

They played the restaurant game.

"Where do you think we should go?" asked Julio.

"Somewhere with seafood, lots of seafood," answered Marta. "Crab legs should come out of my ears. And where do you think we should go?"

"Somewhere with steaks, big ones," answered Julio firmly. "Black Angus." They had read an ad in the paper earlier in the day that advertised a special.

"Red Lobster," she said, even more resolutely and with her lips pushed out.

They couldn't afford any of these places, but they saw the commercials and read the ads and talked about them all the time. The chain restaurants always advertised the most, and their ads always looked the best, whether that was the truth of things or not.

"And what if Red Lobster is closed?" asked Julio.

"Well that would be something, wouldn't it? Chinese food, then, a feast," laughed Marta. "Like at Kin Wah's, with all the birds in the big cage." It was a memory for both of them, Kin Wah's in Nogales, with a floor-to-ceiling birdcage right in the middle of the restaurant, feathers wafting everywhere if you ate there in the late afternoon, the light shining in through the windows and showing the loose underfeathers suspended in the air, the feathers and slight grit and air plankton, everything that came from the business of being birds.

The parrots spoke and called out orders themselves, perfectly in the voices of the waiters. They also talked among themselves as if they were the waiters, reciting whole conversations. Every night at least one parrot-order made it through and the cooks made an extra meal, which the birds later, in fact, got to eat. Their dinner was trickery, but it was hard to say on whom, the waiters or the birds. One would think it was the waiters, of course, but it was the work of the birds everyone came to see, and cheer for.

"No, not Chinese. I think," he paused for a small moment of drama, eyebrows suddenly furrowed, "*italiano*. No bean sprouts. No bean sprouts tonight. We're in the city tonight."

Bean sprouts, and Chinese food in general with all its vegetables, always reminded them both of the *verdolagas* they had grown up eating, which grew in people's front yards here but were treated as weeds. *Verdolagas* always came to mind for them, and other things they could not name from the mountains. Plants. There were so many Chinese in Mexico that Marta and Julio had, on more than one occasion, seen all the greens they had grown up eating sold as Chinese food specialties—*verdolagas*, of course, *tunas* from the prickly pears, and the ears of the prickly pears themselves, de-thorned, these and more, really anything green.

It wasn't just the Chinese, of course. Everyone at one time or another had eaten something at their grandmother's house that they couldn't identify. Everything, it seemed, could be cooked. Whether one would want to eat it, however, was sometimes a question. Then again, it was sometimes and very simply what there was for dinner.

I think you might like doing this. It's nothing. It's easy. Julio, remembering what Hector had said, and remembering that he had winked as well, thought that it was a curious thing to say. But he didn't think for a moment not to do the favor. After all, he thought, look at all Hector was doing for him, and for Marta, too.

"I just have to do this thing for Hector. It'll only take a minute," Julio said to Marta once they got started.

"What kind of thing?" asked Marta.

"I have to deliver something for him, a package that's in the trunk. He must have forgotten. It's something I think he remembered right when he was leaving, so I said I would be happy to do it."

"A package? What kind of package?"

"I don't know what kind of package. A package. I didn't ask him what it was. What difference does it make? I just have to leave it. It won't take long."

"Why didn't you tell me before?"

Marta frowned, but Julio tried not to look at her. He sped up a little to get this over with. The directions were clear enough, and it wasn't far. Some apartments—he thought he had a vague sense of having seen them before. Certainly he had driven past them because he took that road all the time for different jobs he went out on.

"Well, then," said Marta, "all right. But I don't know."

"Don't know what?" asked Julio, but he didn't want an answer. "It's right up there, the apartments behind that gray wall."

"Do you think it's safe?" Marta asked the question that was clearly in the air.

"Don't be ridiculous," said Julio.

He pulled into a dirt enclosure just inside the wall. With that, and without saying anything else to Marta, he got out of the car, went around to the back, opened the trunk, and got out a small package wrapped in brown paper.

It was wrapped neatly, so carefully, thought Julio as he walked by Marta's window with this delivery in his hands, that it didn't look like it belonged in this place. Everything else was discolored and decaying, with trash piled up in various corners, not purposefully but blown there by the wind, which had found enough of it around to make these small piles in various places along the wall and even up against some of the apartments, which had cracked cement stoops in front of them, stoops a little too high and deteriorating underneath into the pebbles and dirt that made them.

It looked to Julio like there were twelve apartments, six on one side and what looked like six on the other, though he couldn't see the far reaches of this building very well. He was just guessing. It was like a duplex, only six. *A sixplex.* It sounded in his mind like one of the new movie theaters, and this darkness only added to the feeling.

Even though it was cold, Marta rolled down her window for a moment and Julio could tell she could hear what he heard—some voices, some music, or rather, several strains of competing music, which collected together into a noise in place of a song. And she could smell what he smelled, the familiar tang of dinners being cooked, their scents—familiar but not specific, like the music. The bouquet of smells blended and was more pleasing than the music. The aroma, he thought, stood out against all the fast-food bags and cups with straws still sticking out of them in the trash piles. Somebody was doing the work of cooking.

Julio rang the doorbell of the apartment closest to them and waited, but nothing happened. After a minute or so, he knocked on the door.

A tall, thin man answered, wearing jeans and an unbuttoned shirt, even though it was so cold. It was dark and Julio couldn't see very much more. The porch light over the door wasn't on or wasn't working—in fact, only one of the porch lights in the row of six apartments was on, which gave the only real light to the whole area, light with a little haze around it in the cold, and it was the only illumination aside from the light that came through the various curtains and blinds and sheets hung over the windows.

Opening and closing the car door had made enough light to feel like a shout here. It was out of place. They were out of place.

The man said something that Julio didn't quite catch. The man took the package while at the same time handing an envelope to Julio. He caught the muted reflection of its stark whiteness as it was handed from one dark hand to another, from this man to himself. Julio shook his head in a slight *no*, but the man closed the door just like that and without any further discussion.

The walk from the front door of the apartment to the car wasn't much. When Julio got to the car, he put the envelope into his shirt pocket to open the door. When he got in and closed the door, which had made the light come on again and made him uncomfortable and, he could see, Marta, too, she said, "Well?"

"Well, what?"

"What's in your pocket?"

"Hector said they might give me a tip for my trouble." Julio took the envelope out of his pocket and opened it. The flap was loose, just folded down casually into the opening. Inside there were ten $20 bills, $200 just like that in his hands. He closed the envelope quickly, as if some of the bills might try to get out like fish from a net. He held it closed, tightly.

"What is that?" said Marta, loudly but not quite yelling, not quite sure enough to shout.

"I don't know. He gave it to me and said to get out of here."

"He gave it to you for what?"

"I don't know. The package, I guess. Hector said they might."

"What was in the package?"

"I don't know. I told you."

"You don't get money like this for nothing. It's not a tip—that's too much. It had to be something in there, something in that package."

"I don't know."

"Well, give it back to him. It's not yours."

Julio looked at Marta, but it was not the look he had given her earlier in the evening, and she was not the Marta he had seen, not in this moment. Her eyes were big and she was shaking her head.

"I can't go back there."

Marta knew this was true, he could tell. She shivered, but it was more than the cold. She couldn't make him go back to that door. Who knew what might happen? Who knew what was happening here anyway? He was right. They had to leave. Staying wouldn't bring anything but trouble.

"Go," she said. "Let's get out of here."

Two hundred dollars, just like that in his hands. The whole event didn't take more than ten seconds. But just like that the whole evening was changed. They could go anywhere with that much money, anywhere at all. They could go somewhere nice to eat, eat all they wanted, and still have plenty left over to pay a few of the bills sitting on the kitchen table, or save it, just save it. Suddenly everything was possible—they understood that, if not much else about what this meant.

They had come here to this country to make money, and here was some money. Julio had promised Marta, and her family, to work hard, and he had worked hard. He had only worked hard and nothing less. Money comes from working hard, or it was supposed to. The process had been slow, excruciatingly slow.

Marta had promised to work at things equally hard, and to take care of things that Julio couldn't. That often meant handling the finances, not because he couldn't but because she had a better grasp of their whole lives, of the house and the car and the groceries and the repairs and the movies and the neighbors and the paperwork and a—he treaded lightly here, in thinking this, *and a baby*, maybe. She had a sense of all these things working together that he admired. She had good judgment. That should count for something, all the careful planning and patience, the small sacrifices each of them made without telling the other. He knew she did it as much as he did. All this should count for something.

People for as long as he could remember had talked about the border and the fence and the crossing over from one place to another. Up to now it had always been a line between two countries. He and Marta had crossed that line and understood what that meant. Everything had been so clear. Suddenly, this felt like the border, this moment. There was something big here.

They had worked patiently at getting their papers and coming across, and it had taken years. This, on the other hand, this was over just like that.

But, thought Julio, this felt like the moment, the thing he always thought he would feel, the line, the crossing over—between what and what he was not certain. But this was it. He could see that Marta felt it too.

They drove off, unsure. The envelope gave them a good dinner, but a quiet one, and a quiet ride home afterward. They were neither happy nor unhappy, though neither one would say so. Marta still looked beautiful to Julio, but there was a haze around everything, including her, the same way there had been a haze around the porch light at those apartments. It was probably the cold, and something about how rarely cold came to the desert. It made the world look strange. Maybe there would be rain.

They didn't talk about the money anymore, not after their discussion in the car that night, but it was sitting there with them nonetheless as they ate in the restaurant and drove home. The cold insinuated itself even further into the later evening, and bundling up into their jackets, which they had to do, kept them from having to talk so much about things.

THE MAP

Once, every map was really two maps, or four, or eight—depending on how many folds. The marks on the fully displayed and unruly paper that one held down against a countertop or the hood of a car showed the places where places were meant to be. The imagination, however, had to be complicit in that figuring.

How thin a layer of truth it is, the thinnest kind of truth, the barest sense of things, a map on paper. No up and down. No wind or dust. No desert heat, which explains the persistence of hats. No lizards. And those lines, those lines don't really exist.

9

Bernardo's Corrido

A car, not carelessly but in following too literally the grammar of the street signs and making a turn that was a little too wide, hit Bernardo the dog. Their meeting made a small but unmistakable sound, and the car lurched afterward to a stop. It was an accident, but like all accidents, there was no taking it back.

Everyone who was in the area stopped to see what had happened, and the driver of the car was distraught, not seeming quite able to work the handle to open the door and finally giving up in an enervated swoon back against the seat. Who was driving was difficult to say, as in that moment the driver's body fell down like the dog's, below the high window. "I'm all right," the person was heard to say, after which all attention turned to the dog. The mystery of the driver would be cleared up soon enough. But the dog, the dog was flat on the ground—not dead, but on the ground. Everyone recognized Bernardo.

"Thank God he's not dead," someone said, but that was all. Nobody was quite sure what to do next, and each hoped someone else would take charge. Bernardo was not bleeding, or did not seem to be, but his tongue had fallen out of his mouth and hung too far down to be right. Bernardo's breathing was not fast but should have been.

A workman brought over an old towel and wrapped it around the dog, who did not seem to notice. It was a kind gesture, and was all that the workman meant to do, but people crowded up behind him so that he could not now back away.

"Call the doctor," he said, to nobody in particular.

"Yes, call the doctor," said someone else. It made sense, or as much sense as anything else. Bernardo was a dog, of course, but surely a doctor could be counted on to know what to do. The new doctor in town, Dr. Bartolomeo, surely he would know what to do next. Several people went hurrying in his direction. His office was not far, and he was brought back to the scene quickly.

Everyone made way for the doctor, and the workman who had placed the towel around the dog was finally able to step away. He simply pointed at the towel, which covered Bernardo.

Dr. Bartolomeo looked down, kneeled, and removed enough of the towel to say, "But it's a dog."

"Yes," people said. "It's Bernardo."

The doctor hesitated. He was just back in town as a newly minted doctor, and he understood the moment to be something beyond the dog. He was not a veterinarian, but he was not unable to help, either. There was nobody else, and he saw as much when he looked up at the crowd. He threw his hands up in a decisive gesture and told nobody in particular to bring the dog to his office.

"I'll look at him and do what can be done. Is there an owner?" he asked.

Everyone simultaneously volunteered Miguel Torres's name, and someone added that Miguel Torres and this dog went everywhere together.

"Well, go find Sr. Torres. Now, be careful when you lift this dog. We don't want to do any more damage."

Through all of this, Bernardo listened patiently. He was in no mood to argue, or to move. Lying down felt all right to him and was where he preferred to stay. When someone began to pick him up, he wished it were not so, but he had no particular energy to resist. Like the voices he was hearing, the feel of being lifted seemed like an echo to him, something far away even though it was happening to him right then and there.

Still, and how curious, thought Bernardo, it all felt black. When curiosity presented itself to him, Bernardo always stopped, and his tail was a barometer of his interest. He stopped wagging and concentrated. Right now, his tail was not wagging, which was good. That was right. Something was happening. In this blackness and in this curious moment, then, where Bernardo should have been standing and looking into what was what, he instead fell asleep.

Bernardo—it was such an elegant name. Names for dogs rarely got so much attention, and even when they did, the quicker "*quítate, perro*" and "*condenado, perro*" and "*get out of here*" and even no name at all, just a hard hand to the back or a kick to the stomach—these were the real names that worked, if a dog knew what was good for it.

Bernardo. Nobody knew where the name had come from, or where Bernardo himself had come from, for that matter. He was just always there. And for a long time he was invisible, or as invisible as dogs are when they survive as best they can, behind buildings and in small corners, always looking for something to feed the animal inside them.

His was a feral existence, chasing rabbits in fields when he couldn't find anything in town, a dog with a dog's limitations, but

finding a way, slower than animals built to be faster than dogs—
animals with long legs and swift wings—so that all that was left
to the dog Bernardo was to think his way into the next day, to be
smart if he could not be fast, to be strong when he felt weakest in
a long chase, and to be kind of heart when he least felt it, having
been struck on the ears by a workman.

Bernardo at first had no story. But through the years he became
part of everyone else's story, and in that way he was always bigger
than he was. He himself, in truth, the real Bernardo, was small and
regular. He had an appetite for chicken and a fondness for warmth.
He gravitated toward people who gravitated toward him, and that
had made a good life.

Miguel Torres, his keeper all these last years, made sure of that.
A good life was what they gave to each other, and Bernardo was
happy.

❖

When he awoke, Bernardo's first impulse was to jump up and run
at all costs, which was a lesson the rabbits had taught him. *Run!
No matter what and no matter where and right now!*

But as he tried to lift himself and find his bearings to make his
big push away, his legs failed him. His legs. His rockets. They had
never failed him before.

His snout sailed forward, and his neck, but nothing else followed. His shoulders tried, but they were helped more by the deep
breath he took into his lungs than from their own strength. His
shoulders instead felt to him as if he had nothing attached to them,
nothing but weights, as if whatever lay beyond them was something he was stuck in.

But it was more that he could not see, not to look at himself.
He had on a big something, some kind of paper, all around his
head, something white that blocked his view. He moved his head

back and forth, but Dr. Bartolomeo shushed him. Bernardo did not know what was happening, but he knew better than to do something nobody wanted him to do. He had learned this much at least over the years. Do what you are told, and then get away as fast as you can where nothing can hurt you.

Bernardo would play along, at least for now. He looked at the window, but it was closed. He looked at the door, but it was closed, too. The doctor was reassuring him, but having all the exits closed was not a comfort. He would play along, all right, because he had no choice. It was not an effort, however, staying still, because moving would have been some work. And his body hurt. Staying still, even if it was not what he wanted, was the better choice for now.

After a few minutes the doctor picked Bernardo up and carried him out the door. Bernardo saw a roomful of children, and they all laughed at him. Laughter was always a better sound than so many other noises. It made him want to laugh as well. He tried to throw a little bark into the mix, but not much sound came out.

Dr. Bartolomeo spoke Miguel Torres's name, and Bernardo recognized it. Miguel Torres! That's where he needed to go. Home. Where was Miguel Torres? He had to get to their house. Bernardo knew that Miguel Torres would be worrying about him. It was time for him to be home. But again, his legs did not move the way legs are supposed to move. Bernardo bided his time. Dr. Bartolomeo put him down gently onto a couch.

Bernardo wasn't sure he was supposed to be on the couch, so he kept quiet.

Dr. Bartolomeo busied himself making something, then turned around and lifted Bernardo onto it. The platform he'd made was like the couch, a little. The doctor waved some of the children over to carry the dog on this little couch. Bernardo wasn't at all sure that this was a good idea, but he was not in a position to argue. His legs, he hoped, were under him, but the big collar that he was wearing hid them. Bernardo would simply have to get through this.

He was picked up carefully enough, though every little awkward and sideways movement made him feel like jumping, even if he couldn't. They carried him outside. Bernardo found a comfortable way to ride, a little on his back, a little on his side, with his neck still able to keep his snout up. He was able, finally, to find enough of a leg to use it as an elbow. And soon enough, he was back on the street where all this had started.

The children carried him with increasing confidence, and laughter. Bernardo seemed to float aloft, above the crowd, with no particular one person holding him. All their hands were in on the effort. Bernardo's markings suggested a big grin on his face, which showed itself best from underneath, directly the way the children were looking at him. They laughed harder and harder every time they looked at him. Bernardo liked the sound. Because they were holding him up, the sound seemed to come from under him, and it tickled. It made him feel better, even in his condition. They walked past parked cars, going, Bernardo knew and to his relief, in the right direction. People everywhere were looking at them. Bernardo recognized them all, though it was more of a general smell that he understood rather than any particular face.

Curiously, Sra. Belmares seemed startled as they went by on the other side of a car that was parked between them. Some adults crowded around her, and Bernardo thought that they should take her to see Dr. Bartolomeo, who seemed very helpful after all. But whether they did or not was not his first concern at the moment. Bernardo was interested in going home.

Miguel Torres was waiting for Bernardo. To be more accurate, Miguel Torres was not waiting for him so much as he came out of his house to see what all the fuss was about. The laughing and the parade of children and townspeople, and—when he could finally make it out—the mysterious center of attention, a conquering hero borne on what seemed like the shoulders of the whole town. It was the return of Bernardo, a return as dramatic as if he had been away for years and had suddenly returned to the delight of everyone here.

Miguel Torres, so used to the dog being around, had not yet missed him, and so he was as surprised as anyone to see Bernardo on this floating bed. The children put the small contraption down carefully, and Bernardo mustered enough strength to stand, however weakly, enough so that Miguel Torres could put his arms around him.

"What happened?" asked Miguel Torres, though almost before he could ask he was hearing twenty versions of the incident.

Once he had the gist of it, Miguel Torres lifted Bernardo in his arms. "Well, my friend, we have some sleeping to do," he said. Miguel Torres thanked all the children, who asked if they could come by and check on Bernardo. "Of course, of course, though I am sure he will find you first," said Miguel. In that moment, in all that happiness that the children felt and which, in turn, he could feel, he was himself for a moment young again. They were all in this moment together. The children returned a saved dog and made the day happy. Miguel Torres had his dog saved and felt that joy, which had grown with each step these children had taken and with each step closer they had come to this moment. It was simple enough, and Bernardo himself felt it all as well.

Miguel Torres took him inside, placed him in his sleeping spot on the small carpet by the bed, and shushed him with his quiet voice and a few strokes of his straggled fur.

"You look ridiculous in that bonnet," said Miguel Torres quietly to Bernardo. "But I see its sense. So do you, don't you?"

Bernardo knew he did not have to answer. With the lingering feel of Miguel Torres on his back, he fell asleep yet again.

❖

The driver of the car had been very sorry and had offered to pay the doctor's bill. The doctor himself, however, had made no charge, so the matter in that regard was settled amicably all around. That same evening, one of the neighbors brought over some chicken soup. It was for Miguel, she said, but she also instructed that he should give some, perhaps, to Bernardo as well. Miguel thanked her, and meant it. Everyone knew how Bernardo loved chicken. By now Miguel Torres had heard the whole story and was glad for the rescue of Bernardo. The event and the parade home were to change the course of Bernardo's life.

But for now, Miguel Torres and Bernardo knew what this meant. That is to say, they remembered another day, the day they met. Many years earlier, Miguel Torres had come limping into town, having been attacked by a pack of javelinas out in the country where he was doing some work. The encounter had been by chance. Miguel simply wandered in the wrong direction at the wrong time, so intent on looking at the ground that he blocked out everything else. His work gave him an intensity that drove him to finish anything he started, but sometimes at a cost to himself.

The javelinas, he knew, did not intend to harm him, at least not at first. He didn't hear their grunted warnings, and their gray coats blended in with the high-desert scrub. But he did smell them, that dark smell that on any other day he would have recognized immediately, and so he should have known better. He was following an arroyo when all of a sudden they came at him, tusks down, slashing and hooking. As he recalled the attack, he suddenly remembered their markings—their white collars not at all unlike poor Bernardo's device now. So the javelinas were still at him, he thought, even now.

The attack was unremarkable as far as javelina attacks go—vicious, muscular, grunted, their sharp, rough, spiky fur cutting his skin as they shoved him around. That they attacked at all must have meant that they had babies or an injured brother to protect, something, because this was not the regular way of things. Of course Miguel meant them no harm. That was unimportant now. How many of them did not matter either—Miguel, shifting that intensity he had brought to his work, saw only the first, and he did what he could with his arms. The animals did what they did best when scared and provoked.

Miguel managed to do what humans do best, which was to survive. The attack lasted no more than several minutes in time, but it was years in Miguel's imagination, a raw edge in his memory. The javelinas moved on, and he crawled away from them. That part of the day was done. Miguel Torres found the strength to stand, finally, and to make his way toward town. Exhaustion was more at play than wounds, but at the moment they felt like the same thing.

This day, however, when he found danger from an unlikely source, he got help just as ferociously from an equally unlikely source—Bernardo the dog, whom Miguel Torres had only seen around town before then. The dog and the man were suspicious of each other, but Bernardo understood what the man could not say to him—he needed help. If Bernardo were fierce, it was not in fighting but in helping. In the same way that Miguel Torres was single-minded when doing his work, Bernardo, too, worked this way.

Bernardo knew the arroyos around here as well as anyone, man or animal, and had spent his first months living in them when people in town would not tolerate him. He came back on some days just to look, to smell the creosote and to wonder at the nature of birds. An occasional small animal would still find its way to his stomach, but it was an uneasy relationship and not one from which he took pleasure.

Occasionally Bernardo would rescue the young cow Paquita, who liked to wander in those years. He would shepherd her home when she lost her way. Paquita was black and white just like Bernardo. Perhaps they were related, though Paquita did not look like much of a dog to Bernardo. She listened to him when he barked, however, and she would go where he said without much protest. She understood him even if he could not quite make out what she said in response, that low, slow bark. Bernardo took it upon himself in general to keep her out of trouble, figuring that she needed the help, especially in light of her not being able to speak for herself. Together through the years they had many adventures.

Today, however, it would not be Paquita. It was this man.

At first Miguel and Bernardo looked warily at each other and began to circle in the way all animals who are strangers do. But Miguel Torres could not waltz, and the moment was done. Bernardo could eat him up or let him go—Miguel Torres had no say in the matter in this instant, weak and unsure on those thin legs, and in obvious pain. Miguel unintentionally made a sound like Paquita, low and long, and was immediately sorry for it.

Instead of continuing to circle, Bernardo came to Miguel Torres and, after hearing that sound and looking in the man's eyes first, licked his hand.

Bernardo knew where water kept itself in this desert, and he knew the fastest direction to town. Both would serve Miguel on this late afternoon.

The dog led and then pushed the man toward the water, which is as far as they got that very late afternoon before the darkness found them. The evening was warm, and the night did not get too cold. After Miguel Torres had drunk his fill and had cleaned himself up, Bernardo was careful to move them both a good distance away from the water so that the rest of the world could have its turn through the night. The man did not argue. As Bernardo watched Miguel Torres, he watched a man asleep. In showing that tenderness to the world, Bernardo knew he had to stay with this man who could not take care of himself any better than that.

Bernardo circled himself, finally, in front of the man and settled right there next to him, carefully, face outward, keeping one eye open and one eye closed, one ear high and one ear low. His nostrils did not sleep.

❖

Old Dr. Cano took care of Miguel Torres, but not until the next day. Even then, he did not do much more than Bernardo. And he did more head-shaking than the dog, though Bernardo had more cause.

Miguel Torres recovered easily because he was still young and strong, and he made his report to the town council, who invited him to speak in an effort to determine whether any further action was needed.

"Not unless you want to declare war on the desert. The fault was mine. Still, the warning is there. We should simply take that for what it is."

The council laughed, but they understood the greater meaning. Miguel Torres gave his report with Bernardo by his side, a condition that was to last for many, many years. It was a marriage of sorts, and both of them were happy.

All these years later, with Bernardo hurt now, Miguel Torres knew what needed doing. Along with the chicken soup, which Bernardo tried to eat but, for the first time, tired of trying, Miguel Torres told him it was all right, that he would save the soup, and that he wanted Bernardo to know something. For the next while, with Bernardo trying to stay awake, Miguel Torres recounted the story of their first meeting.

The dog very soon fell asleep, and Miguel Torres knew what to do. He got a blanket and spread it out next to the dog, then got down on the floor next to him. The dog opened his eyes briefly and knew. Miguel Torres, first with his arm around the dog, but then, his arms wild to the night, slept next to Bernardo, wholly with the intent of allowing him no further harm.

They were sore the next morning, and Miguel thought that maybe sleeping that way was a mistake. Bernardo with his markings seemed to laugh at him, something of a nod in agreement, but the night was done and the next day had arrived. The day was a strong one, clear and clean, with the sounds of the world in full concert. Bernardo would live a long life for a dog, and every day would be like this one, every one of them good.

The recovery was slow but even. Everyone wanted to know how Bernardo was. Children came regularly to check on him, and chickens found their way in all manner of cooked fashion to their door.

Dr. Bartolomeo explained it, asking Miguel Torres a few weeks later to stop by and to bring Bernardo with him, ostensibly for a check-up but really so that the day Bernardo was hit by the car might be reenacted. They would not talk about the accident, of course, not at all. This was about the cure, and everything that followed.

Apparently, Sra. Belmares had been passing by on that same day and had seen Bernardo fly by her on his magic carpet. Everyone had heard the story. Explaining it was easy enough, said Dr. Bartolomeo, but he wanted to show her—to show the town, really— what had actually happened, though in doing so he also hoped to bring back some of the festivity of that day. He was not anxious to clear up Sra. Belmares's version of the story, though in the name of science he felt compelled to set things straight. Still, he was wistful. A magic carpet was a very appealing idea, even to scientists.

Showing how the children carried Bernardo, that he was injured and therefore reclined on his back for comfort, and that the children carrying him were blocked from view by the car that was between them and Sra. Belmares—this was easy enough to demonstrate to everyone, including Sra. Belmares herself, who sniffed and said of course that is how it happened.

But the event took on its own life and its own place in the town's history. Real or not, Bernardo on his carpet flying around town was the real story, with science only a nagging backseat driver. It was not long before people made piñatas of Bernardo on his carpet, schoolchildren doodled that image in the marginalia of their notebooks, and the singers in the establishment on the north side of town—which everybody knew but never called by name—composed the "Corrido del Bernardo," which attempted something of an obscene rhyme with "Belmares." Everyone, or almost everyone, thought it was the funniest rhyme on earth. How people would have heard the song was another story altogether.

And Bernardo, the dog with the elegant name—Bernardo himself for the rest of his days ate what he liked, walked where he wanted, and dug holes whenever he felt the urge.

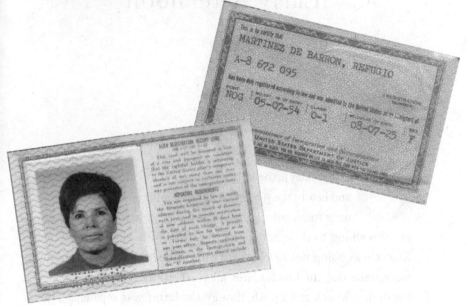

THE GREEN CARD

So often we expect it to be made of gold, and the truth is, it is. But it is a gold mined from the heart, not the ground. It is hope incarnate, possibility, a chance, opportunity, the future made different. It used to be green, but now it is blue. Things change. It is a card in a great deck of cards.

In one country, it is an ace of diamonds. In another, it is a two of spades.

10

One Tuesday in the Early Afternoon

On a Tuesday in the early afternoon, before the cicadas started and before the wood smoke beginnings of the town's evening meal, before the people began leaving work in cars or by walking to their houses on the small hills all around, while Marta was doing not much of anything since the morning chores were done and the lunch plates all washed, there was a knock at the door, a knock and a push, though the latter was accidental, the door in need of some attention, moving every time someone knocked. The knocking startled her but not the movement of the door, which, in the easy way that it followed the knock, was a little like someone saying *bless you* after a sneeze. It's just how things worked.

She got up off the couch where the afternoon had hypnotized her as it often did, as if she were a cat and the afternoon her window, and when she got to the door she looked through the slight opening and into the eyes of a man who was looking back at her, a stranger, a little dirty, she could tell by the way his hair looked, not quite wet and not quite combed. This was not the first time he had knocked, though this man was nobody she knew. This same man, or the maybe six or eight others who looked so much like this, had found this door easily enough in the last several years.

When he saw her looking at him, he immediately looked down and said nothing. Standing that way, she saw his hair all the more, with its three or four parts, not straight but jigsaw-like and angular, the way hair that hasn't been washed flattens when it's been covered by a hat for days, maybe a week. If she had been the afternoon's cat, now he was hers, something animal in the way he stood, and brave in the way that he did not stand back, brave but not bold, not scary. Just animal, and in need—she could not help her feeling, though here was a man.

Of course he was an illegal. That was the new word now, *illegal*. It went without saying or even thinking. It simply was so. Absolute, and not gray at all, though Marta could not say why, only that it was confusing. She knew some bad people, and they should be illegal, no argument, she thought. Maybe he knew them. But she didn't think so. They wouldn't have stood still like this. They didn't know how.

This was one of those others. She opened the door.

She hesitated, somewhere inside herself, but it did not stop or slow her. She unbolted the thin chain they had put on the door, which wasn't really very much protection anyway—it was simply all they could afford at the time. They could put a better lock on now, but they hadn't gotten around to it yet. It was like so many things. And she knew about not opening the door to strangers, of course—even kids know that. Still, all the people inside her from all the years—they, they or something, said it would be all right.

And just like that, here he was, whatever he was. He was dark and not too tall, maybe Indian, or part. Or he was just a hard worker who had made this face in the sun. She couldn't see that he brought anything with him, or that he was hiding anything, not anything she could be scared of. He had simply reached this house by walking. There were no guns, no knives, no karate-chop fighting, no fast car getaways or crashes or fires, no police or helicopters, no parachuting special forces, no Border Patrol jeeps, no rabid mountain lions or rattlesnakes or bats or javelinas, no earthquakes or volcanoes, no high mountains or rickety bridges, no floods, no huge nuclear-accident-ten-foot-high ants or tarantulas, no bullies, no wild-eyed ranchers with shotguns, none of these.

Instead, there was a little water—she could see a water bottle sticking out of his pocket—a little food in there, too, some folded tortillas and a little bit, the last, of some dried *carne machaca* wrapped in napkins and a red bandanna, some dehydrated plums to keep the mouth making its own water, but with the plum meat all gone now and just the fat seeds left for sucking on, a pocketknife to cut oranges from the trees. She knew what he had in his pockets. He didn't have to tell her.

He held an old baseball cap, or what looked like one, in his hand. It had been in use for some time and didn't look any more like the ones in the stores. It was more like a drawing of a hat, with the woven material looking like crosshatched pencil strokes not quite filled in or finished. It was a hat that didn't have time to think of itself.

Some things about him Marta hadn't guessed. He had a few small wounds, just cuts really, not too bad, though there was some blood that had darkened in harsh lines, two on one arm and, though she could not see them on his skin, some more lines on his jeans, soaked through but lightened from dust and wear and moving on. And there was desert—he had it in his eyes, but it was high-country desert, with low scrub and some cactus that could lend you some water if you were desperate, though they preferred not to. This man had taken the route closer to Nogales, not the desert people talk about when they say *desert*, not the land to the west, between Nogales and Yuma, the land that made people disappear or get lost or simply die straightaway, sometimes with their babies. This man had chosen just to walk over these easy, rolling hills and hope for the best.

"Señora," he said, and it was all that he said. The words for what needed to be said were all hiding in that first one, that only one he could manage.

Never open the door to strangers—they said it everywhere. On television, on boxes of food, on billboards. Never open the door to strangers.

"*Entra*," she said, and opened the door wide enough so he could make his way through.

Once inside, standing on the throw rug, he stood as he had stood outside.

He had come from far south. North, he would say. He had come north. It was always funny to hear everyone here talking about being in the West. The West this, the West that. But north, she knew, was his direction. Go north, young man. The thing of it was, however, that they were the same place. It wasn't just two languages that were a difficulty here, two ways to say the same thing—it was two directions as well, both of them pointing to this house, this front room, right here. West and north at the same time and the same place. What kind of compass could find that?

At this moment, however, because of the desert in his eyes and the dirt in his hair, they were both standing at the tip of the great Mexican north, the frontier, the place to find your true self and start over, the place that—who knew?—could make you famous, even.

The cap in his hand and the way he stood and that he looked down the way he did as if his head had no other direction available to it: Together these were a letter of recommendation from his father saying that he was a good boy, this man, that you will know this, and if I were there to tell you myself, I would. Marta could read the letter plainly—her own father had sent her out into the world with that very same letter of approval, written everywhere in her manners. This boy's mother, too, sent her quiet regards, as the man had stamped his feet before entering, quietly but firmly and with the serious intent to make fall off of his pant legs anything that might soil his next steps.

It was this letter handed over to her by his manner, it was this that made letting him in so easy. She knew the authors of his introduction though she did not know them. She knew them because she remembered her own parents, and there was something in that feeling. His parents and hers, they were all standing together at that moment in the room, the four of them and two more, counting herself and this man, so she felt no reason to worry. She ushered him in to get him out of the crowd.

"Lunch is finished," she said, "but I've got something." She pointed him to the kitchen. He wouldn't move at first. Then he moved his hand and arm, something that said *you first*, and she understood. She walked and he followed her.

Marta's husband, Julio, would not approve of this, not at all. The neighbors would not approve either, the neighbors who must surely have seen him come in, Mrs. Gomez especially. Everybody saw everything, which was good and bad both, and confusing, too, just like west and north.

Better not to ask him what he is doing, she thought, and knew why. Knowing too much would be bad for both of them if someone started asking questions. But why did she let him in? Everyone would want to know. Still, everyone would guess the answer as well, and it would be the right answer. They would all know why. He was hungry. He was moving on. Everybody here knew his story, just like they knew the story of the one before him and the one who would come after him.

Marta and Julio had a nice house, if not a big one. It was clean, in good repair except for the front door, which she could not fix and which Julio had promised he would fix last weekend. The walls were freshly painted, and they had not been married long enough or gone enough places together for the knick-knacks to be out of control. There were some things from when they were dating, some onyx fruit in a bowl, some ironwood figures—a roadrunner, a pelican, a turtle. These they had bought on the beach from one of the Seri men when they honeymooned in Guaymas.

With these three ironwood carvings was a fourth piece, a saguaro cactus, which they had gotten on their only other trip, this time to Puerto Peñasco, four hours or so to the south and, like Guaymas, on the Sea of Cortés but a little more to the north, and so a little closer. It had been a difficult weekend, as so many college students had also picked that weekend to visit, though they were at Rocky Point, at the northern tip of the Gulf of California. That's what they called this same place, as if it were another world altogether, a world of their own devising. Marta and Julio had come home early. Both of them remembered the bay from their childhoods and had wanted to recapture it, to share it between them, even the poisonous jellyfish. But that would have to wait for another time.

Moving from the front room to the kitchen took only a few steps, really, but it was their world. Marta thought that it was probably not so different from this man's own world, what he was leaving behind. It was probably only a little better, a little newer. But it was enough. There was a painting of the Virgin on the wall, and that helped.

And she herself was probably not unlike the wife he was undoubtedly trying to help by doing all this, the wife he had left behind, perhaps with kids. He wanted to get Marta's house for them and get them into a town like this, on this side of the border.

He was like her Julio that way, not so different—Julio had wanted the same things and found a way to get them, had worked at it. The way she and Julio had gotten into this house was not so different from what this man was doing. But she didn't want to think about that, about how things used to be, about their parents and all the things they had gone through. And she didn't want to think that Julio would ever leave her behind, either, not for anything. It occurred to Marta that this man's wife might be outside somewhere, but no, probably not. There must be kids, and they must be back where he came from, waiting.

So it was some fresh paint, some ironwood figurines, an old painting of an Italian villa in a gaudy white-and-gold plastic frame, a couple of throw rugs, an old television, a couch, several small lamps, one with an etched-glass base, all of which had been wedding presents—it was all of this that they walked through to get to the kitchen.

She opened the refrigerator, then remembered to turn around and tell him to sit. He would not have dared do so without her permission, of course. She was sure of that. He put his hat on the table and folded his hands in front of him. It wasn't prayer, exactly, the way he held his hands, but it made Marta think it anyway. His hands were rough, but calm in this moment, and at rest, which she could tell was not an easy feeling for him.

Marta took out a soda first, opened it, and gave it to him. She was going to put it into a glass, but as she opened it his eyes opened as well, and the glass seemed the least of things. She would have put ice in the glass, but the drink was cold already, very cold, the way Julio liked. She kept the cans at the back of the refrigerator so that opening and closing the door wouldn't bother them. The soda was a local store brand, something she had never heard of before, but a discovery. They were so much cheaper than regular sodas— she wanted to tell this man all about them but stopped herself. He wouldn't be staying. It didn't matter, but buying them had been a bargain regardless. Finding these sodas had made her happy two days ago in the store, and still did.

It wasn't that she and Julio were poor—he made good enough money in the produce-packing warehouse, moving the crates of cantaloupes and tomatoes and mangoes and watermelons, all the fruit that came through here from Mexico going who knew where, somewhere else. Even the fruits here were tourists. Tourism, here on the border, was of course the other big business of the town, much flashier and filling up all the billboards and signs and store windows, even though everyone wanted to buy their things in Mexico. But it was the fruit that took care of the two of them and made them happy. Still, when she found a bargain, it was like finding money, like a lucky penny. And who wouldn't pick up a penny?

Marta had made a big pot of *sopa de arroz* with chicken yesterday, and she and Julio had eaten some for lunch today. That would do. She had already put the soup and the lemons and the tortillas away and washed the dishes, but it was okay. They were all right there. It was easy enough to make this meal again.

The trouble came not with the rice or the chicken or the lemons, and not even with the tortillas exactly, but with the butter she put on them, butter that was from the other tub, not the one she had used for lunch, though she did not distinguish between the two or think anything of it when she took a generous dollop out for each of the three tortillas she had warmed on the *comal* Julio had made for her out of scrap metal, a perfect fit like a dark metal flat-plate over one of the four burners. It had worked so well they never took it off, though at first it had been a temporary solution to making and warming tortillas faster and better than on a burner, which had no business being near tortillas. One adapts to these things, of course, and letting the tortillas touch the flame sometimes gave them a light burn that made them crunchy and crisp, which was a taste a person might feel like—but only on occasion, certainly not all the time. Still, that's how they built stoves in this country.

The butter somehow had gone rancid, or something worse. While it did not smell bad, probably because it was cold and toward the back of the refrigerator with the sodas so that it was very cold, something in it nevertheless had turned bad. Perhaps something else had somehow fallen into it. Perhaps a spoon or a fork, while trying to get some butter out, had left some of whatever it had touched before on the butter. Sliding a knife into butter also cleaned it, taking off the bacon fat or lamb gristle going in, and giving back the butter coming out. The gristle, soon afterward, would start a party, inviting anything and everything, all of them germs. That's how gristle was, wherever it went. Only fried, fried to the end for hours, made into *chicharrones*, and eaten still hot— only then could it be trusted.

What she gave him must have been butter like that, butter that seemed happy but which was ready to be sick—and that's the feeling it gave to this man, who at first tried not to show anything unpleasant on his face, any indication of something that might seem rude or unseemly. This woman, after all, had fed him, and that was that. Food was food, and offered in this way was always good. Good, good, good. There was no other way to think about it.

And the food was good, very good, and he said so, except for something he couldn't put a finger on, something he didn't say, something that lived in him as a small twinge at first, like a tiny propeller suddenly turning in him, somewhere inside his stomach. It must have been from the first tortilla, though he didn't feel anything until the third one was finished.

The propeller got worse, and more of them started, a small fleet of aircraft, all lifting off the ground, propellers turning, but with nowhere to go except around and around in the hangar of his stomach. Though the man had already said his thank-yous, and his opinion that God would look on her with kindness that same way she had treated him, the noise in his stomach as he readied himself to go was louder, almost, than the sound of the chair he slid backward from the table in order to stand.

"*Señora, mil gracias, Dios nos cuida*, and I will tell Him about you in my prayers, though he has seen your kindness already, no doubt." These were the most words he had spoken, and they were sincere. He looked down with his eyes but forward with his heart. His face, however, at the end of his statement of gratitude, twisted itself for a second, involuntarily she was sure, so much was it a second of theater. He tried to turn his head, but it was over before he could.

"Are you all right?" It was a clear and gentle question, not an accusation. She had the kindness of the food in her, and meant only to help, regardless of what had happened.

"Yes," he said, and nodded his head. But the mask came over him again. He tried to pull the grimace into a smile, but it wasn't very convincing, not to either of them.

"I'm sorry," he said. "It's nothing."

They stood in the kitchen in this half-moment: he was getting up to leave but he could not move.

"I'm afraid, I mean, I'm sorry—I hate to bother you, but I need to use the bathroom." The request made him look as mortified as the physical pain he was also feeling.

"Of course, of course, don't worry. It's right there. Go ahead." She pointed, and hoped she had remembered to flush. With her by herself all afternoon, and drinking coffee, she didn't always feel like it was worth the waste of water. She couldn't remember.

But too late. When she pointed, he almost fell in its direction.

❖

After a while, when he was finished after a false start in which he had come out of the bathroom but had to go back in, she asked him if he wanted something to drink or to eat. He drank some water but said that it was all he could swallow down—he couldn't even look at food—and thanked her. They both attempted a small laugh.

"I don't know what happened. Forgive me," said the man.

"Oh, no, it's nothing. I hope it wasn't something I gave you."

"No, of course not. It had to be something I ate, I think, this morning. I'm certain of it."

She remembered him standing at the door, not an hour ago. He hadn't eaten in some time. It wasn't that.

"Maybe today is not the day to keep moving," she said to him finally, after a small silence, giving him a moment to steady himself. "Maybe you should start tomorrow." She couldn't really ask him to stay in her house, but if he could manage, starting tomorrow was still a good idea.

He smiled at her, but this smile was different from the others, the smiles of thanks, of good food, of being at rest—the smiles in place of words. This smile, instead, was weary. There was no stopping, not for a stomachache.

"Yes," he said. "Maybe tomorrow would be better." He picked up his cap from the kitchen table, where she had been waiting for him and where they were now talking. "Thank you, señora." He started moving to the front door.

"Well, you're welcome. I hope it wasn't something I did," she said. It was clear what she meant.

"No, no. Everything was very good. Very good." He nodded his head in a *yes*, up and down, and it took the place of him putting his hand on her shoulder. "I will tell my wife about you. She thanks you as well."

Marta walked with him to the front door, which was closed but still a little ajar.

"You should have this fixed," said the man.

"Yes," said Marta. "My husband has been meaning to fix it. This weekend."

With that, he stepped outside and put his cap on and his hands in his pockets. It had been a short visit. Maybe nobody had noticed. Would she tell Julio? He would just get mad, but it would make him fix the door. She would have to decide. And what had happened, anyway? She knew now it was something she gave him, of course. How could it not be? She didn't want to believe it. She had filled up his plastic water bottle. She had thought of sending him away with some food but thought better of it. She would have to throw everything away. Something was wrong, but she didn't know what.

It was confusing. She held her hand up and moved her fingers in a small good-bye, to which he nodded and turned. It sent him into the world on even more uncertain terms than when he arrived, shaky and with a weak stride.

She closed the door and gave it an extra push to make it seem right.

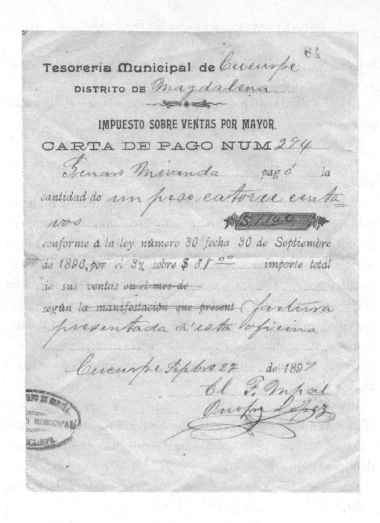

THE BILL

This is the cousin nobody wants to have come to visit. And so often, that cousin comes with the whole family, and will not leave, will not even talk about when they are thinking of leaving. They just stay and eat and talk and think about inviting some other cousins to come and visit.

Even centuries later, a family keeps these documents because of what it took to get beyond them.

II

Licenciado Ubaldo Dos Santos, at Your Service

Licenciado Ubaldo Dos Santos, the lawyer, went to work every day as if it were neither his first nor his last day on the job. He neither began nor finished any business at the start or end of the working day. His successes, instead, came after lunch or after late-morning coffee, and his new clients were almost always his old clients, so old that neither he nor the client could remember their first encounter, the both of them able to presume, therefore, and entirely to Ubaldo's benefit, that this encounter would certainly not be their last.

People counted on Ubaldo Dos Santos, and he counted on them. He was the town's lawyer. The town was small enough that the townspeople never knew a time when they did not know each other. Even their parents could not remember a time when they, too, did not know each other, and their parents' parents as well. This was how things were, Ubaldo thought, and inasmuch as experience taught anything, how things would be as well. The thought neither comforted nor bothered him, as his feeling was that the world was simply the world. The good part was that he didn't have to worry about it.

And his feelings about the world and this town were true up until this day, this Tuesday, this day different from all other days.

Ubaldo adjusted the fan this morning in his comfortable office. Summer was close, and he could already feel its breath on the back of his neck. He did not mind the heat but did not go looking for it, either. The fan would help to keep summer away for another week or two.

Ubaldo Dos Santos was still young, but that didn't mean much here. He was still young or already old, he was thirty-four or forty-six—given the way life was lived here, and his life in particular, it was all the same. One did not count life this way, not with days and years and other sorts of arithmetic. One counted only the day at hand. To predict tomorrow was too easy, and to remember yesterday was to take the fun out of today.

And this time of year, one needed all the fun that could be found—within reason, of course. Everything within reason—that was Ubaldo's training as a lawyer, after all. *Licenciado* meant something in the world, after all, and Ubaldo did his best to uphold his training in all things. Too much or too little—these were the dangers of the world.

So that when the knock came at the door, unannounced and unexpected, Licenciado Ubaldo Dos Santos wasn't quite sure what to do. Answering the door might have seemed to be the thing to do, just like that. *But just like that*, thought Ubaldo, *is how dangerous things happen.*

He sat at his desk hoping that whoever was on the other side had gone away until he heard a second knock. His office had a window in the door, but the pane was pebbled, as if someone had put the end of a pencil eraser into the hot glass, over and over. Ubaldo could see the shadow of someone standing there but could not make out who it was.

Life seemed suddenly precarious when someone came to the office without an appointment, even though Ubaldo Dos Santos—like his father before him—was always fond of saying "no appointments necessary" whenever anyone asked. His father had always added, and Ubaldo followed suit, seeing even as a child the astuteness of suggesting personal service, "and certainly not for you" to whomever was asking. Asking, however, was itself an appointment of sorts, so that when the person showed up, it was no surprise. And in asking the question, as well, the person anyway was no stranger.

This was different. He expected no one, not today. Ubaldo had planned to catch up on some professional reading, which was always such a nuisance. It was always his plan when there was nothing else to do, though something to do almost invariably showed itself. That was all right, and he was never particularly sorry. The law should be the law, simple and finished. It shouldn't always be turning on this change or that. Ubaldo often wished he had a lawyer himself to explain each little emendation, clarification, reiteration, and palpitation. It was so much easier—and made more sense, really, if the law was the law—not to worry so much about all these changes. These laws that changed would change again, after all, so what was the point. They would come full circle, he was sure, so that waiting was just as good, really.

His catching-up corner of things he needed to read had grown considerably, but neatened up and put on shelves, the books and serious-sounding journals all looked very impressive. When speaking to clients, he would always find a way to draw their attention to these materials, suggesting that a lawyer's work—and here he took a deep breath and lowered his eyes, with high seriousness tinged with a curious and touching sadness, or heroism, perhaps—was never done. He would take an extra second or two to let the person admire this large collection, which could not be ignored. It suggested that all of those books were the reason people needed him. Had he known what was in them that might have been true. But it was true anyway, if they thought it, and he was a help to the town in his way. Nobody complained, or knew to.

❖

The knocking on the door was not going away. After a third time, Ubaldo finally said, "I'll be right there." He did not say it with eagerness, but his voice was not timid either. He was a lawyer, after all, and used to theatrics. If the knock scared him, he would scare it back.

Ubaldo opened the door to a man who stood with great patience, not about to go away.

"Ubaldo Dos Santos at your service," said Ubaldo, shaking the man's hand and waving him to a chair in front of Ubaldo's large desk.

He was a stranger.

What that meant was that he would not understand the laws of this town. Once explained, if he was agreeable to them, then that was one thing. But if he was not, or if he brought some kind of other town's laws with him, that would be another thing altogether. One answer would mean an easy afternoon, a good dinner, and a restful night's sleep. Another answer would mean work.

"Sr. Dos Santos, I have heard so much about you. Everyone has said that you are the one to see in all matters regarding the law. And I'm not surprised, not now, seeing this office and that library."

"You flatter me, señor. I did not get your name, I'm afraid. Do I know you? Please forgive me if I have forgotten. I do not intend to be rude."

"No, please, it is my fault entirely. Here is my card. Allow me to introduce myself, which I hope, let me say it right now, will be a happy circumstance."

"I'm certain of it," said Ubaldo, hoping it would be true. But it was a good beginning, and he was, in fact, feeling good about the meeting, even though nothing had yet been said. The bookshelves were always the test.

"But what is this?" asked Ubaldo. He looked at the card, then back up at the man. "You are a Belmares?"

"Ignacio Belmares."

"Don Cayetano's son?"

"Yes, yes."

"But I know your whole family. Have we met?"

"Yes, but long ago. We were kids then, and interested in different things."

"Ah, I see, I see," answered Ubaldo, understanding in those few words their greater meaning. Ubaldo had lived a privileged existence thanks to his father, Martín Dos Santos, who himself had suffered a difficult upbringing and would have no such thing happen to his own children. As such, Ubaldo very often knew people whom he had known as children, but perhaps not as friends, exactly. So many people had to work, even at that age. Ubaldo understood that kind of life to be hard, and always felt an involuntary shudder when he came near it.

"The thing is, Don Ubaldo, I have five jobs for you."

It was curious for Ubaldo to hear this phrasing, because now, though it did not impress him as meaningful, Ubaldo Dos Santos was the one for hire. People were still very thankful to him, and his life was not a life of service in the sense of hard work—that is, hard work in the fields or in the factories—not that kind of hard work. This was very different.

"Five jobs, you say?" Five jobs? That was quite a number. One job was usual. Two jobs often happened as an afterthought, something else that needed doing now that the big thing was being done, say a will along with a business transaction. Three jobs sometimes, for the same reason, perhaps a wife's will as well. But five was simply five. That could easily amount to—he did not want to get ahead of things—but it could amount to several months' worth of work, if they were the right kinds of jobs. And Ubaldo knew how to make jobs last—*done correctly*, is what he called it, though the truth was that the joke fell on Ubaldo, because taking more time did in fact, perhaps by accident if not by true design, end up with things being done correctly, eventually. In this way, he was meticulous and had earned something of a reputation for being thorough.

When a job needed to be done quickly, however, given the right circumstances—which meant the right fee—he could be counted on to do the right thing. Miguel Torres was counting on exactly that, the right fee and their many-year friendship, both of which would be considerable when doing what Miguel Torres wanted done, which was everything in the world. But Miguel Torres was another story and another worry. This man stood in front of him now.

It was laziness, then, that made Ubaldo's reputation. Or rather the inclination not to proceed too quickly, nor to give too much weight to one thing or another, nor to say *yes* or *no* when asked a question about the matter at hand. Once it was his, it was his for a long time. It was his automatic and abiding assumption that there was always more to consider before one could bring a case to closure. This suited the courts and the bureaucracy well, as they worked in much the same fashion.

In this world and in its systems of operation, he was a captain. In interpreting his captaincy to his clients, however, he was not quite as successful. People grumbled. But several decades of success, or of what might be called eventual success, had made its mark and defined his reputation. After all these years, things simply arrived at his office, little mysteries, things he had filed with the courts sometimes a decade earlier, completed and finished at last all this time later. He often had to wade through his files to see what the matter being settled was, and he had to hope as well that the applicants or litigants or claimants were still alive so that he could show them this success, small as it might be.

Waiting out the last form, no matter how minor and no matter how many years—this was his strength, even if others were not as certain of things. That he never particularly tried to move things along any faster or stir the waters, this was a kind of strength, too, though there were many other words that might work in defining the circumstance. And people were not afraid to use those words.

Through all these years, however, Ubaldo's secret was his secrets, which were not secret at all—they were anybody's business who had simply known where and how and why to look. But had he told them, well, quite simply, *they would have known*, and his secrets would not be worth much then. He would not have been necessary to the town, or appreciated. *Anybody could do that,* he imagined them saying. Ubaldo would have had no job, or at least not this job, which was a job with an office and a place in the scheme of the town that suited him.

So Ubaldo kept things to himself, neither telling nor not telling, which is what explained his general quietude, which people mistook as dignity, which he very much liked. If he did not tell people what they might find useful, neither did he not tell them, which is what allowed him to keep his head more or less high, believing, as he often said he did, in the great resourcefulness of people to learn what they needed to know if they wanted to. But they never looked, of course, and instead always came to him. So what Ubaldo knew was that he knew what others did not know, and this was something. He was careful, therefore, to shepherd that gray area, to corral it with his arms and to make it his. As a lawyer, he guarded his recipes.

In this way he was not at all like his sister, Guillermina, who told everything she knew to anybody she saw and even took the trouble to wave people over and tell them what she was certain would be true if they were simply to do what she told them to do. And all at no charge.

But it didn't matter, not to Ubaldo, who held his head high and explained to anyone who would listen that regular people simply did not understand the workings of the legal system, and that the fault was not his. He understood their frustration, of course, he would say, but he was frustrated himself, and there would throw up his hands in a gesture of despair. After a while, he began to skip the explanation and just use the gesture, which saved time.

And it was indeed true that the people themselves were not lawyers, any more than they were scientists, and so they had to believe Don Ubaldo, had to take him at his word whether they liked it or not. It was an uneasy circumstance, but a charmed one for Ubaldo, who lived just slightly beyond the understanding and grasp of the town, in a framework of elegance and sincerity, because nobody could say otherwise. But they did grumble. They did grumble.

He says a lot, now if only he would say a lot, was the old joke about Ubaldo Dos Santos. And curiously, it was both an old joke and a new one in that what was true once upon a time was just as true so many years later. At the end of the day, the world in his office even after all those years had rarely moved more than a half-inch. But that's how he measured success.

Behind it all, behind his demeanor and his gruffness, there was a simple truth. He did not want to know what was farther than he could see, for fear it would be something bigger than he was—and then what? The truth was, he didn't care for change, not if it meant that his lunchtime would be changed, or that dinner on Thursday night would be enchiladas instead of tostadas, which is what he always had on Thursday nights, the same way his family always had tostadas on Thursday nights, and which they did because his grandparents always had tostadas on Thursday nights. *Who would not understand that?* he wondered, and would shake his head at the nonsense of enchiladas on Thursdays. How did that make sense?

People dying, well, of course that was different. That was the natural order of things, as long as it wasn't Ubaldo himself, or his mother, or his sister, more or less in that order. He missed his father, Don Martín. He missed him so much that, when he died, all of these feelings became clear to Ubaldo. His father had taken care of things, for the family but for the town as well—he was a lawyer, which is why Ubaldo had become a lawyer—and he missed that man.

But he still had tostadas on Thursday nights. Some things did not have to die. This was the thing about Ubaldo Dos Santos—a little thing or a big thing, neither mattered much because Ubaldo took them both in stride, making much of the small and little of the big.

This gave him something of an even temperament, but one did not need to go far to get a second opinion of him, even if it did make him a good lawyer.

❖

Ubaldo did not like when Miguel Torres, who was like an uncle to him, having been such a good friend to his father, he did not like it when Miguel Torres on his darker days talked about how everyone in town looked like an animal, and even worse, an insect. It only confirmed Ubaldo's worst fears that all the noises he heard in the night were, somehow, a gathering of the townspeople, hungry and wide-eyed, coming to his door. That Dr. Bartolomeo only confirmed the idea that human beings were, in fact, animals, and did indeed share many traits, if not most, with those things out there in the world, those things in the distance, in the woods and

176 | CHAPTER 11

in—could he say it—other towns, no, this he did not like at all. Not at all. It kept him quiet at the meetings of the Forward Science Society, which he attended only in order to make sure they were not talking about him.

He would never say such a thing, of course. It sounded crazy. And he was not crazy. He was, as anyone could see by looking at the frames hanging on the wall of his office, quite the opposite. Quite the opposite.

These distractions on the part of Ubaldo were noticeable to Ignacio, who said again, "Don Ubaldo?"

"Yes. Forgive me. I was thinking of an important case, a detail. You know. Now, let's see. You have five jobs for me?" This was good. It meant, first of all, that he could never be working on more than one job at a time, not if he was to do a good job. This would be the first thing to say, or rather, he would find a convenient time some weeks down the line when the shadow of a complaint would show itself, and then he would say this. *One thing at a time, if it's to be done right, and one part of one of the jobs at a time, carefully done.* Ubaldo could not get the sudden mathematics of this man's statement out of his head. This sort of job, or jobs, could last a long time, five jobs, with many parts each, certainly, and certainly the requisite understanding that they were to be done well, which took time, as anyone could easily understand.

Five jobs, though—on the other hand, Ubaldo didn't like the sound of that. It sounded like something getting done. Like progress. Like industry. Like movement. What was this man Ignacio up to, anyway?

"Well, let me be quite honest with you, Don Ubaldo. I have one job for you right now. But I intend to use your services quite a bit, and I wanted to give you that impression, so that you would understand that I mean business. I want you to be the company lawyer, with the understanding that at least four more jobs lie ahead—you can be sure of that. I know your father's reputation through my father. So, please trust that it's important to me that you be the one who takes care of this."

Surely this man is going to be mayor before long, thought Ubaldo. Ignacio wanted to get things done, and to get things done as well that didn't yet need doing. It was something of an interesting thought, not new, of course, but so firmly spoken. The future had cause to listen.

All that, and he seemed not to have heard of any of Ubaldo's— what would he call them—*difficulties* with the town.

"You have the words, Don Ubaldo, and I have the energy."

Ubaldo nodded. He wasn't sure if that was an insult or not. Ubaldo pushed his chair back and turned the man's attention to the wall and all its frames, "Well, as you can see . . ."

"Like your father, Don Ubaldo. He was very proud of you, I'm sure. And I am proud to know you as well."

Ubaldo cleared his throat. He liked this man.

"I have a company, or rather I think I have a company, but the town does not yet recognize it. I need to register my company with the town and see what else needs to be done. I want to do what's right, after all. I want to be a company like all the other fine companies in this town. It should be a simple matter, I think." Ignacio spoke all this earnestly, so honestly it was hard for Ubaldo to believe.

Ah, thought Ubaldo, *so the man knows nothing*. That was a relief. Ignacio didn't know the first thing about what he thought he wanted. Ubaldo wasn't at all sure that there even was any required paperwork, or anything to file, but then again, that would be something to investigate, certainly. Surely Ignacio was right that it should be a simple matter. But just as surely, Ubaldo was certain that there would be prudent and reasonable paperwork to be filed, just in case, and official stamps to be obtained, which always took months. If done correctly, of course. Ubaldo would make the time in the coming weeks to get started.

Ubaldo in that moment understood that he and Ignacio were going to be good friends after all. The better part of that understanding was that they would have to be good friends—there was no getting around it. This suited Ubaldo. The niceties would be put in place overnight, without all the years that might have had to go into building such a relationship. They knew people who knew each other, and in this way they were already best friends. Just like that. But the good kind of *just like that.*

"Well, of course, when it comes to the town and the courts, there are no simple matters. But that is not your concern. Leave it to me."

"Then you'll take the job?"

If Ubaldo had been thinking about Miguel Torres and all his troubles, he was now giving Ignacio his full attention.

"Don Ignacio, rest assured I am at work on it already. First thing in the morning."

GOVERNMENT OF THE STATE OF SINALOA

In the name of the Republic of Mexico, and as Offical
Civil Registrar of this population, I hereby acknowledge to
whoever views this document, and certify as truth, that on
Page Number 265 (Two Hundred and Sixty-five) from Book Number I (One) of Births in this year 1953 (Nineteen Hundred and
Fifty-three) from this Office of the Civil Registry, which is
in my care, the following entry is noted:

ACT 265 (Two Hundred and Sixty-five). BIRTH OF THE
FEMALE CHILD REFUGIO MARTINEZ, indigenous race mixed
with white. Union of the parents: Civil Union. Regis-
tered at the OFFICE OF THE CIVIL REGISTRAR in Los Mochis.
In the City of Los Mochis, Municipality of Ahome, Sinaloa,
at 11:00 A.M. on September 2, 1925 before me, Jesus Osuna,
Official Civil Registrar, at this place appeared citizen
Jose Martinez and his wife Rosa Valdez, the former born in
Culiacan, Sinaloa, married, 35 years of age, carpenter,
and the latter born in Alamos, Sonora, 32 years of age,
housewife, and presented before me a live female child
who was born at their place of residency on the 7 (seventh)
day of this past August at 1:00 A.M. to whom they gave
the name REFUGIO MARTINEZ, legitimate daughter of those who
now appear; the presented child is granddaughter through
paternal line of the deceased Jesus Martinez and Refugio
Anaya and through maternal line of the deceased Adelaido
Valdez Toxps. The witnesses of this act were citizens
Joaquin Martin and Octaviano A. Rodriguez, both of legal
age, of this area, married, and employed. This act was
read by the offical subscriber to the parents and witnesses
who agreed to the veracity of, and ratified by their signa-
tures, these contents.   Official Civil Registrar--
J. Osuna. Person here appearing: Jose Martinez (underlined in red).

--- I certify this is a faithful copy of the original which I
send as requested by the interested party today on October 19,
1953 from the City of Los Mochis, Sinaloa, Mexico.

Official Civil Registrar

(Signature)

Aurelio B. Escobar

THE BIRTH CERTIFICATE

I was born. You were born. Until the turn of the century, being born was a story. Until the 1960s, birth certificates were written by hand in a stylized manner. The story told had characters, a narrative, plot, secondary actors, and a writer who captured it all, sitting in front of a typewriter at the civil registrar's office and trying to listen to everyone speak. So many of these narrative birth certificates have been lost—to fire, to neglect, to already-yellow paper gone brown. Sometimes you can write to find out. Sometimes they will write back.

Sometimes, in earnest, they will try to tell you what happened, and in whatever language needs to hear it.

12

Curandera

The front room of Armida Castañeda's house was like anyone's—a coffee table, some chairs with crocheted doilies placed nicely on the arms and backs, vanilla-colored curtains, some clay animal figurines, a small rug, a refrigerator, and a small forest of fat-leaved plants in colorful pots on the floor. The plants thrived around the refrigerator, which leaked water, too old to keep ice very well anymore. The little bit of mold that grew between the plants and in the moisture on the floor was also green and gave the room an even more verdant sensibility. Because this town was in the high Sonoran Desert, one walking into this room breathed in the air of another place.

People ascribed so many things to Armida Castañeda, calling her simply the *curandera* sometimes, or just *la señora*, as if she had no name at all but simply a job nobody wanted to know too much about. But in fact, hers were the habits of the tangible. When something succeeded and when something failed, even when something had no effect at all—she took careful notes through the years, and lived with them. That is, those words she wrote down were people's lives. And if not their lives altogether, then their comforts and their fears, their small pains and great loves.

People. Perfect feet or twisted feet, thought Armida—people were all trees if they grew, and were strong if they were happy. Their differences were the distinction between the oak and the black walnut, the paloverde and the mesquite. She had known so many Alejandros, so many Noés and Angelicas, Mariquitas and Adolfos. So many of them had shown themselves to her, had stood and sat and talked in her front room, that she could not remember their names—she left that to Guillermina Belmares, who remembered everyone by their family. But their arms and their feet, their red sores and dark dreams, Armida Castañeda remembered them all, every last one.

She loved to watch how an elbow bent or how a limp defined someone. If something hurt a person, it hurt her, too. Headaches brought themselves to her hands. Rashes came to her as little mysteries, and she was their Sherlock Holmes, a book she had read many times and which she kept next to her bed. Toothaches called her name. So often she was in between, the step after something happened and before somebody went to Dr. Cano or Dr. Bartolomeo or to the dentist, all of whom she recommended when it was appropriate. There were, after all, so many things that she could not fix.

But just as often she was the afterward as well, which she wished were not the case but where she so often did her best work. People came to her after having their immediate problems fixed by the doctor—their broken bones set, their bleeding stopped, their wounds stitched. After that, however, when there was no more blood to be seen and the bone seemed well positioned, after that, when the smaller pains began, they came to her for the long term. They came for the days and months and years following the loud thing that the doctor fixed but which needed more attention, more of something the doctor had no name for, the quieter thing that nobody else could hear.

So many other *curanderas* she had known lived nervous lives. They guessed at the world. They tried to remember what they knew and what their mothers had told them. They tried their best to listen to the world but did not know what questions to ask of it.

The language they spoke, finally, it was so simple. A red bougainvillea flower for a red rash. For pus and infections, the yellow chamomile flower. For white skin, onion peels. Hard for hard, warm for warm, salt for a grimacing face. It was a dialogue, but not always a conversation.

That language, she understood, did not speak the truth. It was instead a cruel vocabulary, beautiful but without any particular further understanding or reverberation. Its grammar was selfish. Red wanted and required and functioned best and made the most sense next to more red, the more red the better.

She, too, had spoken this language as a child. But she was no child now, and the children she knew needed her to say more, the children and their parents as well.

There had been a beauty in simplicity, however. She sighed as she thought about it, about all the times she had seen this language spoken. She sighed at its beauty, even if the mystery of complexity was what charmed her now. One aches, nevertheless, for that first time. Her first time was red. It was a room full of bougainvillea leaves and rose petals, butcher stains on white paper, coals glowing, sleepless eyes, tens of *ristras* of chilies tied to the rafters, strings of red chilies hanging everywhere. Christmas yarn wound in between everything, and there were knickknack Santa Clauses, a bowl of pyracantha berries next to a bowl of *chiltepines*, some old dresses and socks, a cut watermelon and some tomato wedges, a row of open lipsticks, a nail polish bottle, a borrowed Coca-Cola sign. Don Fausto the red-bearded man had been invited and sat in the room, sticking out his bright tongue, comfortable on the straw-matted chair enameled with roosters. Several bottles of ketchup were arranged around him, along with a big bag of *jamaica* blossoms for tea, the three bowls of chicken blood, some sticks of dynamite (on loan), a checkerboard with half the checkers, a bandanna, and some bottles of *tinta*.

Together all of these articles made a powerful argument. Their sheer force at having gathered, their compliant juxtaposition, all of it seeming to suggest understanding that one thing carried something of and to the other, and so to her. Red drawn together in this way was impressive, magnificent even. But for all of that, this circus was nevertheless relatively ineffective in actually countering even the simplest malady. This collective did bring awe and made a music in response that was sometimes joy, which sometimes worked to cure a thing, if only by distraction. It was the trick of magicians and the medicine of the centuries. Distraction.

All that single color made a radiance. As she looked at all of it, the spectacle of its color reached into her as a single sound, a surprise at first, a startled sound, and then a deeper voice, steady in the moment, a red voice, speaking a single color syllable. All these things, their red connected to the red of her lips, to the insides of her eyelids, to her tongue. The color touched her. It drew her red, the reds of her own body, into the ruby of the moment.

She understood, and felt something strong in the moment all those years ago. Gathering a single color from all its work in the world, marshaling it into one place, a person had to feel impressed, and connected to the world by this overwhelming attention, each small thing pulled away from its regular work to be here. In the end, however, such an event did not cure a cold, at least not very well.

On the other hand, this gathering of the things and attentions of the world did make having a cold more bearable in that moment.

This medicine of distraction, this simple language, could not be ignored altogether. One color suddenly assembled—it felt like concern. It felt like the world, for a moment, had stopped to listen.

Armida Castañeda knew that. She knew what people expected, and how much their expectation mattered. The green of her front room was a testament to her own first time with red. So much color drawn together, however, this was not normal. One did not see or cause to be made a gathering of colors every day, nor did one want to. It was dangerous, an upset of the world, like a great wind or a very bad storm. A little bit of color and texture in everything, balance, this was normal. But in putting many reds with a red illness or a great helping of the world's full scale of yellow with a yellow skin, one spoke to imbalance with imbalance. Wars were fought this way, many soldiers to many soldiers. This is how she thought of illness, a great imbalance, and her way to fight it was to find an equal footing.

But her work was more than that. The doctors did that part well, anyway, taking care of the immediate things. She herself expected more now, wanting to help people beyond one afternoon and into a second and third day, into the months and years of their distress, if she had to. She wanted something more in her cures and made her life a search for it.

So many notes all these years, so many questions—she had learned that this was half the cure to people, paying so much attention to them. Whatever questions she had, as long as she had enough of them, everyone answered willingly and enjoyed joining her in the pursuit of the culprit, which was inside them. The more questions, the closer to a cure they seemed to get.

When someone was sick, she would bring that person in with her first words, her understanding welcome. *La sopa cayó en la miel,* she would say, *the soup fell into the honey.* They would nod *yes*, and the visit had started. *La lágrima es hermana de la risa*, she would continue, *a tear is sister to a laugh.* With the simple word *laugh*, people would, and the cure had begun.

Armida Castañeda remembered all the sayings her mother had used just as much as she knew how to use all the herbs on the hillside and from gardens. They themselves were sometimes the herbs but in words, a medicine that helped people's thinking. And when people despaired, they needed attention everywhere. The herbs were one thing, but what Armida said to people, she had learned, was like sugar in the tea. It gave people something extra, some reason to go forward. *La esperanza no engorda pero mantiene*, is how she always thought about it, and optimism was the first ingredient in all her cures—*hope doesn't fatten, but it nourishes.*

Armida's chest of cures went well beyond the fragrant wooden cabinets she kept in the back room. But those cabinets were impressive nonetheless. Over the years, she had personally gathered much of what they held, and now they gave a fragrance to her house that made it, if not sacred ground, then special ground at least. It smelled like a church on some days, but did not stop there, calling on the full orchestra of smells to play the song of her rooms.

The cabinet was locked, but not with a regular lock. All the drawers were easy enough to open. The little drawers were all labeled with what they contained, but Armida herself was the key to opening up their meaning. The herbs were locked with what they could do, and Armida knew how to open them to their use. People came to purchase the herbs, which was half of her work for the town. They came to ask for one thing or another, and she knew right where to find it. And with each purchase she gave a detailed instruction.

One day she would write it all down, she thought. Armida's life, however, never gave her a place to begin, and finally she gave up the plan, not consciously but by practice. To write what she knew would take a lifetime, and she was too busy with all her notes about everybody else. Still, some things needed someone to know them. She tried her best to pass on some of her thoughts to her son, whom she had named Perfecto. People sometimes laughed at his name, but she was sure it was right. The name was a medicine she gave to him before birth. *Buen principio, la mitad es hecho,* she remembered her mother saying to her, and she believed it: *Well begun is half done.* Sickness and sadness would have to think twice when looking at someone named Perfecto.

She tried to show him more, of course. Not everything—there were things nobody should have to know. She would take those things with her. Their cures came from the night, and she would wander into it, into the countryside, very late, and she would find what she needed. On those occasions, what she held in her hands made her hands nervous.

She showed Perfecto what she brought back with her, but only the white spiders and occasional twisted roots and soft acorns with worms. The rest she kept to herself, and gave them names in her cabinet that were from the alphabet and not anything more. To speak them, and to speak the core and manner of their service—she hoped these things would die in this century, and that people would have no memory of them. Some illnesses did too much.

Everything else, however, she showed to her son when he had an interest or when she needed help with her gathering as they walked through the hills, or on the more leisurely walks past the gardens in town, where she reached in and always came back with something useful that nobody would notice was missing. Some herbs and flowers needed to be replenished every season, but she was very discreet. Indeed, some people liked her intrusions because they had less weeding and cleaning up to do after she had taken what she needed. The ugly roots and dried stems, she could have them all. It was a happy arrangement.

In this way the world gave Armida her ingredients and her live-lihood, and sometimes her dinner—everything she needed. When people marveled at her chest of cures, which became through the years cabinet stacked upon cabinet, Armida would laugh.

"These are nothing," she would say. "Look out there and you will see a thousand things more, all of them good for something. That is where the cure is," she would add, pointing outside. "But finding the right thing, one must be careful." The caution spoke for itself. People had heard stories of what happened in the hills.

Much of what she gathered she turned into teas when the need arose. She could make a hundred teas, a thousand if she blended things, and so many of them were pleasant enough taken with conversation and reassurance. *Manzanilla, hierba buena, hierba mate*, and all the rest, all with rules for drinking them correctly. Armida and her son both drank them as well, the regular teas, and they ate as well from the things they gathered in their travels, on their long afternoons, the *tuna* prickly pear fruits, which she de-thorned, and the *verdolagas*, which so many people thought of only as weeds. How many meals the world had given her, she often marveled, and she gave that sense of wonder to her son as well.

The teas were not everything. Armida had just as many herbs as teas, *romero* and sweet basil and all their first and second and third cousins, which gave Armida and Perfecto so many ways to taste rice and chicken and rabbit. Her son would remember that delight, a different dinner every evening, but he would have the complaint, as well, that he would never again taste something that he especially enjoyed on any particular night, as Doña Armida never repeated herself. Perfecto himself later on in life would not be so bold, but not because he did not know boldness.

❖

So many notes. If anything became clear, it was that each person required a separate note, and to try and use one person's cures on another was more often folly. Armida's mother had said it so easily—*Con lo que sana Susana, cae enferma Juana. What cures Susana makes Juana ill*, she had said, though she was talking about why Armida was so meticulous about her breakfast when others were not. But if Armida's notes were to be useful, she would have to write down the story of everybody, one person at a time, with nobody left out. How did the doctors do that, she wondered?

When she asked Dr. Cano, he laughed very hard. "We don't. We don't do that. We're just the opposite, really."

"How do you mean?" she asked.

"The truth is, we know things about how a body should work, and we try to help people get their body to behave like the best of other bodies. It's not anybody in particular. We just try to help people get better when they're sick, or when something bad has happened."

"But what if they're not sick? Or else, not very sick?"

"Then why would they come to a doctor?"

Armida was surprised at the answer, even though it made perfect sense in its own way. If the lamp falls to the ground and breaks, picking up the pieces and putting them back together again, well, of course this makes sense. But if the lamp wobbles every time the door closes, shouldn't one make an effort to either move the lamp or fix it more securely to its table? She asked him this.

"Yes, yes, that's true," he said, but quickly and with a wave of his hand. "But we have too many of the first kind, people with things broken or with fevers. Nobody can expect me to come around looking at every little thing in a house that might cause an accident."

"Or make them sick," added Armida.

Dr. Cano wrinkled his brow. "I take your meaning. Yes, of course, we could do more of that, but there is no time, really. No time at all."

"Ah," said Armida, and they had a pleasant talk otherwise, about their families and the surprising warmth of the day, even as fall was coming to a close.

It was the end of October, and the town was full of yellow flowers. A small rain had raised their scent, which was strong. Armida did not care so much for *cempasúchiles*, those marigolds that people placed near the dead. It was thought that the flower's strong scent drew the dead back, helping them find their return to loved ones, if only for a visit. During the last days of October and the first days of November, before and during the *días de los muertos*, and for the weeks of the flowers' decay that followed, the scent was a cloud on the town.

Armida did not work so much with the dead, not like other *curanderas* she knew. Some of those ladies in some towns made a good living fostering that conversation between worlds. Everybody seemed in a mood to say to the dead things they should have said when they were alive—that feeling did not go out of fashion. But, she thought, it was as the doctor said—there was no time, even if one might find such conversation pleasant. Besides, she thought, why not say these things now and save some money and heartache?

"You know," she would say when someone asked her to help, "*más vale atole con sonrisas que chocolate con lágrimas.*" *It's better to have gruel with a smile than chocolate with tears.*

Armida's work, she saw clearly, was in doing whatever the doctor could not, which left her in charge of most things in town. If the doctor was the doctor, he was only the doctor, important as that was. Armida, on the other hand, was something of the unacknowledged town councilmember in charge of how people felt. She did her best work addressing people's smallest disquiet. The big concerns, she thought, let the doctor have them. All that blood was unsettling, after all. But the small things, the secrets and the aches, the sudden shivers at the sight of something odd, all of this, all of it, she took pains to compose and repair.

Dr. Cano first, and then Dr. Bartolomeo, both of them liked Armida and held her in high esteem, even if they did not agree with her methods. Her results, these were what impressed the doctors, even if they supposed there was nothing to cure to begin with. Still, they knew, however grudgingly, that what people believed could be just as important as what was wrong with them, even if they themselves did not have the patience to sit the many hours with someone that a cure like this might require. Dr. Bartolomeo, especially, liked having her in town. Even though he was a fervent believer in science and had founded the Forward Science Society, he knew enough not to dismiss history in his quest to move into the future.

But if Armida did not understand the ways of the operating table, she believed wholly in the church of the kitchen table. Talking, eating, drinking coffee, crying. The operating table was fine, and she had a healthy respect for what it had to offer, but she was greedy, for herself and for others. She knew there was more than the operating table in the greater field of medicine, a small corner of which she claimed.

People came to her to cure things the doctors did not want to cure, the things they waved off as superstition or bad education, but which everyone knew happened. There were the diseases that the doctors said were not diseases but which everybody knew were diseases—the *mal de ojo*, the *empacho*, the *caída de la mollera*, and all those others, with their symptoms that doctors could not find in their books and could not set straight so easily like bones. Their answer was to ignore them, or to treat something else. That's when people went to Armida Castañeda.

The litany of curing these things was easy enough. Learning the cures took some time, but anyone could learn them, with a little patience. The full list comprised three different areas of illness. The first area covered all the natural illnesses: *aire de oído*, the earache; *caída de mollera*, the fallen fontanel, which is the soft spot at the back of the head; *cólico*, the colic; *mal aire* or *sereno*, which was the bad air; and *mal de latido*, which were the palpitations that people got. These were the regular ailments.

The second area of illnesses she did not care for and chose not to address if she could help it. These were the illnesses of the supernatural, and were dangerous, not because of the supernatural but because of people themselves, and of what they imagined the dead to be doing. When these came to her as conditions she had to help with, she did it only at night, and people had to come to her back door. But they were real illnesses, all right. She had seen them wreak their havoc, sometimes destroying a person who was not brought to her soon enough.

The most insidious were the most purposeful, the *embrujamiento* and the *hechizo*, which were witchcraft and curses and hexes and spells, all the same but with slight variations, all of them up to no good. The more common condition, especially with babies, was the *mal de ojo*, the evil eye. The *mal puesto* was a lighter hex, and was often simply a fluster of the moment, a frustration, a spoken curse that took on a small life of its own. Once spoken, someone heard it and spoke it to someone else, who in turn spoke it to someone else. Those few words quickly grew into something else. The last was *susto*, which was fright or shock. Some people thought of it as a loss of the soul, and to Armida it was the most interesting.

The third area of illness was made up of the extremities of emotion. The most common of these sorts of illnesses were the *bilis*, which was bile in the blood, brought on by anger, or gall. Its opposite, and the one that interested Armida the most, especially in that its symptoms resembled the *susto*, was *tristeza*, which was all the varieties of sadness and melancholy, a depression from which one could not easily withdraw, as if it were a quicksand in the mind.

Many of these conditions from all three areas exhibited common symptoms, such as *empacho*, and one had to work hard to sort out the cause. *Empacho* resulted from foods that get stuck inside the stomach, which often meant vomiting or diarrhea or constipation or other unpleasantness. The doctors were always irritated by this symptom because it could be so many things. People thought it came from poorly mixed powdered milk, or still-grainy baby formula, or swallowed gum, or grape skins, or green bananas—things that were not done correctly. The cure was a massage with grease, or any of a variety of oils, depending.

Some conditions were interesting more for their cures, however, than their causes, which Armida sometimes thought curious herself. *Caída de la mollera*, for example, people thought happened to infants when the infant was bounced too roughly or tossed around by a boisterous father, or if the child drank a bottle while in a moving car, or if the child pulled away from the mother's breast too quickly and without letting go. All of this could cause the soft palate at the top of the mouth and the fontanel both to sink in, which led to all manner of difficulty, especially in feeding and swallowing. Children became overly fussy and had fevers or diarrhea.

The cure, however, was a carefully orchestrated event. To realign and reposition the fontanel, the thumb was used to push up on the soft palate inside the mouth. This made a kind of sense, and provided a sculptural effect, though the thought of sculpting a baby was not a good one. The condition could also be treated by pulling hard on the hair covering the fontanel, thereby raising it. But this was just the beginning. One might apply a poultice with ingredients that would cause this lifting to occur. One might clean the fontanel with a new bar of soap, or with a whole egg, or by rubbing alcohol on it.

Some people had been known to suck on the fontanel, or even to hang the infant over a basin of water and tap its feet, though that added much to the infant's displeasure. Armida had done them all, sometimes with the help of a person who was a twin, which some people believed was necessary to the process. Armida thought they just got in the way, since this was not their normal job and they were always willing but nervous—and sweating. More than one helper had started to drop the baby, a circumstance Armida took care to look for.

Other illnesses had their cures, too, of course. *Susto*, which occurred after a frightening or startling experience, had symptoms that included insomnia, or nightmares if one could fall asleep. Sometimes it came with diarrhea or fever and always with a loss of appetite. People who had it never wanted to be left alone. The cures included prayers, which Armida left to Padre Nacho, who helped her when he felt he could. He would suggest other religious practices as well, but people would sometimes go too far. Wearing an *azabache*, for example, a charm that seemed like wood and was about the size of a peach pit, protected a child from illness caused by the *mal de ojo*. Armida had made many of these *azabaches* and knew their secrets, the first of which was faith, though she could not tell this to Padre Nacho.

And all the rest. *Sereno*, for example, occurred when a child was exposed to suddenly cold air or water, which brought on a stuffy nose and runny eyes. Sometimes the face became paralyzed or twitched with pain. The answer for this was warm clothing and cleaning the child's eyes out with mother's milk. The better cure was not to let it happen to begin with, which explained all the layers of clothing that folded over onto a child's face, and sometimes even a light blanket, being careful of course not to smother the baby, but understanding as well that the illness was not kind. The blankets always worried Armida, who tried to change that particular practice.

❖

When someone brought a child in, they were not who they were. They were not the person one might see shopping in the *mercado*. They were not the person one might see doing a job in town, fixing pipes or streetlights. They were not even the person one might see in the front yard of their house grooming the garden, planting a tree. It was the same person, of course, but they had stepped out of their private lives, which gave them a different face. They were instead the people farther inside their houses, in a small room with a small child coughing and crying. These were people bringing with them their despair.

They had already seen the doctor, who had given them what a doctor would have. But now the months were at hand, the time that healing asked. A few weeks, several months—they were easy phrases to say and to hear, especially followed by, *and then he'll be all right.* The months themselves, however, the weeks, the days and minutes, they did not disappear so easily. They were not unmitigated misery—that would have meant going to a hospital a long way from here—but they were misery enough. When someone brought a child in, they were a mother or a father, and only that. They were not the barber or the butcher, not in that moment.

Prayers and teas, one could count on these as a necessary starting point. And a family might know more, as well—but if not, Armida would teach them. She would always begin the lesson the same way, with the simple ones—*manzanilla*, the chamomile flower tea, for chest problems and colds. *Oregano* for coughs. *Hierba buena*, peppermint leaves, for distresses of the stomach. *Canela,* cinnamon, for dehydration. *Escobadura*, the little plant that looked like a broom, for *empacho*.

In whatever way they were conceived and whatever the name they carried, the illnesses of the people who came to her said something about the fears of the town. Armida's kind of medicine, more than being a cure, spoke against that fear. Modern science did too, but Armida believed that the town could not forget the first sciences, which tenderly matched, and continued to match, help to hope, imagination to the human condition. She thought this but did not say it. The words were big, but just words, and she had other things to concern herself with.

The boy Baltasár was brought to her. Guillermina and Cayetano Belmares, this was their moment, tender as when the boy was born, to be his mother and father once more, mother and father and nothing more, looking only at him, worried only about him.

Guillermina would later find a way to pay Armida back, but today there was no talk of that. They were friends, and for a long time, after all. It was a favor, and a hard one to ask. Guillermina and Cayetano were always hard at work and in charge of everything. But even if it was a favor, Guillermina would remember— she remembered everything—and she would help Armida's own son, Perfecto, years later. With that, the favor would be repaid. Right now, however, the world was Baltasár, and all these weeks and months, now, of his curious behavior. With so much work to do and so many other things going on, understanding that Baltasár had gotten stuck in time took everyone awhile to figure out, and even longer to believe.

The boy had gotten stuck in life, in a moment, and could not find his way beyond it. His body grew and the years went by, but he lingered in that one day and would not budge, or could not. He

lived that day every day. It was a Thursday, which he could say
easily enough. Wednesday had come before it and Friday would be
coming. The day was cold, and he knew to put warm clothes on. He
knew all the things he knew—nothing from that day was gone. He
ate and drank and laughed and everything else, as he had on that
day. But Friday would simply not come.

Nobody could explain it. Baltasár had seen his friend, the boy
Oswaldo, have an accident on their ranch, to be sure, but that was
now a long time ago. The boy had died, quite unfortunately, and
Baltasár had seen everything. What else it could be, nobody could
say. He had been quiet since then, but he had always been a quiet
boy, so not much was made of it.

"Was it that?" asked Guillermina.

"Perhaps," nodded Armida, listening to the story that she
already knew. The whole town had heard the story of the other
boy's tragic fall from a horse. It had been one of those things. A
simple accident, even though accidents are never simple when it
comes to their aftereffects.

"Perhaps *susto*," offered Guillermina.

"Perhaps," answered Armida. And indeed, Armida thought, perhaps it was. But this was not the kind that went away, not a case
like this.

"We've been praying, of course," Guillermina said, and crossed
herself. "And we've taken him to the doctor, who can't find anything wrong. We tried to explain, but in his office, Baltasár did
seem fine. It just wasn't the truth of things, though. It wasn't.
Something's wrong."

"All right," said Armida. "I understand." She took the hand of
the boy, a holding of the hands that would last for years, as they
would see each other all that time. This cure was not an easy one
and might take their whole lives. Not to try, however, would end
things right now.

There was no magic in any of this, not that she believed in. The same way that a butcher was good with meat and a ditch-digger was good with the earth, one herb was good for one thing, another for something else. This was simply the magic of hard work. Armida was not a witchcraft *curandera*, not a *bruja*. She was, instead, interested in the things of the world she could hold in her hands and understand. People all knew this, and even if, now and then, they came to her for advice on the other world, they respected her position—someone even going so far as to say that Armida herself should be a member of the Forward Science Society that Dr. Bartolomeo and that group were always talking about.

"It's you," people would say, behind the doctor's back, "it's you who knows things about the world, things more than just how to fix it with bandages."

But Armida would laugh off the suggestion, even as it hung in the air. "I have no time to talk like that with those people," she would say, understanding for herself that she preferred to use talking as one more kind of herb. Still, it was a thought that did not go away so easily.

She gave Baltasár the calming teas to begin with, the *manzanilla* and the sugar, which he liked. Armida also gave some tea to Guillermina and Cayetano, who needed it even more than the boy did at this moment. She motioned for the adults to stay in her front room, and she took Baltasár to the kitchen table.

They did not talk, not in the regular ways, but in the silence that Baltasár loved. They spoke this way for years, all the times he was brought to visit or when Armida visited him. It was as calming as the tea, even if in his quietude he was saying very loud things. Armida, he understood, listened intently to all the things he could not say. She knew what he was saying, and she nodded her head to him in a *yes* every now and then, which made him feel better. She knew what he was saying in general, even if she could not say what words he used. When he was finished for the day, it was clear that they needed to meet again, even if no words had been spoken aloud.

Guillermina and Cayetano arranged to return, and Armida began the preparations for what she knew needed to be done. It was the simple language of her childhood that Armida needed to call on, not the big words everybody liked to speak now as adults. And for Baltasár, especially, the red he had seen in the accident needed an answer. The red in all things, the blood of the world as big as it was, and not just the blood of the damaged body, this would be a starting place, something that Baltasár could see was not just trapped in that one moment. It would show him that the boy Oswaldo, that something of him, continued in the world.

Armida gathered the red of their town, all of it, everything she could find. She tried to remember what she herself had seen gathered when she had first seen this, and she brought all those items to the room—the chilies, the ketchup bottles, and all the rest. Don Fausto, the red-bearded man, had long since passed away. In his place Armida had found a large cutout of the devil that someone had used for a party along with a piñata—take a swing at the piñata with your eyes blindfolded, then take a swing at the devil with your eyes open. The idea was a good one, even if it never caught on. The fact of it being the devil was of no particular interest, but that he was painted red was everything. She exhausted the town of its red. It was a stroke of some luck that the late afternoon turned the sky just the right color at sunset. Armida opened the window.

To gather a magnificent showing of red made finding that color in the regular scheme of things much easier. To have seen it, to have been struck by it and been awed by it, big as much as small, a lot of red along with the memory of a single incident—this made remembering red painless, effortless. It was everywhere.

Baltasár now looked for red in everything, and to find it made him happy, or at least calm. For Baltasár to have seen red, red in such a way, made him look for red now every day in things—red instead of black, which would have been the end of him. To have let him be, or to have sent him in search of black, would have led him to closing his eyes, finally, closing them and not opening them, looking with great success for the darkness inside himself. Red was his distraction now, and it kept him alive. It did not cure him, but it did save him.

"*Contigo, pan y cebolla*," Armida would say to Baltasár every time they met. "With you, bread and onions." It meant that she would stick with him through thick and thin. It made him smile every time as the years wore on, and in that moment he felt good.

Baltasár looked very far and very well into red, and learned to see it even very far away. When Armida came to visit him through the years, she wore something she knew he would recognize.

Armida's personal favorite was the gathering of blue, so rare, so breathtaking in its small appearances, except of course for the sky. She herself saw its hue most, however, in the hummingbirds, which spoke to the soul, the tips of matches, which spoke to the stomach as the beginning of a fire first thing in the morning for warmth but then for breakfast, so many thousands of breakfasts now in her life. She saw the color in the farthest mountains, so far they were almost imaginary, just the idea of mountains, so that when she looked at them it was as if she were looking at the edge of dreams.

Some things were blue just for a little while on their voyage toward what they would be—the *mora* berries, for example, hung blue in the trees for a few days on their way to live their lives as purple. Some old bottles turned from clear to blue on their way to being broken glass. That moving blue was in the color of the Virgin's robe, which sometimes looked more blue than green on the prayer cards she kept to remember the passing of her family and so many friends, her parents, her aunts. Bruises themselves had this shading, hard bruises, which made their slow way to yellow having come from purples and reds. They were blue in between.

The sky by itself was something singular. When she looked hard at the sky then closed her eyes, it entered her. Something of its color found its way into her darkness, shimmering and wandering around inside her, in the deep shadow of her being. In this way, she saw herself when she opened her eyes and looked at the color of the workers' pants in the morning, at the occasional swirls and filigree on the peso notes she kept in her purse. It was what made the fringed paper that was glued to the piñatas and the *papel picado* decorations hung at all happy occasions. It was the color of some people's eyes, a few, and some cats, and a dog, once, named Bernardo.

But if her favorite thing to see had been blue, nevertheless, white was her lot, and it was not a bad one. In spite of all her cures, cures for everyone except herself, as Armida got older her own eyes began to change color on their voyage toward what they would be. They turned white. It was as if, she thought, they had a mind of their own and were now looking at things she was not, or not ready to.

Her eyes were taken by clouds, which gave Armida a sense of heaven the way it had been described to her as a child, along with the further refinements of how children imagine it. Everything white, everything uncluttered by detail. What she had was a white blindness, someone had said to her, and she agreed.

Armida could still see the regular things of life if she looked hard to the left or to the right with her eyes and tilted her face, but when she looked straight ahead, it was into another world. If she had seen red gathered, and had herself gathered green and loved blue, now it was white making its noise, white and gray speaking a language to her, and she listened. It was the quiet song of herself and her long life.

THE PHOTOGRAPH

When presented with a photograph, *Who is that?* we ask. Don't we always ask? It is a requirement, part of the grammar of human behavior. *Who is that?* and *What were they doing?* and *Is that a dog they're carrying? See how young they looked.*

This is the fate of photographs, finally. They carry so much and we listen so little. We like the frozen moment, but to have it come to life means a kind of work.

Yet, sometimes we make the leap, right there into the scene, right there with everybody pictured, everybody who used to be a stranger. We make the leap, into the photograph, breaking into the frozen moment and pulling up a chair to listen, pulling up a chair and the afternoon.

13

The History of History

Guillermina Belmares was smart. She was not scientist smart, or doctor smart, even though she tried to tell everyone how to cure everything just as much as Sra. Castañeda the *curandera* and Dr. Bartolomeo himself. It was family smart that she was. She knew who married whom, who died when, who went away, who was missing a finger and the two reasons why—the one reported in the newspapers and the real one. She knew all this and more about her family and everybody else's as well, whether the things happened or not.

Doña Guillermina knew the rumors and the stories as much as the facts, and now that her mother and father were dead and her brother was so shy, she could not be argued with. Whatever she said happened is what happened. She was the family now, in every way, the family and eventually the town. Her husband, Cayetano, tended to the fields and all the things that needed to be done, but she remembered things, or said as much, which was equal to the fact, given that her voice was more persuasive than that of her brother, the town's lawyer. If Doña Guillermina said it, then it happened, and that was that.

The dairy her family owned and had owned for a hundred years did not benefit from her talent—the cows and the pigs did not care. But the people to whom her family sold milk and cheese and cream and butter and sometimes ice cream—they benefited absolutely, in that Doña Guillermina not only knew her own family's history but everyone else's as well. Having been hard at work in the *mercado* all these years, she was simply at the center of the universe.

That she remembered every transaction, every conversation, no matter how small, and every raised eyebrow, this was Doña Guillermina's blessing and her curse both, as she would often say to anyone who would listen long enough. If Doña Guillermina was small on the outside, this knack for remembering made her very big on the inside. Everyone who spoke with her knew her talent to be a fact, because Guillermina could say the most casual, almost off-handed thing, and that person would suddenly know something more about a lost grandfather.

But the remark would always be something that they would have to come back to hear more about, because Doña Guillermina was always busy. She was busy with all the others who had come back to learn more, themselves having had to wait to hear details regarding a previous comment. To see Doña Guillermina was like seeing the serials at the movies, a little bit and then come back again next week for more. The cheese and the cream she sold had their charms, but the bits of information she gave to her customers as well, and taking these home in the same basket, made for the best dinners in the world, because people brought home news they did not know about themselves and talked about it with their families.

And as more people died, the old ones particularly, Guillermina seemed to know still more about their families, even more than the families themselves. People whispered that it was as if Guillermina were receiving information directly from the dead.

This could not help but be good for business, as her mother had pointed out many years earlier, encouraging her to remember small details and then to tell people when they came to buy something. It was very funny in those early years, but as Guillermina grew up and then grew old, remembering details simply became her habit, which was not a power any more than someone who is good with leather makes a perfect saddle. Still, Guillermina enjoyed her role, so much that, when the moment was right, she corrected a few things here and there in people's lives, making the town a better place and making people thankful to her. It was the least she could do, she thought, and was even an answer to an occasional prayer. Time helped her with things, but Guillermina quietly took the lead when she thought she could do some good.

Whether what Doña Guillermina said about this or that was true, nobody else could say for certain, but nobody could say it was not true, either. So in this way, by living the longest and by remembering the most, or claiming with great authority to remember the most, María Guillermina Belmares became the history of the town, and occasionally its patron saint, arranging marriages and helping to baptize children when there was nobody else to step in.

Guillermina did not know about the business of being a saint, but what she could indeed say until the day she died is that she never hurt anyone. In that regard she compared favorably to the one saint who had passed through here, Santa Teresa. But regarding her sense of history, Guillermina Belmares Dos Santos simply took a fluid view, seeing herself sometimes as its keeper, sometimes as its maker, or perhaps as its simple cementing authority. Certainly she was at the center of things, but history was history, and whatever little part she played in it was of no consequence, she said.

The truth was the truth, wherever it came from, even if she had to help sometimes by sorting out what other people remembered from what she knew to be the case, whether she'd been there or not. Especially as she grew older, Guillermina knew enough to know what should have happened, regardless of what people thought, or perhaps even said. And this, as she often said, was good for the town because it kept everyone from being confused.

Guillermina's conviction in all things is what first attracted her husband, Cayetano Belmares, to her, and what most impressed her children, so that as life moved on she took to the business not simply of the dairy but of the town, working for the common good in the same way that Cayetano took care of the town's needs, running the dairy and the orchards and the fields. Her father, Martín Dos Santos, had died some years ago, an early death, and it was her brother, Ubaldo, who took instruction now from her manner—*Certainty in all things.* Her father and her brother were both lawyers—the only lawyers, in fact, taking care of whatever was left to be settled that she had not gotten to first.

Guillermina was always strong for her family when she was growing up, understanding how her strength served them, and of course by extension the town itself, and she continued in this vein after she married and had a family of her own. In these things of her character and of its service to the town, Guillermina felt very good about her lot in life, and about life generally.

While her father and her brother were lawyers, her family concern was still the dairy, which her parents and grandparents had run until they got too old and then passed on. She and Cayetano had taken things over and expanded the farm's operations substantially on her advice, of which she felt quite proud, as things were going very well. The workaday success of their business was

Cayetano's doing, but Guillermina understood what was needed in the greater picture.

In these last years, with the *rancho* and dairy and orchard and all the rest going so well, Guillermina had taken over the *mercado* part of the dairy business. Everyone agreed that she knew how to sell things. And it was not so much that she knew how to sell things as that she knew when people needed to buy what she was selling. She remembered everything, and it was a talent that served her and the family dairy both.

The truth of things was, however, that she liked the *mercado* because it was the heart—and voice—of the town. By midday when she closed her stall, Guillermina would have seen almost everyone. If not, then by the end of the week she certainly would have. And they would have seen her, which she didn't think was to her disadvantage in things.

Why her father, Martín Dos Santos, died Guillermina was happy to tell anyone who wanted to hear, which she assumed was everyone. *Why would they not be interested?* she thought, and that was that. He was practically the founder of the town, after all, or at least he was by the end of the first year of Guillermina's telling the story.

"Overwork," she would say. "We're all like that in the Dos Santos family, and the Belmares, too, now that I'm there." This made her the common denominator in all things related to work no matter which family one was referring to, which secretly pleased her but scared her brother, who was not similarly inclined. "Doña Guillermina," people would say—"go see her." It didn't matter for what.

Her strategy was simple enough and unflagging. She always started with overwork, feeling that it was a good ethic to instill as a foundation for all things, if not necessarily in the town, then in the town's understanding of her family. "They're such hard workers," people would say. It would help when she explained other things if they started by first thinking that. Knowing that someone was a hard worker immediately defined whatever happened next in a conversation, hard work being more important than money.

But it was underwork that got her to where she was. Underwork—it was not a word she used, but one she thought, and furrowed her brow to mean that one should not mistake that idea for laziness, as they were not at all the same thing. Underwork took just as much work as overwork, but instead of focusing on the task at hand, the focus was on the impact of the task at hand—that is, it meant not simply serving a person but watching the person being served, asking one thing or another about their family as they waited to have their cheese wrapped or their eggs settled into a carton.

Underwork meant taking into account everything else along with the thing that needed to be done. This could slow things down considerably, but there was as well the chance of everything to be gained. Everybody knew about overwork. But underwork was the real trick. It was the work under the work that was so often the most important part of her day. And of her customers' days as well.

She was like Ubaldo in this way, paying attention to details and respecting them. Everyone said this. She saw and understood the comparison, and tried to think the best of it, but she knew Ubaldo. He was just lazy, no matter how good he was at explaining that he was working, *and working hard*, he would always add. The way he would throw up his arms to say to people that the fault was not his—she knew better. The fault was perhaps not his, but the solution was not his either. He steered his ship down the middle and hoped for the best.

This was not at all how Guillermina felt about things, and she was always ready to do whatever amount of work might be required regarding any particular circumstance.

❖

Guillermina did not simply know the town as it was now and had been before. She remembered as well how it reached out into the world and beyond. She remembered all the children who had left, children who had died or who had grown up into wanderers and gone north to find the next part of their lives. Those who went north always seemed to go in twos, Marta and Julio, Mariquita and Adolfo. Others who seemed to leave by themselves in truth did so for marriages, like Magali, the young woman who had moved to Guaymas so quickly.

Regardless, all those who left, they were out there somewhere, all of them. She knew it and she remembered them, expecting no less than to see each of them again one day. In fact, when anybody came back to visit, it was never a surprise to her, because that is how she presumed the world to work. And in that way she did not have to worry, only to remember.

In that regard, there was much to do, as so many were so hard at work forgetting.

In her work, she was made fun of—she knew it. People laughed just a little after she went by these days, her brow furrowed in concentration so hard that concentration and the wrinkling of old age seemed to have come to some agreement on her face, in spite of how she might feel about it. Her ears were not so old, however, that they could not hear at least that much, the little side laughs of those she passed. And besides, her ears were well trained after all these years to listen for the smallest word about the smallest thing. She wondered that they were not two meters big, each one.

But laughing at the old, in general, she had done it herself when she was young. She'd giggled with her friends at the hearing devices that made people look like they were carrying around whole phonographs or which made them look like deer with antlers, or like

Vikings, which they had seen drawings of, with those kinds of hats that had horns on them.

Old people looked funny, so laughing at them wasn't hard. It was harder not to. She understood that and did not take particular offense, no matter how hurtful it might have seemed to others, who always shushed the children. They need not have bothered on her account. Children know what to do, and they're not afraid to do it. There was something to be said for that part of being young.

There were many things to be said about being old, too, however, and they were good things, even if sometimes they didn't seem that way. Guillermina could not put out of her mind one of the things one of her ears had picked up as she walked by, something about her, about how she delighted in her dislikes. What a thing to hear, that she liked what she disliked—that is, that she was happiest when she was complaining. Well, the longer she thought about it that might be true. If she was complaining, then something was wrong, and what was wrong with trying to rectify that? Of course she understood. Complaining, complaining—had she become one of those? She hoped not.

Her whole life, however, had indeed been devoted to fixing things. The marriages she helped to make—Berta and Perfecto, for example. That was fun, and great theater, the two of them walking around town so long in search of the next part in their plays. And how good they turned out to be, and without having to act at all. It was a blessing, that wedding. And the other things she had done, the more delicate ones.

Guillermina thought of the Parque del Elefante, the town's plaza, which commemorated the story of the lost elephant that came through town, how it had left its tracks at the river and how everyone had gone to see. Or at least that was the story the young man Adolfo had told everyone. Everyone knew Adolfo, and Guillermina best of all. It was some story. But she knew what he was up to, he and Mariquita, fooling everybody with that story, which may or may not have been true.

And while everyone was down at the river looking for the elephant, didn't Guillermina know what the two of them were up to, with all the houses, and all the bedrooms of all those houses, empty and to themselves? Well, it was a good story, and Adolfo was a good boy. A plaza dedicated, really, to love—she was happy to be part of it. And though they had gone north together, Adolfo and Mariquita had made a good life for themselves, which was the most important thing.

But an elephant! Surely he could have thought of something better, something easier. It had taken some real work on her part, claiming to have seen the elephant, to make everyone believe the truth of it, which for her was the magnitude of his love. It was all right. It was a good story after all.

All those things, all those stories. And now this incident of the magic carpet, which had everyone laughing at her. It was a simple mistake, and she wished she could take it back. She wished there were some Doña Guillermina for her to turn to. She was sure people would forget. But for now she was the talk of the town.

Still, no matter what else might be said, the moment at the center of all this had been compelling to her. She had closed up her stall in the *mercado* and was walking down by Dr. Bartolomeo's office on her way home, when all of a sudden she turned to see a dog, the dog Bernardo, whom she would have recognized anywhere because she had secretly been feeding him for years, the dog, big as anything, relaxed on his back riding by on a magic carpet high up in the air and smiling at her, one paw flapping as if to wave.

The Forward Science Society has gone too far this time, she thought, *making cars for dogs*. Dogs did not need cars. Imagine that, with the

cars people had already causing so much noise and dust, not to mention adding the smells of oil and grease and gasoline to the *mercado*,
which had gotten along very well for decades on the smells of cinnamon and creosote and breakfast foods and lunch foods and tortillas.
And if dogs were to get cars, what then? Cows on motorcycles?

Though the dog car was easily explained away when Dr. Bartolomeo brought her back to demonstrate what had happened,
showed that a group of children had hoisted the stricken dog, who
had been hit by a car and needed medical attention, on a platform
and were carrying him home to Miguel Torres's house, and that
a parked car had simply prevented her from seeing the children,
leading her to believe she had seen Bernardo floating along in the
sky—though this was easily explained to her. Nevertheless she
felt that the Forward Science Society was capable of anything if
left to their own devices. Maybe it was not a dog car this time, but
anything was possible once imagined.

Well, the dog car, or flying carpet, was perhaps not *scientifically* possible. At least, that's what Dr. Bartolomeo said. But that
was exactly what was wrong with science. It was never quite big
enough for all the things the world had to offer. If she had seen a
flying dog, then it was possible, even if, just to start, it was possible in that moment only as an act of the imagination. What did
not start out that way? And that act of imagining was just the
first step on the ladder—for anything. Everything started with
that little moment. Looking at the blouse of a young woman and
imagining—she had seen the results many times.

Doña Guillermina had an open mind, just not a particularly
scientifically open mind. The Forward Science Society and its members made claims to open-mindedness, but they were last in line in
that regard, every one of them.

She understood all the science she needed. Whatever else science might invent, it still had not dealt with sadness. It did not help

her bring her parents back. Science simply told her what to do, but it did not listen to what she wanted. The doctor had told her how to bury her parents, but that was not the problem at hand. She did not want them to go. What was to be done for that?

The Forward Science Society could have their science. Guillermina knew that she had a more open mind than they did and would say to anyone who would listen that they should not get stuck with those ideas, which were too small. Science was little, she would say, but the world was big. Science would be followed by something else, and soon enough, too, given the speed with which the world was moving.

Some people prayed, and that was good. It was a comfort and a glimpse of something bigger, something very big. But it did little in the short term, she had to say, if a little wistfully. She was not opposed to praying, certainly. She herself prayed and had said more rosaries, she felt, than anyone else on the continent. She never missed a funeral. But prayer, too, was in need of something new. Faith in the Virgin was good, but Guillermina's faith was more democratic than the church's, which was all about big things. Guillermina was far more interested in small things, in people things, in daily things—all the things the church told a person not to worry so much about.

Science and religion, she thought, they were two steps on the ladder. What came next, she wondered? Or would it be one of them?

Had the last two wars been fought without science, for example, well, those wars would have been different. Medicines, small cures and large ones, they were good, of course, but the guns, the weapons, and those bombs. What were they except people screaming? And all her prayers, who was she praying to, or against? It was confusing, to say the least. The town needed to find something better than what it had now, and soon, she thought. The town and the world both.

❖

If people went to the Forward Science Society for answers about what to do next, they came to her to hear what had been done before. It was a good arrangement, even if it meant people sometimes laughed at her. Her own son Ignacio teased her on occasion, believing in the way he did that science was the answer to all things. He had built a whole company and a whole life based on that ideal, bowing to science in all things. But her son, and all the rest of them, they confused her ability at remembering with her believing that things should still be like they used to be, which was not the case at all. But few people, these days, listened to her long enough to understand that. She wanted what they wanted but simply felt they were too slow getting to it.

When all was said and done, she remembered to do what nobody else had—she took pains to trace events in detail. She traced events back so that she found the driver of the car that hit Bernardo. The person, as could be imagined, was very nervous, given all the attention paid to the dog and how all the children were talking about Bernardo's great adventure. He had even heard about the incident in which Guillermina herself was involved, though she immediately waved it off as not being important.

"Have you heard the song about me as well?" she asked.

He sheepishly answered, "Yes."

"That's all right," she said with a laugh. "So has my husband, who thinks it's very funny."

With that act of generosity, the man looked up and knew Doña Guillermina could be trusted.

Guillermina moved closer to the man. "I'm the only one, I think, who remembers for now that it was your car. And I will try to keep it that way, just so you know."

"Oh, señora, if you could do that."

"Think nothing more of it. After speaking with you I am certain that of course it was an accident."

"Oh, it was, it was, señora. And I've already been to see Padre Nacho."

"I'm sure you have." Then she made the next part up, but for the greater reason of reassurance. "And my brother, do you know him? Don Ubaldo Dos Santos? The lawyer? He says you have nothing to worry about as well." She would tell her brother later.

"Thank you. Thank you, señora. It means a great deal to me." The man understood why she would mention her brother and was clearly relieved, though the thought had not previously occurred to him.

"We can all just be glad that the dog survived."

The man nodded vigorously. "He is a good dog. I've seen him many times."

"Not another word, then."

With that, they drank some *café con leche* together, which the man's quiet wife had fixed, and in the fading afternoon light they ate some gingerbread pig cookies and laughed about other things.

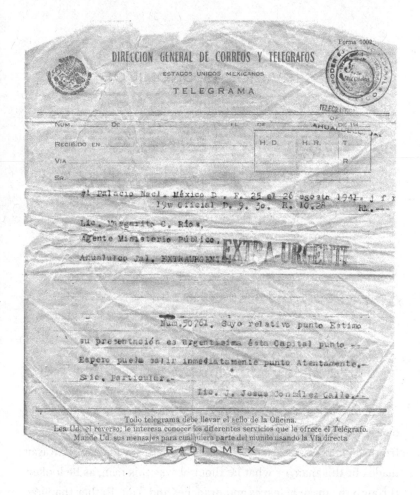

THE TELEGRAM

EXTRA-URGENTE. Written in capital letters and stamped in purple ink. It didn't matter the language, one knew what getting a telegram meant. Anything in a telegram was either news—bad news—or *do this right now.* That was its universal language.

Reading over an old telegram, even today the old purple urgency makes us feel something. It stops us.

Urgency never gets old and never apologizes.

14

The Five Visits of
Archbishop Oswaldo Calderón

To Baltasár, the red bird that was bobbing on a low branch in the tree at the end of the yard looked like a bishop coming to visit, a rotund, high-chested man making his way laboriously down the road toward this house, which was at some distance from the main street, set far back into the front garden. Baltasár made out this man, or what he thought was this man, as he looked through the maze of leaves and branches and fruit. Rather than joy, however, what Baltasár felt on seeing this man was foreboding, a feeling of something to come, if just a conversation.

The curious thing was that in actual matters of the church, it was cardinals who wore red, not bishops, at least not normally, and the bird's own name was *cardinal*. Everybody knew that. But this easy moment of clarity escaped him at present. People might say that it was a bird he had seen, but he was certain it was a man, and Baltasár had learned to trust himself more than others in all such matters. There were so many things that people did not see, so they could not be trusted to understand them. And anyway, people called him names when he tried to tell them stories like this. *Estúpido. Retardado.* Worse.

He had been in school long enough to learn that much. After that, though, they had made him leave school, saying to his parents that it was better that way. It did not matter. The orchards were his school now, and they had much to teach him. He learned there what nobody else could, nobody who was in a regular school. For that he was glad, though nobody would listen to him about it. Well, he knew about cardinals, certainly.

But this was a man. That much he was sure of.

And it was not simply a bishop Baltasár had seen, not any bishop, but *the* bishop. That's how people always said it: The Bishop. Our Bishop. Archbishop, some people even said, promoting him right there, right in conversation. Everybody knew who he was and spoke so readily about him that one might think he owned this place, thought Baltasár. The Bishop. The Archbishop. Ha! It was as if he had no other name, nor did he need one, this Mr. Big Shot.

Baltasár wrinkled his forehead and narrowed his eyes in order to get a better look at the Archbishop, who must have come all the way north from Mexico City, or farther, all the way south from New York City—or maybe even the Vatican itself, for all he knew, wherever the Vatican was. Whatever place the man came from, it was somewhere very far from here—Baltasár knew that much.

Here, a person might see a carpenter on the street or the butcher. Even a regular priest, on occasion, Padre Nacho. But priests wear black, not red. This man was coming from wherever it is that bishops live, a place certainly where people who wore red like this, red in broad daylight, did so in some regular fashion, so much that it was not uncommon. Baltasár imagined it must be a bishop city, full of bishops and archbishops and wheelbarrows and cabooses and fire engines. Here, however, in this town, wearing red like this was news, and especially when it was uncovered, all red without a sweater or a jacket over it. Blue or green or white were just colors here, whereas red meant something, something serious.

The man, this particular bishop, or archbishop now, had a fancy name these days, a fancy name and a fancy title, and people would come to him with *oh Bishop* this and *oh Bishop* that, and *Archbishop Calderón will take care of it—he's such a good man*, kissing his ring and bowing in front of him. But who could forget that he was still Oswaldo, thought Baltasár, Oswaldito, whose pants were always too short because they were handed down from an older brother. A shorter older brother. Even at a distance Baltasár thought he could see the dark socks under the bishop's cassock. Perhaps that red robe, too, had been passed down to him from an older, shorter bishop. Some things never change.

Oswaldo was not scheduled for a visit, however, so the vision was stranger all the more. It was simply a moment, a finger-snap, a picture of something he wasn't meant to see and which was not there the next time he looked. Instead, a look into the distance showed him a cardinal, sitting in a tree, plain as anything. And that's all. Seeing the bird, remembering its name, and staring at its color did not clear up the moment for him. This was so often the case for Baltasár. Some might call it confusion and had pointed things like this out to him, but his mind was set in each of these matters and not at all unclear.

But if the Bishop wasn't now there to see, then what? Was this some new trick he had learned at the bishop city, or something perhaps even lent to him by the Holy Ghost? Where was Oswaldo? Baltasár looked all around and could only see the bird. In these few moments Baltasár had already lost the connection between the bird and the bishop, that one had made him think of the other. Instead, the bird now appeared and the bishop now disappeared. That was simply a fact, and he could attest to it with certainty. That is just what had happened.

And furthermore, should anyone have asked, it was not the first time Baltasár had seen this sort of thing. People seemed to disappear all the time these days. It did not surprise him, then, when the man would not be seen. He would turn up sooner or later. Baltasár didn't need to get all excited over this. He had been fooled too many times now. *Relax,* he told himself. *Get on with things.* The last laugh would be on Oswaldo. These cheap magic tricks didn't impress him, not anymore. He was no child. But Baltasár thought he would nevertheless add this to his notes, to the things he was careful to remember.

The thing to do would be to start his day the regular way, undisturbed by what he had seen, so that when Oswaldo showed up, all smiles and with a big *Boo!* at his back, Baltasár could just shrug it off and pretend it wasn't anything at all. He would not be fooled so easily, certainly not by Oswaldo of all people. When he showed up to try and scare him, Baltasár would simply shrug and ask him what took so long to get from the road to the house, say that perhaps Oswaldo was getting older and that Baltasár would have helped him if he had simply asked.

The reason I couldn't see you, he would tell him, *was simple enough. You think you're so smart. I just didn't look. Once I saw you, that's all I needed to know. I'm not your mother, having to watch you every minute. You're a big boy now, too big, even—I see how your dress isn't long enough. How big do you think you're going to get, anyway? Are you ever going to stop?*

That's what he would tell him. And Oswaldo would laugh— Baltasár and Oswaldo were friends, after all, or at least friends of a sort. But the part about Oswaldo growing and growing and perhaps not stopping: that part Baltasár wasn't so sure about. What if that was the truth? So many things seemed possible these days.

❖

The day was warm, the air was calm, and the bees were out. Baltasár could hear them and their one-note song, that hum music wafting in through the always open window of his small kitchen. He had for years been trying to hear something in that song, the slightest inflection, a moment in which one of the bees would let down its guard and sing some word, something more than the hum, something beyond it. One word, and then he would know he had been right all these years to listen. One thing, at the right moment, and everything would make sense.

The bees did not cooperate today.

So much of the world worked that way, Baltasár thought. He was always struggling, trying to be nice, to understand, to keep his ears sharp and his mouth closed and his heart open, but nobody let him in on anything. It had always been like that, even though he had found his way through life well enough. But a glance here, a small gesture there, the sudden turn in a bird's movement, a glint of sunlight reflecting off something, as if that something were trying to say something to him, trying to signal him: Baltasár had taken careful note of them all. Someday, any moment, everything would add up and his job in life would be made plain to him, and he would do *it*, this thing that life had been saving him for all these long years.

But for now, Baltasár sat at his kitchen table and looked out the open window into the garden and, beyond that, into the orchards he was charged with keeping. He would wait for Oswaldo to show himself, just as he had on his first visit so many years earlier.

Oswaldo Calderón had come to visit with his whole family, with his five brothers and five sisters, all of them hungry for the fruit in the orchards, and in particular the *granadas*, the pomegranates that were growing thick in their bush-trees that year. All the red seeds, the red juice, the red skins on the fruit—Baltasár noticed how Oswaldo had looked at them, how he could not hide from Baltasár the peculiar way in which he held the fruit in his hands, their color reflected in his eyes. But that red color in Oswaldo's hands, slight and rough and barely noticeable, was Baltasár's to see. The boy had quickly looked up at Baltasár and smiled. Something in that moment, something quiet, was as loud and plain to Baltasár as the songs played by the town's civic band in its Sunday mood. That smile meant something, as if Oswaldo were speaking some kind of words directly to him.

The red from the pomegranate, from its skin and its seeds and its juice, all of it moved from the fruit to Oswaldo. It was as if the redness were suddenly a rush and then a swell of water, water all around, but an invisible water because there was no such thing present—except to Baltasár, who could see it plainly and was surprised enough to step back quickly with a startled step. This is what made Oswaldo smile, the jolt backward and the big-eyed look on Baltasár's face. Water everywhere. The water and its redness filled Oswaldo and clothed him at the same time, as if he were swimming in it. In retrospect, it occurred to Baltasár that Oswaldo, in that instant, wore the color even then.

Well of course if Baltasár had told anyone what he saw, he would be taken to the priest, Padre Nacho, who would say with his foreign accent that it was the color of Christ's blood, and that it meant something of course and beyond any doubt and all of that, but such an easy observation was beside the point—it didn't take a priest to point out that this boy was, in that moment, destined himself to become a priest. Even Baltasár could have said that.

But as Oswaldo stood there, Baltasár saw the other thing as well, and that made all the difference.

What it was called, Baltasár did not know. What it sounded like, he could not make out, drowned as it was in the ocean of voices all fussing loudly in that moment, Oswaldo's family and Baltasár's own, everyone laughing and talking and offering suggestions for how to clean the boy up. What it tasted like, Baltasár could suppose, the pomegranate giving him a sweetness to think different from all others. This was not sugarcane, or pears, or cantaloupes, or candy. This was something that spoke for itself in the midst of so much noise. What it felt like, Baltasár could only think of as fruit within fruit, all the pomegranate seeds spilling out of the larger gourd of itself, container inside container, asking of its holder some work at getting to the gift it had to offer at its core.

What it smelled like made no immediate difference. It smelled warm, like the day that had yielded this pomegranate, the day and the tree and the earth itself, everything in concert, everything held firmly in that warmness, that feeling becoming a place in between the hot of the summer to come and the cold of the winter that had been.

All of this was simple enough, easy news from the five senses and the four seasons. But there was something else in the moment, something only Baltasár and Oswaldo understood: Baltasár imagined—or was made to imagine—the sixth thing, which was something else, something not of the senses.

It gave something to the imagination as well. Whatever happened in that moment, it was as if time stood quietly and walked slowly and carefully like a cat between one minute and the next, taking its time and looking straight at Baltasár. It—this feeling, this vision, this sense that Baltasár felt unmistakably—well it was like a cat at first, but in the next few moments the feeling simply grew, unchecked, and in that moment as it stretched out and became bigger, Baltasár now imagined Oswaldo riding a horse, which made a sound as it galloped, each of the seeds inside the pomegranates a gift of the gallop of the horse, every one. A hoofbeat, a seed, a hoofbeat, a seed, as if they were one. When everything was finished, when the moment came to calm them, to count them all, every pomegranate seed in this orchard would tell the tale. Toward what destination Oswaldo in this vision rode, Baltasár could not say. Toward what further end, Baltasár did not know.

Not yet. But this story was all something about Oswaldo.

❖

The counting of the seeds in order to decipher the meaning of this vision regarding Oswaldo would take some time, and the direction of the horse Oswaldo was riding was equally uncertain—getting one's bearings in a vision like that is always difficult. Baltasár was looking at the horse, after all, not at the compass or the sun or the stars, even if they had been visible.

Oswaldo's second visit would help Baltasár to understand what had happened but would still not answer his most basic questions. What did this thing he had seen—or imagined or felt—mean? Oswaldo would never have words to offer in exchange for this question. Baltasár, in fact, never asked. But that did not mean that something was not happening.

When Oswaldo came to visit a second time he was by himself—and on a horse. This second visit was not long after the first, and was something of an afterthought. Oswaldo's father had misplaced his machete, and though he had several, was looking to find this particular one because it was his favorite. It fit his hand.

Oswaldo was sent to inquire if perhaps his father had not left it somewhere on the premises after cutting fruit. The loss was something Baltasár's parents took quite seriously. They themselves would not have wanted to lose such an item, as these things lived in people's lives almost as friends. A thorough search ensued, and indeed the machete turned up, at the farthest end of the farthest row of plum trees. It was found stuck casually into the wooden fencepost, lonely at the far northeast corner of the orchards. That it was lost was of no consequence to Baltasár, but that it had found itself placed at such a pivotal extremity—this was everything. Exactly northeast.

Oswaldo, in fact, was the one to find it, with Baltasár not two seconds behind him. The instrument itself was handsome, an eighth of a moon wedged into the fencepost, but perfectly, as if the moon itself were in the moment, resting. The shine, slight but full, of the low sun on the polished metal made the story tell itself, and while Oswaldo said nothing, Baltasár understood that to grip the handle of that machete was to hold onto something bigger than all of them combined. Oswaldo nevertheless drew it out and hefted it with ease, then holstered the machete as if the whole affair were nothing.

He thanked Baltasár's parents, nodded to Baltasár boy to boy, then rode off on the horse, both the horse and Oswaldo turning for a moment in a wave good-bye as they left, followed by a small cloud of dust. Baltasár would not see Oswaldo again for many years, during which time, as if swept into that turn of risen dust, they both moved from childhood into what lay beyond.

This was the second visit as Baltasár thought it would have happened.

❖

Baltasár could not remember the third visit, or had lost count, because he knew the next visit to be the fourth. He would think of the third later. The fourth visit was not so much a visit by Oswaldo as it was a visit from everyone in the town, in the town and beyond, as far as people could walk or ride in a day. The necessities of the fields this time of year, a particularly bountiful spring, disallowed anything more. People were happy to see what may have been a miracle, but the crops, too, needed attention. One day was what people could afford.

They came to see what Baltasár had done. Oswaldo was one more of the hundred or two hundred people who made their way to the orchards from all directions. In truth, Baltasár was not precisely sure Oswaldo had come, but he knew the chances and felt confident in believing that it was so.

One Sunday afternoon, after church and having done the chores for the day save the evening feeding of the horse and the chickens and the general inspection of the grounds, Baltasár climbed onto the lowest branch of the tallest *mora* tree in the orchard. And what he started he could not stop, even as the chachalaca birds all made such a rude fuss, whistling and shouting at him in their high voices. Along with the bees, he had always suspected them, as well, of speaking, and what they said now was plain enough. Baltasár did not stop. He climbed to the second branch, then the third, then farther. He was neither slow nor in a hurry, but precise, and what had taken everyone aback is that, as he was inspecting the orchard, he had not gotten off the horse to start his climb, but had stepped up, drawing his feet easily out of the stirrups and standing himself up straight on the back of the horse as if the horse itself were the first step, the first branch. And he simply stepped from the horse to the tree.

He did all this in front of his family—they could see him in the small distance, and his father shouted at him as loudly as he could, *¡Balto! ¡Balto! ¿Qué estás haciendo?*

Baltasár didn't know himself what he was doing, only that he could do it, so he said nothing and continued climbing upward, as easily as if he were moving forward, step after step. He had simply, at that moment, found a new direction. Up.

The horse took care of itself, wandering back and making rounds as it would on any other late afternoon. The particular tree Baltasár climbed was not one of the regular fruit trees but an old being, a tree that had been there for as long as anyone could remember. It gave shade to the young fruit saplings when they were first planted, and removing it would have been more trouble than anyone had to give.

It was an old *mora*, a mulberry tree, which too had found and followed this new direction, up. Because it had given its small but particular fruit in such abundance, everyone had looked only at that, without noticing what else the tree had been attempting. Why stop, it seemed to say to itself, why stop and not keep going? Baltasár understood its sensibility the moment he had passed under it, and he wondered how he had never comprehended this tree's map before. He was used to noticing so much that not having noticed this tree's height startled him. And that a map the tree offered might be thought of as an up and down thing, not simply here to there—that by itself took him further by surprise. This was a new map.

It made him think that the tree had found its direction suddenly, just in the way he had discovered the tree, and that perhaps it was calling to him, and that he was lucky to be there the moment the tree was moving. The tree had found something, and he had found the tree.

In the moment he stepped from the back of his horse to the first low limb of the tree, it felt to Baltasár that he was doing nothing different from continuing to ride his horse. But instead, now he was riding the tree, and each branch he stood on and then leapt from was simply the spurring of the horse, until together they rode faster and higher than anyone ever had, but up.

Nobody in this town had ever climbed so high in a tree, nor had anyone from the surrounding towns. Up in the hundred arms of that *mora*, Baltasár had in fact climbed higher than anyone there knew of anyone else climbing, anywhere. He climbed to a point higher than the tops of any of the other trees, and on up to the point on this tree where the topmost limb began to bend with his weight. Had the limb been strong enough to hold him upright, he would have been even three feet higher. But no matter, even after it bent a little and the gathered people gasped, he was as high as it was possible to be in this world, in a field and without any other help.

Even when the crowd assembled underneath him shouted in unison it took time for their voices to reach him, and time for his voice to reach them in return. That was the nature of his remarkable distance. It would have been the same had he been that far away across a field, regular and flat.

Why did you do it? they were all shouting up to him. *Why?*

But in his remoteness, and at the whim and mischief of the breeze, Baltasár did not hear *why* but *high*, and nodded his head in agreement, moving it vigorously and in an exaggerated fashion so that they might understand him.

"Yes!" he shouted back, "yes!"

Everyone looked puzzled.

"Yes!" he yelled even louder, to help them understand. "High."

Baltasár stayed in his tree for several weeks. Weeks or years, he lost track. It had been an impulse at first, something from his heart moving into his legs and his arms, pushing them with a marching rhythm, something from his lungs, breathing hard, so hard that the breath leaving him propelled him upward as much as his muscles—he could feel it all, the muscles and the air and the pulling and the pushing that moved him up through the branches. If he had been riding a horse, now he was the horse.

He worked so hard, his effort was so great, that a fire—something like a fire—finally came out of his nostrils and burned his lips. At least, that's what it felt like. And when he could feel it he breathed even harder, feeling that it lifted him, this hot air. It propelled him. It told him he was alive in a way different from other days. And the higher he got, the hotter and harder the air that left his nostrils got. If the tree had been another hundred feet tall, he would have had no trouble reaching that height either, or more. He was unstoppable.

And he was so certain in his direction that he could not come down, could not understand why anyone would want to go down. In *up* he had found something else, something so clear.

So he stayed as high as he could, finding a balance and a support in the bend of the topmost limb, which bowed just enough to make him feel comfortable, comfortable enough, no different from sitting on a wooden bench in church.

Nobody could persuade him to come down, and he could persuade no one to follow him up, so that's how things stayed. What was special to him, however, became less special as the days went by. A person up in a tree on one day is everything. A person up in a tree for seven days divides the news into seven parts, so that any given day is only one-seventh the news, one-seventh as strong. After the event got to be one-fourteenth as strong, even Baltasár tired of it and came down. He had felt what he had felt, but now he wanted to go home.

Going up was a very good thing, he thought, but the road runs out. He had tried, stepping tenuously into the air in order to move higher, but it didn't work very well. A slight gust fooled him for a moment and lightened his heart, getting him ready to start moving again, but no. He tried to step out onto the air, but even he could see the error of it.

So Baltasár came down, as slowly as he had climbed quickly. By the time he reached the ground, he had taken so long that everyone had gone home. Nobody was there, and after he reached the final step, recognizing the ground and the whole world of forward movement, understanding that he was changing dimensions, moving into the regular, he slumped against the trunk of the tree and sat there for another hour in order to adjust.

His parents were dead now, he thought, and the orchard was his. Whether they had died while he was up in the tree or after he had come down—had he just come down?—he was not sure. No one would be waiting to see him home; that much was clear. He tried not to think about his parents, not anymore.

So he got up and walked in the old way, not up and down but forward, and went home to a house full of two-week-old spider-webs and dust and old leaves, let in through the open window. Two weeks or two years—which was hard to say.

It was night when he got there, but he made himself some coffee for comfort. He lit a candle and sat at his kitchen table, wondering what had happened, what it all meant. But the feeling of it all was too much for him now that he was on the ground. It made him dizzy. Nothing made sense down here.

He steadied himself and got ready for bed, and wondered for no reason in particular if Oswaldo had seen him up there. But why Oswaldo? Why think of him?

That must mean something, he thought. He would add that thought to his mental notes.

❖

These days, thought Baltasár, everything seemed to mean some-thing beyond itself, and just beyond his grasp of understanding, though he could see the signs and was always careful to note them. The time would come when everything made sense.

The color red, for example, red among all the other things in the world, red meant something here in this town, on this ranch. Crowds meant something, too—danger usually, some accident, someone in need, or, once or twice, the circus. Even the circus, which sounded like fun, was predicated on danger, all those people up high on those wires. The wires, Baltasár now knew, were like the thinnest branches at the top of the *mora*. It was as if those circus performers in their red suits walked on the top of the world and could see everything, and could thereby understand the world. They were better at this than he was.

Understanding the world, it seems, was not his experience when being up so high. If anything, being up at the top of the world had made things even harder to see. That's how it was with so many things. They should add up and make other things clearer, it only made logical sense, but things never did add up, not quite. They did not behave as they should, even though he knew himself to be so close, so close to understanding.

Perhaps that is what made Oswaldo's visits so difficult, and so complicated to predict. Oswaldo might live far away, it's true, but far away might be up and not straight into the landscape. Wherever that place was, Baltasár thought, it certainly wasn't heaven—nothing he had experienced up high felt like heaven. But it was a place. Baltasár himself, had he been able to get more water, and after having eaten all the fruit he could reach, wishing that he could have been able to get more food, those things, and going to the bathroom, which he had to do at night, all that—if he could have gotten all that straightened out, he himself might have stayed up there, however, on the chance that he was closer to something rather than farther away. Where he was, was not heaven, but what he was close to might have been.

The boy Oswaldo had of course died many years ago, falling from that horse on his visit to these fields that first time. The boy had not found the lost machete so much as it simply turned up where he fell, which is why Baltasár always thought it was him coming to visit, Oswaldo, no matter who told him different. Oswaldo would want to know what had happened to him just as much as Baltasár did. After the fall from the horse, the blood that coursed out of Oswaldo stained him, and even as a crowd gathered and carried him away, they could not wipe the color off of him or out of his hair. *That he died here is why he keeps coming back to visit,* Baltasár thought. And he, Baltasár, who was a boy then but who was a man now, was patiently waiting his turn. No one had let him near the boy Oswaldo after the accident. So, all these years, all this readying—Baltasár was simply waiting his turn to say good-bye. Good-bye and with maybe a few questions.

Though they had tried not to let him, Baltasár had seen enough of the boy, enough to remember.

That the boy Oswaldo had an accident was tragic but not uncommon. These kinds of things happened, especially on ranches where the work was hard and the dangers were many. It was a sad accident, but that wasn't the story, not for Baltasár, anyway. It was the other thing.

The two boys looked almost exactly alike, head to toe, but nobody ever called Oswaldo names, not in the same way—Oswaldo who was clever and who could always explain things. But while there was no question that they came from different families, they nevertheless looked uncannily alike.

Their hair, black and like a mop, so thick, was the same. Their eyes, which were perfectly round and wide open, were striking. Their noses, which had the capacity to move a little like a rabbit's, were startling, especially when they smelled something. Their bodies, which were the same size and build and shade of color, the shade of a potato, moved similarly, even when they ran. Even the small scar each of them had at the back of the head seemed to be the same scar, though they derived from very different stories.

Oswaldo was always falling, the end result of adventure after adventure. He never tired of trying new things, looking into dark places, or tasting anything that could be tasted. The scar on the back of his head was simply one more on the list of scars he had accumulated through his early years, each a small white stripe of bravery.

Baltasár's scar was never talked about and was a mark of a different sort altogether. The several times he had asked about it, his mother had come to tears straightaway. His father said that he had fallen when he was still an infant, fallen out of his small bed and onto the floor.

"You must always remember, Balto, that when this happened, it not only changed you—it changed all of us," said Baltasár's father one day, very quietly. "But it's okay."

Baltasár nodded his head and tried to comfort his father as best he could, seeing that he, too, seemed troubled at the questions about the scar. He wanted to know more, but he didn't want anyone to cry, so he kept quiet and shrugged his shoulders and went out to play. But he knew it meant something.

He could see his scar, sometimes, when he looked at the back of Oswaldo's head in school. They looked so much alike that their scars must also be similar. But when he felt the back of his own head, Baltasár always thought that his scar felt much bigger than what Oswaldo's looked like.

❖

It was not much, but because they would not let him it became everything. Baltasár simply wanted to say he was sorry, that he felt this all the time, and that he had tried to do enough for the both of them, to carry on as best he could, so that if people thought well of Baltasár, then they would think well of Oswaldo, too. And as he grew, people could see how Oswaldo would have grown, too. But Baltasár was sorry, he wanted to say, because he had not done very well for the two of them. If it had been Baltasár who had fallen from the horse, he was sure Oswaldo would have done a better job for them both. He would have become something more than a fruit seller in the world. And that would have been better.

For Baltasár, it had been the best he could do. But Oswaldo, Oswaldo would have been different. He would have become something great, something important, something like the archbishop title that Baltasár imagined for him. And in that way Baltasár could have been something, too. Seeing Oswaldo the Archbishop made him feel better about himself, even if he could never tell Oswaldo.

Through all these years, which he counted only in days, Baltasár had looked for the boy everywhere and was always ready to give him a nod of the head and an "I'm sorry," but Baltasár up to now had not quite been able to see Oswaldo on his visits, even though he was sure of them. Baltasár knew that he had been there, the same way he knew that the boy had become a bishop, and even an archbishop—the boy had no choice, really, not after having turned that color. This boy's skin had to add up to something.

Well, at least after all these years Baltasár was sure that Oswaldo was here now, that he was finally on his way. It was no bird he had seen, not this time. There was no confusion. At last they would find each other, if just for the few moments it would take. Baltasár made some coffee for the two of them and guessed that because he was a boy still somewhere inside himself that Oswaldito would want some sugar.

CORRESPONDENCIA PARTICULAR DEL
C. AGENTE DEL Mo. Po. FEDERAL
TAPACHULA, CHIS., MEX.

Octubre 26 de 1929.

QUERIDISIMA MAMACITA:

No te imaginas lo desesperado que estoy por que no he recibido carta tuya,pues se me figura que estas en un estado de completa imposibilidad para escribirme,cosa que,como tú comprenderás,me causa mucha mortificación,por el estado en que sé te encuentras,y con este motivo te recomiendo que cuando tú no puedas escribirme,recomiendale a Antonio o a alguna de las muchachas que me escriban dandome razón de como estás con tus hijos,a quienes tengo grabados en mi mente,sin olvidarlos ni un momento

Te adjunto un giro por cincuenta dolares para tus gastos,y en estos dias te mandaré otro,pues no he cobrado todavía mi sueldo.

Te participo que Susana se salió de la casa del,licenciado Spindola,y se vino ayer para acá,mientras encuentra trabajo, y en estos momentos ya la estoy despachando con el Dr.Casanova que me dijo que la podía ocupar,así es que creo que hoy mismo se irá a trabajar.Te manda esa fotografía para que la veas vestida de juchi.Salomé sigue bien hasta hoy,pues aunque Anita me la quiso quitar ofreciendole veinte pesos para la finca,parece que no se resolvió a irse.

Para mañana nos está preparando un menudo al que he invitado a todos los del Banco,y al General Méndez,pues debo de decirte que vino como Gerente del Banco Nacho Santacruz,a quien ya tú conoces,y como no ha traído a su familia todavía,lo más de los dias viene a comer conmigo.

Tengo en mi poder un estuchito conteniendo un par de aretes que doña Elenita me trajo el día 15,para mi hija,dime si te los mando a Nogales,Soh,o los guardo para cuando vengan o yo se los lleve,pues creo que para diciembre o enero me voy sin remedio,sino me cambian,tiro el empleo.

Todos los dias que viene el trimotor,que es el que trae la correspondencia que viene del Norte de la República,espero recibir carta tuya,y cuando me convenzo de que no me llegó me desespero mucho,así es que te recomiendo que me escribas siquiera cada ocho dias.

Dime si ya llegó a Nogales,el Lic.Azuela,pues aquí no se tienen noticias,y ayer me dió un consuelo Peñaloza,diciendome que de México le había escrito diciendole que cuando mucho para el primero de noviembre estaría por aquí,pues que estaba consiguiendo la permuta con el Procurador,para que yo vaya a Nogales.

Saludos para toda la familia en general,y dime como estan mis hijos,cuantos dientecitos tiene ya el chiquito,qué tan despertado está mi Guilito,mi hijita santa,en fin dales muchos miles de besitos,y tú recíbelos de tu esposo que con todo su corazón te adora y no te olvida ni un momento.

THE LETTER

We write to each other, and have since ancient times. Epistolary writing has been a way of being together without being in the same room—or country. It is a way of hearing someone's voice as if they were there. A letter says things—for good, for bad, as instruction, as information, as testament, as witness. It can declare both love and war.

A simple piece of paper, speaking. Through all time and space, we sit to listen, and hope every time that it is love. Red ink love.

My dear dear dear dear girl,
You cannot imagine how desperate I am not to have heard from you . . .

ABOUT THE AUTHOR

ALBERTO ÁLVARO RÍOS is a Regents Professor and Katharine C. Turner Endowed Chair in English at Arizona State University, where he has taught since 1982. He was designated the inaugural Arizona Poet Laureate in 2013 and was elected to the Board of Chancellors of the Academy of American Poets in 2014. He was appointed director of the Virginia G. Piper Center for Creative Writing at ASU in 2017. Ríos is also the author of twelve books and chapbooks of poetry, four collections of short stories, and a memoir.